T0128937

COUSINS AT WAR

A CIVIL WAR NOVEL

RALPH BEEBE

"Their tears washed the stones their blood had once stained."

iUniverse, Inc.
Bloomington

COUSINS AT WAR
A CIVIL WAR NOVEL

iUniverse books may be ordered through booksellers or by contacting:

iUniverse
1663 Liberty Drive
Bloomington, IN 47403
www.iuniverse.com
1-800-Authors (1-800-288-4677)

ISBN: 978-1-4759-8625-9 (sc)
ISBN: 978-1-4759-8626-6 (hc)
ISBN: 978-1-4759-8627-3 (e)

Library of Congress Control Number: 2013906848

Printed in the United States of America.

iUniverse rev. date: 5/2/2013

Aaron and Joel Haskins, both born May 24, 1840, called themselves "twin cousins." Their fathers cooperatively farmed land on Antietam Creek near Sharpsburg, Maryland. The cousins were closest friends who did everything together. Then came the Civil War and their lives changed forever.

This is a story of how war made enemies of those dear friends. Through their experiences we learn of those who seceded from the United States, and of those who clung to it. The war brought tragedy that would permanently change their lives, but deep love offered hope of renewal.

Cousins at War, written by an historian, teaches us about both sides in the Civil War. It was a war that cost America about 625,000 lives (the American Revolution, War of 1812, Mexican War, Spanish-American War, World War I, World War II, and wars with Korea, Vietnam, Afghanistan and Iraq killed a total of about 675,000 Americans).

Cousins helps us understand that although the closest of friends can become enemies, deep love can combat the hatred brought by war. But can it win? Aaron and Joel would say "yes, love can win." But how?

Cousins tells the story of the American Civil War from both the Confederate and Union perspectives. It teaches history through fact-based fiction. Every newspaper article and sermon quotation is real. The battles fought by 56th VA and 71st PA, the regiments of the two main characters, are real.

A few things are fictitious: The specific story itself, and the location of the family houses are devised by the author. Two of the 30 songs used in the novel were written later: *I Heard the Bells on Christmas Day* (1864) and *Precious Memories* (1923).

One incident in the book seems implausible: one of the characters is on the winning side of a major battle, but is captured by the retreating enemy. Strange as this seems, it actually happened, as after that battle 19 victorious soldiers found themselves in the losers' prisons.

Theodore Roosevelt was likely mistaken when he said if it hadn't been for the Civil War we would never have heard of Abraham Lincoln. Still, it's the war that made Lincoln famous—a war that was fought because the eleven southern states seceded in fear of losing their slaves and power in Congress, and Lincoln insisted on forcing them back into the Union with or without their slaves. Lincoln set up the conditions for the13th Amendment that did free the slaves, and is the basis for the film, *Lincoln*. This leads to one of the key questions this book brings to our minds: Could the slaves have been freed peacefully, and would their descendants have been better off if that had occurred?

DEDICATION

In appreciation to Wanda, my wonderful wife of 60 years, and our three children (Diane, Lori and Ken), ten grandchildren, and five great-grandchildren (so far). Also, special thanks to Dick and Kathryn Eichenberger, our close friends who were major helpers in the early stages of the book, about 30 George Fox University students who helped along the way, and ten close advisers.

CHAPTER 1

Sharpsburg, Maryland, April 20, 1861

Aaron Haskins raced the mile and a half from Sharpsburg to his home on Antietam Creek. He rushed into the living room and gasped to his parents, "We're going to war. It's true. It's true. Lincoln's invading us. Virginia's going out. We'll be next."

Still puffing, he thrust a newspaper at his father. "I saw Johnny Williams in Sharpsburg, and he said they're going to form a Maryland regiment." He took another quick breath. "They're calling for volunteers—men who can come right away."

Sucking in air, he barked, "Joel and I are gonna go! We'll leave when the Maryland regiment forms at Harpers Ferry." Joel was Aaron's cousin; the boys shared the exact same birthday and had been almost like twins—twin cousins—all their lives.

As his father scanned the newspaper, Aaron's grin widened. "It looks like there will be fighting soon."

His mother gasped.

Abigail looked into her son's face. Her eyes swam with emotion, but Aaron could not decipher all that dwelt in that look. He knew she feared war, but he didn't comprehend the depth of her pain. He could see shock and anguish mounting inside her, expanding with each shallow breath.

"Are you sure, Aaron? Shouldn't you leave the fighting to older men?"

Aaron drew back his shoulders and gave her his most charming smile. This was a battle he must not lose. He slid onto the worn couch next to her and squeezed her cold hand. "Ma, we're almost twenty-one. I know you're worried about the danger, but I'll look out for myself. No Yankee can catch me—you know that. We'll get it over and be home for harvest."

Aaron looked back to his father, who was examining the article closely. Robert lifted his head, and their eyes met. Aaron felt reassured that his father understood and was proud of his son. Aaron looked again to his mother, who remained silent beside him. He had to make her understand too.

"Ma, I can't just sit here and let Lincoln take away our freedom and destroy our way of life."

His brow furrowed with concentration. Perching on the settee's edge, he left one hand in his mother's, while the other gripped the wooden armrest.

"Pa, *you* know that Joel and I are doing the right thing, don't you? Somebody has to stand up against evil."

Abigail released his hand and fisted her own deeply into the folds of her apron.

Aaron's hopes sank as Robert said, "I'm not sure, Son. The harvest may be early this year. I don't know if we can afford to let you boys go."

Abigail responded quickly. "Yes, yes, you two have to stay for the harvest. By then the problem will be settled." She picked up her crocheting and changed the subject. "Aaron, would you run upstairs and get my blue ball of yarn? I'm about out. How do you like this sweater I'm making for you?"

"But, Ma, don't you see? What if the war is over before we get into it? I don't want to miss the action. It'll be the greatest adventure of my life."

Aaron paused for a moment and then continued. "Ma, you just don't understand what it's like to be a man. Men stand up for right. My great-grandfather was a hero in the American Revolution. I want to be a hero too."

Abigail wasn't done. "Aaron, my father fought too. He told me what it was like. You think that just because men do the fighting, they know more than women. You're wrong. Think what it was like when mothers lost their sons, and wives lost their husbands. War is hard on women too."

"Yes, of course," Aaron said. "But what if we don't fight? What if Lincoln takes away our slaves?"

They all were silent for a moment. Aaron's last words hung heavily in the air. He felt sweat trickling down the small of his back, and his heart was beating wildly. He found it hard to breathe in the heavy, humid air of early spring. He saw his father's expression change as though he had made up his mind.

"Abigail, our boy might be right. It's a good cause, and we can be proud to have our boy defend it. Let's let him have his moment."

Aaron's face lit up with excitement as his father continued. "We can find a way to make do without you boys for a while. We've always been proud of you, Son, and when you fight for freedom, we couldn't be prouder."

Robert removed his spectacles and then added with certainty, "I remember what my grandfather said about the war for independence from England. He said that freedom isn't free. Right now, Lincoln wants to take away our freedom to own slaves, and somebody has to pay the price; somebody has to do the fighting. I'm proud of our son, just like I'm proud of my grandpa, who fought for freedom in 1776."

The words were barely out of Robert's mouth when Aaron shot forward to grab his father and pull him into a strong hug.

"Thank you, Pa. Lincoln will find out we mean business, and in a couple of months, the whole thing'll be over and our new nation will be free. Great-Grandpa was right. Freedom isn't free. If I have to, I'll give the whole summer to make it happen."

"Grandpa would be proud of you," Robert said, releasing his hold.

Aaron moved to his mother and bent to kiss her pale cheek. "I'm going to tell Joel right now." He snatched the newspaper from his father's hand and was out the door before his mother's tears soaked the sleeve she held before her eyes.

She listened to his pounding feet as he ran for his cousin's cabin across the stone bridge on Antietam Creek, and then she looked painfully at her husband. Robert sat gently beside her. With a small sigh, she buried her face against his shoulder, clinging to him in her fear and sorrow. He rocked her gently, as he had done with their babes. With time, she regained some control and moved away from him, retreating into herself. He kissed her forehead and then went out to do his evening chores.

Abigail walked to the door and closed it softly behind him. She glanced down at the doily still clutched in her hand and noticed it had begun to unravel.

Aaron sped across the stone bridge and soon stood at the open doorway of his twin cousin, who had been married to Amy for a month. The run had been less than two hundred yards, but the excitement had left him panting.

Amy greeted her husband's cousin with "What do you have there?"

"It's something I want to show Joel. Where is he?"

Aaron had barely finished speaking, when Joel came up the back steps, carrying an armful of firewood. His blond hair was askew, and sweat dampened the plaid cotton shirt that hung loosely on his lanky frame. Everybody said the two looked alike, right down to their pale blue eyes and fair complexions.

"I'm right here," Joel said. "What's going on? Is something wrong?"

"No! It's *right*! Read this. Virginia has left the Union!" Aaron shoved the crumpled paper into Joel's hands and faced his cousin with a wildly beating heart.

A frown crossed Joel's face as he scanned the words on the page. "But just a few weeks ago, they voted not to secede. I guess Lincoln's call for volunteer troops spooked 'em enough to reconsider."

Aaron moved about the room with excitement. "That's just what the *Gazette* says—Lincoln called for seventy-five thousand troops to invade the South and force the seven seceded states back into the Union, but it worked just the opposite. Virginia joined the Rebels and became the eighth state to secede. See, it says the Virginians have already taken over the US arsenal at Harpers Ferry."

With trembling fingers, Aaron pointed to the paper. "Johnny Williams told me they're forming a regiment in Maryland to help Virginia defend the arsenal and keep it from going back to the federal government. Johnny and Lawrence Williams are going. We can join! It's going to be great, Joel!"

"Now, wait just one minute," Amy protested. "We've only been married a month." She glared at the bearer of unwelcome news as she moved to stand between her husband and the enemy. "I need him here." She wrapped her arms possessively around Joel's waist and pressed her cheek against his heart. Joel closed his arms around his pretty wife's shoulders; he looked warily at Aaron while gently stroking Amy's curls.

Aaron couldn't contain himself; his eyes blazed with frustration as he gazed at Amy. She was no better than a cat with her fur up. It was Joel's job to soothe her; he was the husband. All Aaron had to do was keep away from her claws.

"A lot of wives will have to let their men go for a few weeks. Sometimes you have to sacrifice for what's right. When a monster is at your door, you defend yourself!" His voice rose, and he looked toward Joel. He hadn't come prepared for this kind of opposition. He could depend on the men, but the women were bewilderingly difficult.

Yet Aaron knew this wasn't the real Amy. She would understand later why her husband needed to be gone for a bit. "We'll be back before she knows you're gone, Joel. You have to do this with me. This is the most important thing we'll ever do. We may never get a chance like this again."

Aaron wondered why Joel was even hesitating. This was going to be a war as great as any they had read about in school. Of course Joel wouldn't choose to miss it.

Still, Aaron realized Joel had been caught unprepared and had no answer for cousin or wife. "Amy and I need to discuss this, Aaron. You gotta understand that. I have to think about her too. It's a little sudden, and we'll just have to think it over."

Aaron gritted his teeth. He wasn't sure he could control his anger and disappointment, so he turned on his heel and headed for the door. "Come find me when you've convinced her, then," he barked over his shoulder. He lunged for the wooden door and pulled it shut behind him with such force that it rattled on its hinges.

As the door banged shut, Amy's hands tightened on Joel's shirt. He held her closer. There was no way he could leave Amy—yet, as Aaron had said, thousands of husbands were leaving their wives. *Every soldier who goes to war has to leave his family. Maybe Aaron is right—maybe the cause of Southern freedom is worth it. Maybe …*

He was still holding his wife close when the scent of burned dough drifted across the room. Amy shrieked and rushed to rescue the blackened biscuits. Joel watched her wave at the smoke with a towel. Chuckling, he went to wash for dinner.

He paused and stared at his reflection in the mirror. Growing up, he and Aaron had always complemented each other. Their looks and temperaments worked together to create a perfect match. He laid his hands against the counter and lowered his head. In all this time, he couldn't remember failing to support Aaron. Aaron always supported him too.

"Joel, supper's ready."

He felt a headache forming and grimaced. "Coming. Smells good," he joked.

Amy nodded but kept her back turned as she ladled the soup.

Later, Joel lowered himself slowly onto their bed, his neck aching with the tension Aaron had brought. The ropes beneath the feather mattress creaked, and Joel reminded himself vaguely that he needed to tighten them in the morning. As he searched for a way to resolve the unfamiliar strain with his bride, his fingers traced patterns of blue and green on the new quilt Amy and their mothers had pieced together before the wedding.

As Amy braided her hair, Joel noticed that her mirrored eyes reflected the fear she felt. With a sigh, he sat up and swung his legs over the side of the bed. Their eyes locked in the mirror.

"Amy, I hope I don't have to leave you. Aaron just naturally expected me to go with him. You know how we've always done everything together." He paused and then added, "I love you more than the whole world, but lots of men protect their wives in wartime. I just don't know what I should do."

He laid his head against her bare shoulder and softly rubbed her neck, pressing his thumbs into the knots of tension. He stroked her softly.

"I'm so glad I have you." His hand trailed down her cheek and onto her lovely brown hair with its captivating curls.

"I'm so glad I have you too," Amy whispered. She slowly brought her arms up around his waist and moved with him onto their bed, where the dark shadow of war was hidden and the cares of life melted into the joy of togetherness.

Afterward, the newlyweds clung to each other. The spell of their love hung in the air, leaving a flush on their cheeks. Neither spoke of the decision ahead, but it slept between them. That night brought little rest as they both reviewed their young lives—their childhoods growing up near Antietam Creek, the joy of their mutual attraction, their wedding, and the glory of two being one, body and soul. In her fitful sleep, Amy's hand sought Joel's. Finally, they slept peacefully until the morning sun awakened them to life's harsh reality.

CHAPTER 2

Sharpsburg, April 21, 1861

In the early morning light, Joel took a short walk along the creek. The dew was still heavy on the grass, and it looked to be a pleasant day, but his thoughts were a tumult of troubles. His feet led him of their own accord to his parents' kitchen door. Unlike the original house where Robert and Abigail lived, this one had no summer kitchen—only an extension of the house itself. No matter how long he lived, that warm kitchen drew him like a divining rod to a source of refreshment and love.

He entered to the smell of breakfast coffee and bacon. Nattie, the family's slave, bustled around the kitchen in a brown cotton dress that had once belonged to Fannie, Joel's mother. Nattie had embellished it with a white ruffle from some fabric scraps. Joel watched her turn from the stove.

"Lan' sakes, Massa Joel! You liked to scare me to death!" She clutched at her well-starched white collar in a melodramatic gesture of fear, although he had no doubt she'd known he was there. He chuckled at her joke. He had long been thankful for the close relationship his mother had with their slaves. Joel shared the friendship Fannie had created with Nattie—a relationship that, to an extent, seemed to eclipse the difference in color and rank.

Nattie smiled. "Did your pretty little wife feed you good this morning?"

"Yeah, she made her buttery biscuits, eggs and bacon, and a stack of pancakes so high I couldn't see her sitting across from me."

"Well then, all you'll be getting from me is coffee—and maybe one of these cinnamon rolls." Nattie turned and poured the brew into a mug. As she passed it to him, he noticed again the shades of brown in the rich brew and in Nattie's hand. He watched the colors swirl in the cup as he leaned back, content for now to simply be in his mother's kitchen with the sound of Nattie softly humming "Run, Mourner, Run" as she worked. Joel had once asked her about the song she hummed so often, and Nattie had said it meant he should always run from evil. He wondered if the song had a hidden meaning.

As he was finishing the cinnamon roll, his mother entered. On seeing her son, she smiled, but Joel noticed dark circles rimming her eyes. Something had stolen her sleep too. He watched as she poured herself a cup of coffee and sat beside him.

Joel moved quickly to the purpose of his visit. "Aaron is joining the Rebel army. He expects me to go with him. I guess a lot of Sharpsburg men are going."

"Are you going to go with Aaron?" Fannie asked, her breath seeming to catch and hang suspended in her lungs.

"I don't know. I kept hoping I wouldn't have to decide."

"I hoped so too." The words fell from her lips, and it was as if all the air in her body left with them.

Fannie slumped, holding her fingers over closed lips as though that would keep her opinions behind them. Joel reached for her hand and held it. She never said much about her peace-loving Quaker convictions, but they were an ever-present thread that had mended many problems in the everyday life of the family. What he suggested went against that thread. He knew she could not bear to see her son aiming a weapon at another man and feared another man's weapon aimed at her son.

"I feel like I'm betraying our state if I stay behind—and, maybe even worse, that I'm betraying Aaron. Since Virginia seceded, Maryland will follow." He paused a moment, clasping his hands on the scarred table. "But most important is Amy. I don't want to leave her alone, Mama. I love her with everything I am. I just couldn't bear to leave her."

Fannie squeezed her son's hand. "Of course you don't want to, Son. You love her. I know that. *She* knows it too. But you have to decide what Jesus wants, not what Aaron—or even Amy—wants."

"It's hard to tell what Jesus wants."

"Sometimes it is. But we have to keep trying."

"Maybe some things are worth fighting for, but how do I know if this is one of those things?" Tears fled from his closed eyes.

Fannie buried her nose in her white handkerchief. "Do you think you could kill a man?" The question was no more than a whisper.

"No, Mama, but I might have to." Joel shuddered behind his fisted hands.

"I can't hide what I believe, Joel. Jesus asks His children to be vessels of love and peace. I don't think any quarrel justifies hating and killing. It's easy to convince people that their enemy is bad. It's so easy to start a fight but so hard to end it." She paused and lowered her handkerchief. "But you have to find out for yourself what's right. No one can decide for you. Not even Amy. Only Jesus."

Then Fannie added a memory. "You know, Joel, I remember an important thing my father told me. He had read a lot of history, and he said that Christians totally rejected war for the first three hundred years after Jesus's time on earth. Then a man named Constantine took over the Roman Empire and said they should use the cross of Christ as an instrument of conquest. 'By this sign, conquer,' he said. He succeeded, and all western European nations after that became 'Christian nations,' fighting in the name of Jesus. In war after war, both sides said Jesus was on their side, fighting an evil enemy."

"Yes, Mama, I see what he meant. In every war, both sides think they are fighting for God and the enemy is fighting for the devil." He then added, "I think in God's eyes, all people are equal. Even Gabe and Nattie and their children. I just don't think I could fight to keep slaves in bondage."

Fannie understood this shocking revelation. "I agree, Joel. I'm so glad you feel this way."

Joel knew his mother struggled with the issue too but had become part of a family that owned slaves. He had noticed how lovingly she treated their servants.

Joel added, "I think those big slave owners are wrong to make it such an issue. Besides, Lincoln promised they could keep their slaves if they came back into the Union."

The two sat silently hand in hand, each thankful for the other. Joel could feel his mother's pride, and he sighed. He felt as he had when he was thirteen and had taken a great fever. The family had feared for his life and prayed much. He remembered the feeling of draining heat and exhaustion and was deeply aware of his mother's loving presence. Right now, as then, she stood as a rock against the storms of life.

"You know how much I love you, Joel. And I know you love Jesus and want to do His will. Depend on Him, and He will lead you in His way. But before you and Amy make a decision, I think you should discuss it with your father."

Later that morning, Joel found his father getting ready to feed the animals. As they walked toward the barn, he said, "I just don't know what to do, Pa. Aaron wants me to go with him, and it would be a great adventure, but I'm just not sure."

"Why aren't you sure?" Glen's keen blue eyes studied the top of his son's dark head.

"Well, partly it's Amy," Joel admitted, meeting his father's gaze.

Glen's response frustrated his son. "Amy's a strong woman. She can do without you for a few weeks. The most loving thing you can do is protect her from the Yankees. Think how many wives stay behind when their men fight. And don't worry about the work. We'll get it done. You surprise me, Joel. I would think you'd want to have some adventure with your cousin and to defend your homeland doing it. I know it'd make me proud."

Joel suddenly realized his father's dilemma. He couldn't stand for his son to be considered a coward. *Yes, this is hard for Papa. Coward just isn't a part of his vocabulary.*

Yet, for Joel, the issue wasn't merely bravery versus cowardice. He stopped abruptly before entering the barn and blurted, "I have another problem with it, Pa. I'm not sure fighting is the right thing to do."

Glen drew a deep breath as he looked over to the sparkling Antietam. "Joel, I don't know if war is the best answer to this mess either. But I think an honorable man would fight when his way of life is threatened." Glen placed a weathered hand on the graying barn door. "We gotta protect what's ours, be that farm or family. As soon as Maryland secedes, Lincoln will attack us. We have to defend ourselves."

Joel nodded. "I'm not saying we should sit around while the North destroys the South. I'm just not certain killing is the only choice."

Glen banged his fist on the barn door and then relaxed. "Joel, I respect you very much. You're a fine young man, and I'm proud you're my son. I believe you'll make the right decision. Just keep in mind—this is an opportunity like no other. When Maryland secedes and Lincoln invades, someone has to defend our new country and our home. But I can't decide for you." Glen placed a loving hand on his son's shoulder. Joel took the meaning well enough. Glen had his opinion, but his son was free to do what he and Amy decided.

Joel spent much of the evening lost in thought while Amy sat in her rocking chair and braided a new rug from scraps of fabric. Somewhere in Joel's deeper being, family members debated.

People fight too easily, his mother said. *Most problems can be solved without hating and hurting. We need to quit looking at others' faults and realize they're our brothers and sisters. God loves them too.*

Aaron then took her place. *I need you, Cousin. I can't do the most important thing in my life without the one person I've shared everything with. You have to come with me.*

Then it was his father. *Your cousin made us proud, and we know you will too. The righteous person will fight for what's right. Don't be a coward.*

Finally, Amy spoke. *I love you so much, Joel. I don't know how I could live if anything happened to you.*

Joel finally broke the silence. "Since the North will invade us, isn't it only right that we defend ourselves?"

"I suppose so," she said, swallowing thickly.

"But if I join the Confederate army and Maryland doesn't secede, won't I be guilty of treason?"

Amy jerked as if she had been stung by a bee. "Why, yes, I guess you would be."

"Most of all, though, above everything, I have to do what our conscience tells us."

Joel fell again into silence. Then he looked into her pale face. "I don't even know if it's ever right to kill a man. Mama said it's so easy to start a fight but so hard to quit. She's right. Amy, I can't go with Aaron. I have to stay here. I just think there must be better ways to solve this than by killing each other."

Amy breathed a deep sigh of joy. Yet at that moment, the couple heard some men singing outside, coming across the stone bridge. Aaron's strong baritone led out. Joel barely knew the song, but it carried a powerful message: "Hurrah! Hurrah! For Southern rights, hurrah!"

Joel lay back and tried to relax. He thought he had made the decision. Still, it was hard to be certain. Somewhere, down deep, it sat strangely in him. Again he faced a night where sleep would have to fight off a host of tensions.

The morning sun brought a firm decision. He must live with the conviction he and Amy had felt. He must not go to war.

CHAPTER 3

Sharpsburg, May 22, 1861

Aaron and Joel would be twenty-one years old Tuesday, May 24, but since Aaron would muster in on Monday, the family decided to hold a combination birthday party for the twin cousins and an induction party for Aaron on Sunday afternoon.

First, though, Joel wanted time with his best friend. Shortly after breakfast, he went to the barn, cupped his hands, put his mouth on his thumb knuckles, and, with vibrating fingers, blew the special signal he and Aaron had shared since they were boys.

"Whooeee." Then a long "Whooeee-ooeee-ooeee." Then another short "Whooeee."

He listened a moment and then heard Aaron's response from behind the barn. "Whooeee. Whooeee-ooeee-ooeee. Whooeee."

As they fed the cows, Joel assured Aaron of his personal support, even though he couldn't support the war. They affirmed their deep love and respect; each knew they would be lifelong, loving twin cousins. Joel almost shed tears.

"Aaron, you know I'll miss you, and I'm worried about your safety too. But when I was in Sharpsburg yesterday, Mr. Kuhn showed me an *Alexandria Gazette* article about how the invention of gunpowder many years ago made war less cruel and saved lots of lives. The article said that when a ball strikes a man in the throat, it most likely will just make a circle and end up close to where it entered. It doesn't go clear through and really damage his neck. Then a layer forms around the ball and protects the person. It doesn't even hurt very much."

"Really?"

"Yes. This is the safest time in history to go to war."

"Of course, there's not much chance that I'll get hit, because the guns don't shoot very straight, and I'll be watching out for them. And the doctors are learning so many new things that, even if I did get hurt, they'd be able to patch me up, good as new. But thanks for telling me."

Aaron then added, "Oh, I got some great news yesterday. I can take my guitar! It'll be a little awkward to carry maybe, but we probably won't have a lot to do most evenings, so I think it's likely that I can just sit around the campfire, singing."

After church, Joel felt on the edge of the crowd as family and friends had dinner on Robert and Abigail's lawn, outside the original Haskins house on the Sharpsburg side of the Antietam. He enjoyed a family tradition, as Uncle Robert led in a strong prayer of thanksgiving for the family. Joel winced a bit but mostly enjoyed hearing words of praise over Aaron's upcoming service to his new country, and prayer for his safety. Then they sang the Haskins family's traditional song:

> Nearer, my God, to Thee, nearer to Thee!
> E'en though it be a cross that raiseth me,
> Still all my song shall be, nearer, my God, to Thee.
> Nearer, my God, to Thee, Nearer to Thee!

Then, with my waking thoughts bright with Thy praise,

Out of my stony griefs, Bethel I'll raise;
So by my woes to be nearer, my God, to Thee.
Nearer, my God, to Thee, Nearer to Thee!

Robert told the Genesis 28 story: "Jacob had just left his home and family. He wasn't sure what was in store for him. When he stopped for the night, he took a stone, put it under his head, and lay down to sleep.

"For all of his life, Jacob had been surrounded by his loving family. Now, for the first time, he was alone. And that's when God gave him His promise: 'I am with you and will watch over you wherever you go.'

"When he woke up, Jacob took the stone and made it into an altar. He said the stone would be God's house—Bethel. So that's the key to the verse in the song: 'Then with my waking thoughts, bright with Thy praise, out of my stony griefs, Bethel I'll raise.'"

Robert then approached his son. "Aaron, we're going to miss you while you're gone. We'll miss you so much, but we know that God will be with you and protect you."

Robert then handed Aaron a small stone. "My son, I want this to symbolize Bethel. I got it out of the Antietam. Please carry it with you, and whenever you touch it, you can think of your loving home and of God's love and protection."

Father and son and then the rest of the family embraced as Robert said a brief prayer. Joel felt comfortable with the focus on his cousin, who deserved it.

After a delicious dinner, cousin Obadiah Manning moved to the head of the table, holding court over the entire party. The old gentleman hobbled from two musket balls he had carried since the War of 1812. He told tales of his heroism and of Aaron's late grandfather who had fought beside him. He leaned on an ornate cherrywood cane he claimed had been presented to his father by George Washington himself. The family rumor said that the cane actually had come from a secondhand store in nearby Hagerstown, but everyone wanted to keep Obadiah happy, so they oohed and aahed as they listened to the story for the hundredth time.

"Well, Aaron, now it's your turn. I can't say that I agree with the side you chose, but I'm proud to see another family member in uniform. You can't do anything greater than fight for a cause you believe in." Obadiah spoke in a gravelly baritone, motioning with his cane and prodding Aaron in the knee. The cake in Joel's mouth turned to sawdust as he watched pride radiate from the old man's eyes.

Eventually, Robert cut in. "We're proud of Aaron, aren't we, Abigail?" Joel squirmed, knowing his father wasn't proud of him. Robert continued, "We brought him up that way—anxious to defend his loved ones."

By the early evening, most guests had gone. While Gabe did the chores and Nattie cleaned the kitchen, the family moved into the living room, where the floor gleamed from rich orange shellac and cast ghostly red shadows onto the plaster above the hearth. The fireplace stretched ten feet across the south wall. Most sat on the tapestry couch or the nearby floor, enjoying the leaping red-and-yellow images on this cool springtime evening.

Aaron loved a hungry ear. He pulled a black leather case from behind the couch, flipped open the center clasp, and raised the lid like a jewelry salesman displaying his wares. He lifted his trumpet and breathed life into its body. Abigail made the piano shout for joy, while Aaron's brother Devin found his fiddle and joined in the fun. LaVonne, Aaron's seventeen-year-old sister, sang a beautiful soprano, while Joel played his harmonica. Aaron then took his guitar and sang, walking around the room. First he bowed to his little sister Julia and his cousin Elizabeth. His cousin Kylie shook her golden curls and threw her tiny hands above her head, and Kylie's twin brother, Kylan, joined her. Each step landed Aaron in front of another person, who felt the performance was meant just for her or him.

Late in the evening, Grandma Hazel asked Aaron and Joel for a duet. Abigail remained at the piano while the twin cousins sang Longfellow's great poem:

I heard the bells on Christmas Day
Their old familiar carols play,
And wild and sweet the words repeat
Of peace on earth, goodwill to men.

I thought how as the days had come,
The belfries of all Christendom
Had pealed along the unbroken song
Of peace on earth, goodwill to men.

Then in despair I bowed my head;
"There is no peace on earth," I said,
"For hate is strong and mocks the song,
Of peace on earth, goodwill to men."

Then pealed the bells more loud and deep,
"God is not dead nor doth He sleep,
The wrong shall fail, the right prevail,
With peace on earth, goodwill to men."

After finishing the song, Aaron and Joel enjoyed a long, close hug. Each knew he would miss his cousin more than he could say.

Grandma Hazel enjoyed the evening but knew she would miss Aaron while he was gone. As the party ended, the family gathered around her soldier grandson, and she led in prayer. When everyone left, Aaron followed her upstairs. He asked her to tell the family history one more time. She gestured to the few pictures on the bedside table as she told him the stories he longed to carry with him. It was a tender half hour, until she grew weary and he rose to leave.

"Grandma Hazel, I love you."

"I love you too, Aaron. I love you so much."

"I'll be home soon. It may take a couple of months."

Grandma knew most wars lasted much longer, but she said nothing as she gave him her closest hug. After he left, she pondered her grandson's future and her past. She reminisced on happy times when her husband, William, was still alive. He had been gone for twenty-four years, but she still remembered everything about him, especially his big, rough hands tenderly holding hers. William's parents had emigrated from England before the American Revolution, eventually settling close to Hagerstown to be near the Mannings, their only relatives in the New World. Family had always been important to them, as had their church and their faith in Jesus Christ. Grandma Hazel delighted in this heritage.

She picked up William's picture and thought of their marriage and the twenty-six years they had been together. She looked out the upper window at the moonlit creek, remembering how they had first purchased land along this side, the west side of the Antietam, toward Sharpsburg. They had grown wheat, corn, alfalfa, and other crops and raised several horses, cows, and pigs, along with dozens of chickens, turkeys, and geese. She recalled the days before they could afford slaves. She had enjoyed milking on winter mornings and how the cows' teats had warmed her cold hands. Those were good memories, but she was glad she didn't have to do the chores anymore.

She sighed as her gnarled fingers stroked the faded quilt on the bed, a wedding gift her mother had stitched so many years ago. She had lived in this house and slept in this room since her marriage in 1810—over fifty years past. On this very bed, she had conceived and delivered seven baby girls and three boys. Tears filled her eyes as she remembered the two unnamed girls who had died in childbirth and Joshua, who had drowned in the creek when he was only six. She gazed lovingly at the sad picture of her little Alice, lost to the measles epidemic so many years ago. Her surviving six children were scattered from Texas to Ohio, except for the two sons who lived here on the family farm. A tear escaped as she remembered one Christmas when they couldn't write to the children because they had had no money for stamps.

Grandma Hazel's heart still ached at the saddest memory—when William was thrown from his horse and died. She shuddered and thanked God that Robert and Abigail had been there to help her through her grief. Robert had soon taken over the farm, and he and his bride had remained with her.

She smiled at a boyhood picture of Glen, who, at twenty, had decided to seek his fortune in Pennsylvania. Happily, he married Fannie Nutting and returned after his father's tragic death. She looked out the window, feeling blessed that the two brothers got along so well. They farmed cooperatively and raised their families together, dividing everything equally, including the labor of the slaves. She sighed and closed her eyes, thankful for her happy family.

Aaron felt restless as he left Grandma. He strode across the yard and around the barn to Nattie and Gabe's cabin.

Aaron knew the slaves retired early, but candlelight still showed through the cracks in the walls. He knocked and waited. After a few moments, Nattie opened the door. "Yes, Massa Aaron, can I help you?"

"Can I come in?"

Nattie stepped outside, pulling her shawl tighter over her nightgown, not wanting to act above her station by having her master's son in her shack, but Aaron repeated, "Is it all right if I come in?" Nattie relented and pushed the door open.

The slave family's cabin was a rectangle of rough logs, hewn in half so that the inside walls were flat, but there were many cracks and crevices where the logs didn't fit. Gabe had patched most of them with bits of mud and old rags. Half the cabin was partitioned from the main room with planks, creating a bedroom for the children and one for Gabe and Nattie. Sheets hung from each opening as makeshift doors. The floor was hard-packed dirt.

Gabe stood, bobbing his head in deference. Two curly dark heads peeked from behind the partition. Aaron grinned at Carl and Sunny, who returned toothy smiles. Nattie shooed the children back to bed.

Aaron didn't stay long. His parting words rang with purpose: "I expect to fight, and I might fall, but I'm going to protect you from the abolitionists who want to steal you and send you far away to Africa or up north, where no one loves you or will take care of you."

Nattie expressed a quiet thanks. "We'll pray that God'll protect you and bring you home safe."

Gabe said nothing until Aaron was well out of hearing, and then he muttered only a low, guttural "Huuumph."

The following day was hard for Joel. He and Aaron saddled Smokey and Buck and rode to Sharpsburg. Along the dirt road, the twin cousins encountered friends from school, many mustering in. Joel sat stiffly in the saddle as Aaron shook their hands and slapped them on the backs. The friends looked from one cousin to the other and bit their tongues as they learned that Joel wasn't going.

Joel was surprised at the large crowd of early morning well-wishers. Women gave gifts of pastries and flowers; girls gave kisses. Joel checked his stirrup leather for the twentieth time and kept to the rear of the party. The men were mostly young, some teenagers, but included a few who were at least fifty.

Joel smiled as Aaron set his gaze on one girl, whose straw bonnet with buds of silk roses framed her face. Swinging down from the saddle in one swift move, Aaron tossed the reins to Joel. Helen smiled as Aaron came to stand with her. She lowered her eyelids and shyly glanced from the side. Aaron grabbed her elbow and guided her to an alleyway apart from the crowd. Holding her dainty gloved hands, he reached up and lightly tipped the bonnet from her head. It slipped to her shoulders, held by thick blue satin ribbons.

"Hello," he whispered. Joel was near enough to hear. "Thank you for coming. I didn't know if you would." Her hair sparkled like fine threads of golden sunlight.

"I wanted to see you. I'll miss you," she said, tilting her face up to him in a way that made Aaron's heart leap.

"Helen, will you wait? Will you let me court you when I come home?" Time stopped in that instant as he gazed at her. Her white teeth flashed in a smile as she breathed a delighted "Yes, yes, I'll wait for you." Joel smiled as he listened intently.

Aaron threw back his head with a jubilant yell as he lifted her and swung her around. When her feet touched the ground again, he gazed at her with complete adoration.

"I'll be back soon," he vowed. "Every day I'll think about you and want to be with you, my Helen of Troy." He pulled her close once again. Joel smiled at the medieval reference, which their teacher, Mr. Arthur, had so often included in his classes.

"So will I, Aaron." Helen closed her eyes and memorized the feel of Aaron's strong arms wrapped around her. Her hands dug into the fabric of his coat, and she turned her head into the crook of his neck.

"I'll be back soon," Aaron repeated.

The noises in the street beyond the secluded alley grew louder as the men began to mount. Lawrence Williams yelled for Aaron to hurry up and kiss her so that they could be off. A round of ribald male laughter rang out.

Joel chuckled as Aaron cupped Helen's face in his hands and placed a gentle kiss on her lips. She responded enthusiastically. It was over in an instant, but Joel knew his cousin's memory would last forever.

The soon-to-be soldiers mounted and then waited while Reverend Nathan spoke a prayer of blessing, calling for God's protection and a victory that would bring freedom from Lincoln's oppressive government. The pastor included his disdain for the federal occupation of Baltimore a few days earlier.

At Harpers Ferry, a ceremony was held in the open space near the former United States military arsenal, recently captured from the Federals. Wearing an old gray officer's uniform sporting several patches and shiny brass buttons, Captain Herbert called each man forward by name. Joel knew Aaron had hoped for a uniform, but the captain explained that those would come later. Each recruit raised his right hand and swore to uphold the honor of the First Maryland Infantry Regiment, Confederate States of America. He could see how Aaron fought to control the swell of emotion as the glory of the moment overpowered him. *First Maryland Infantry Regiment, Confederate States of America!*

Joel watched the mustering-in ceremony with mixed emotions. Then, alone and lonely, he mounted Buck and started the journey home, with Smokey tethered behind. As he passed over the nearby ridge, he heard a "Whooeee! Whooeee-ooeee-ooeee! Whooeee." Joel smiled as he turned in his saddle, cupped his hands, and answered, "Whooeee! Whooeee-ooeee-ooeee! Whooeee."

The farewell call cheered Joel's downcast spirit, yet his mind clouded as the evening's darkness draped across the familiar hills. Down deep, where reality struggles against naive optimism, he wondered if he would ever hear that sound again.

CHAPTER 4

Private Aaron Haskins,
First Maryland Infantry Regiment, CSA
Summer 1861

First Maryland Infantry Regiment, Confederate States of America. Aaron tenderly tasted the words as he marched south from Harpers Ferry with comrades from all over Maryland. Already they seemed bound together by some invisible bond. They were a band of brothers on an important mission—one that had become much more important when Lincoln's federal troops occupied Baltimore.

Aaron loved to see where the Shenandoah River met the Potomac at Harpers Ferry. He didn't know the song well, but hummed "Oh Shenandoah, I long to see you. Away, you rolling river…"

Gesturing far to the south, a new friend, Steven Johnson, remarked proudly, "It's a long and narrow valley." He had grown up in that area but had moved with his family to Baltimore two years earlier. "A beautiful valley sits between the Alleghenies and the Blue Ridge

Mountains ahead. And in the middle, see that mountain? That's the Massanutten Ridge. The valley is full of limestone caves 'cause of all the water. My brothers and I used to hide in them. Not many kids get so great a fort as one built by God Himself."

They trudged on through the heat until the evening's breeze washed over them, making them feel more like humans and less like pack animals. Birds and insects conversed in the air around them, while the crickets warmed up their legs for the evening concert.

The men slept in the open. Then, after a second day's walk they reached their camp near Winchester, Virginia. A welcoming officer stood on an old wooden crate.

"Men, I'm Captain Herbert. This is going to be your home while you're learning to be soldiers. Divide yourselves into groups, and get some fires going. You'll sleep on the ground. We'll get tents and uniforms in a few weeks. Now go get some meat and cook it for supper. The patriotic farmers of this area gave it to you. Tomorrow you'll get hardtack, so enjoy yourselves tonight. Remember, reveille is at five o'clock, and drilling begins right after breakfast."

Aaron groaned but knew being a soldier was like having to do the early morning milking every day. The men broke into organized chaos as groups set up their individual campsites, which Aaron soon learned were called "messes." The Sharpsburg group banded together and included in their ranks an older man who asked to join them.

Later that night, Aaron walked stiffly through the camp, unable to sleep, and then sat against a tree and let his mind ramble off into oblivion. As he slipped into a lonely half sleep, he heard a voice in the thickening darkness.

"What?" He looked up to see an older man standing a few feet away.

"I just said, 'Hello, son.' You've got a nice, quiet spot here, but I wondered if you would mind a little company."

"Why, no. I was just sitting here thinking," Aaron answered, recognizing the man as the one who had joined the Sharpsburg camp. The stranger sat down and leaned against a tree trunk.

"You missing your kinfolk?" the man asked. There was something about him that invited confidence, and Aaron opened his lonely heart and told of his home, of Helen, and of his disappointment with Joel. He ended by mentioning his cousin's marriage. "Sounds like a good reason to stay home," the new friend said slowly, plucking at the grass by his leg.

"Well, maybe. I'd have liked to stay home and court Helen, but I couldn't. What we're doing here is too important. But I'll be home in a couple of months, and she'll be waiting for me."

"Well, son, I hope you're right, but I have my doubts. I was in the war with Mexico a few years back, and I know that sometimes it takes a whole lot more time than the officers and politicians think. My name's Thomas, by the way," he said, extending his hand.

"Aaron Haskins. It's good to meet you, Mr. Thomas."

"Just Thomas is okay. That's my first and last name both." After a glance at the surprise on Aaron's face, Thomas Thomas's eyes twinkled. "I guess my mama and papa didn't have much imagination. My school friends called me 'Doubting' Thomas Thomas." Aaron laughed.

"At least it's biblical," the older man continued. "Some of my friends tried 'Peeping' Thomas Thomas, but my mother said she would skin them alive if they called me that."

"What were you saying about the war with Mexico?"

"Oh, I was just thinking about how long it took us to chase Santa Anna back to Mexico City. We lifted half of Mexico for the United States, but it took over a year, maybe two. I saw a lot, though—and we won."

Thomas Thomas rose and dusted himself off. He wished Aaron a good-night and disappeared into the darkness.

Aaron walked back into camp softly humming a song about "the girl I left behind me."

He drifted to sleep with thoughts of that girl, fighting to let the crickets' serenade drown out the snores of the men around him. All too soon, the bugle blew him out of his bedroll, and he shivered in the cool morning air that had coated everything with a thick blanket of dew. Darkness gradually surrendered to the light that spread over the beautiful Blue Ridge Mountains. Though still tired and stiff from the long walk and short night, he felt ready to prove himself a soldier.

Dressed in his tattered, richly buttoned gray uniform complete with a brimmed hat, Captain Herbert addressed the men assembled in the clearing. Aaron imagined the sparkling uniform he would soon wear.

"You are now members of the Confederate army. You are on a great mission to gain freedom for a courageous people. First you'll learn to be soldiers. There'll be roll call every morning; then you'll drill. You'll break for lunch around noon, and then you'll spend the afternoon hours drilling. The evenings will be yours to do as you please. You can't leave the camp without permission, but you can get permission to go into Winchester if you wish. Keep the rules and do as you're instructed and you'll be fine. Disobey and you will learn how our army treats troublemakers. You're dismissed for breakfast."

Aaron dug through his backpack for hardtack, a thin biscuit that seemed designed to last till Armageddon.

"They call this food?" grumbled Johnny Williams. "Teeth-dullers is what I call these."

Aaron agreed. But the coffee was strong, and when dunked in the hot brew, the hardtack was edible.

After breakfast, the men marched as Sergeant Emory yelled, "One, two, one, two, one …" Drummer boys and fifers followed the company, keeping them at a brisk 110 steps per minute.

"Company, halt! About-face!" Over and over, a gangly young man failed to turn correctly. The sergeant screamed into his face, "You dunce! You'll get this right, or I'll break you!" Turning from the man, he shouted, "We're going to work on this day and night, gentlemen, till we get it right! And we will *all* stay until this idiot gets it! Forward at the half step, and one, two …"

Eventually they all got it right—mostly—but endured several more weeks of drilling drudgery. Then, one day, a subtler arrived. Aaron hadn't known what the word meant but discovered he was a salesman who drove a team and wagon and peddled food, sweets, medicines, and all sorts of items the men might want to buy.

Newspapers were popular. One man read a *Richmond Examiner* for a few minutes and then said, "Listen! How about this? It says here that if Virginia and Maryland combined together in an attack on Washington, it would force the Union to give up its plan to attack Virginia. If we succeeded in cutting off Washington's mail and telegraphic communications, we would paralyze the Union and end the war."

"That's what we should do," Aaron said. "But here we sit, drilling, drilling, drilling. It's a waste of time. I say, 'On to Washington.' Let's get it over with."

"Here's a story about a battle two years ago at a place called Solferino in Europe. The Austrian army fired 8.4 million rounds—a total of 700 shots for each of the 12,000 French and Italian soldiers killed or wounded. The story says that that it required an average of 272 pounds of lead to kill a man. If any one of our friends should get into a military fight, they should feel great comfort in the fact that 700 shots may be fired at them before they are hit. And it would require 4,200 shots to kill them." Aaron wrote the statistics down to send to his mother.

Another evening, he sat on a log near the campfire, enjoying the crickets and frogs, wondering how they made such fascinating sounds. He closed his eyes and was home once again, surrounded by his family, with the girl he loved snuggling close. He decided he needed to hear the music that was playing in his mind, so he got out his guitar and sang several songs, starting with "The Girl I Left Behind Me."

One man brought Aaron the words to a new song. "I just got this from my family," he reported. "This was written to celebrate our new nation."

Aaron knew the tune, an old one he used to sing with his mother entitled "The Irish Jaunting Car." He sang all seven verses, beginning with the following:

> We are a band of brothers,
> Native to the soil,
> Fighting for the property
> We gained by honest toil.
> And when our rights were threatened,
> The cry rose near and far;

"Hurrah for the Bonnie Blue flag
That bears a single star!"
Hurrah! Hurrah!
For Southern rights, hurrah!
Hurrah for the Bonnie Blue flag
That bears a single star!

As long as the Union
Was faithful to her trust,
Like friends and brethren,
Kind were we, and just;
But now, when Northern treachery
Attempts our rights to mar,
We hoist on high the Bonnie Blue flag
That bears a single star.

The song then called the roll of the seceded states and finally announced that "the single star of the Bonnie Blue flag has grown to be eleven." Aaron then added in a monotone, "And the twelfth star will be Maryland."

This brought a pleased chuckle, followed by a discussion of why Maryland hadn't seceded. The men expressed a uniform attitude—their state was being held in the Union by illegal actions of the federal government. Lincoln was breaking the Constitution, imprisoning secessionists, and denying their right to defend themselves. It was up to men such as those in First Maryland to solve this problem, and they were ready.

The soldiers didn't drill on Sundays. First Maryland had its own church service, which almost everyone attended, although it was not mandatory. Week after week, the chaplain compared the Confederacy's defense against Northern aggression to Old Testament Israel's wars against the Philistines and Midianites. The men were touched by the assurance that God would be with them in the battle against evil, just as he had been with Israel.

One Sunday, Steven Johnson felt tired and didn't attend. Aaron took notes and reported around the campfire that the chaplain had talked about the battle at Fort Sumter.

"He said our victory there was because of Christ, who regulates all things. He said that we are a Christian land, but the North has forced us into an anti-Christian war, so Christ is now sending not peace but a sword. I remember that he called Lincoln a perjured traitor—I thought that was good—and quoted something in the Bible that says God will deliver us out of the hands of our enemy. It was a great sermon."

Thomas Thomas sat nearby, poking at the fire with a long stick. Finally he drawled, "I joined this fight because I live in the South, but I wonder about all this stuff about God. I read the Bible when I was a boy, and I remember how I was struck with how Jesus contradicted all this Old Testament war stuff. I don't know."

Aaron had learned to respect Thomas but wondered why he said such strange things. His statements weren't exactly argumentative, but they had a sense of uncertainty that crawled into a man's ear and chewed on his brain awhile. Still, Aaron didn't worry much. He felt certain he was fighting for God.

After Sunday dinner, the men usually sat around the camp, writing letters, chopping wood, or napping. Thomas Thomas cut Jacob Petersen's hair. Ben Settles stretched out on his coat and slept, one big toe peeking out from a growing hole in his sock. Others played cards, while Johnny Williams stitched a tear in his shirt. Aaron wrote to Helen. His pencil moved with great speed across the page in a mesmerizing swirl of lines and dashes that formed long sentences and paragraphs. When the sheet was full, he turned it and wrote sideways to get more words on the page.

A few days later, Johnny Williams brought exciting news to the mess. "General Johnson's wife just got back from North Carolina, and she brought our new uniforms!"

It was like Christmas when the men saw the new supplies. "Lookie here," one man said. "There must be at least five hundred Mississippi smoothbore muskets."

"Yes," General Johnson said, "along with twenty rounds of cartridges for each man and uniforms for the entire regiment."

The men jumped like boys but were disappointed that the uniforms were rough and crude. Still, they would be the official uniforms of the First Maryland Infantry, a division of the Army of the Potomac, so the soldiers donned the homespun gray trousers and tunics with pride. Aaron was admiring himself when he heard a disturbance near the center of camp. Dressed in his new uniform, a soldier was bayoneting a flour sack that had been stuffed with straw. He had scratched Y-A-N-K into the dirt nearby. When the flour sack gave way and sent straw in every direction, he let out a bloodcurdling yell. He turned to face his fellow soldiers.

"I'm a real soldier now! Show me a Yank and I'll show him a licking!" The men broke into a victory yell. Many shouted threats as they pranced in their new uniforms with their new weapons.

"Where are those Yanks?"

"Give me a Yank to kill!"

"Come on, boys, let's go get 'em!"

Aaron was thrilled, but he noticed that Thomas didn't join in the celebration. Instead, the old man shook his head and looked a bit dismayed. The creature in Aaron's ear began to nibble again, and he wondered if Thomas might be right. *What if it takes a year before the Federals leave us alone*? But the thought was brief. *Of course we'll whip the Yanks in no time and get the Union to admit we're free men. On to Washington and victory. Then home to Helen. She'll be proud of me in this uniform.*

At mail call a few days later, Aaron rejoiced. He had two letters. His heart skipped as he held one of the envelopes to his nose and got a hint of lavender. He always thought of Helen when he smelled lavender, because she often sewed it into the cuffs of her dresses. *Lavender's blue, dilly dilly, lavender's green. When I am king, dilly dilly, you shall be my queen.* The letter wasn't long, and it spoke mostly of the events in their hometown, but it was enough.

Again and again he read her final line: "I will always remember those moments with you that morning. Come back to me soon."

Aaron's mother said that Bossy had had her calf, a heifer. She spoke of spring planting and how he had been missed. Tucked inside was a note from Aunt Fannie, adding more of the family's love and saying she could see how much Joel missed him. Grandma said a few words of thanks for the fine grandson he had become. The men in the family didn't write, but Aaron understood.

One evening, Colonel Elzey brought great excitement, saying that First Maryland had orders to help other Confederate regiments intercept Union troops that had crossed the Potomac and were invading Virginia. Their intent, apparently, was to take Richmond, the Confederate capital. Elzey instructed the men to prepare four days' rations before assembling the next morning.

That night the camp hummed with excitement and anticipation. The singing, storytelling, and card games had a renewed fervor. The spirit of the early nights of camp returned as the men looked forward to completing their mission. At the campfire, Aaron got out his guitar. Ben Settles joined him on the fiddle, and the men sang "Yankee Doodle." Aaron enjoyed the laughter when he substituted "Colonel Elzey" for "Captain Washington, riding on a stallion."

After that, a soldier handed Aaron a sheet of paper, saying that someone at home had clipped and sent a new song that had just appeared in the newspaper, "A War Song for Virginia." Aaron had no idea of the melody but accommodated the words loosely to the "Yankee Doodle" tune they had just been singing:

> Onward, onward, then, to battle!
> For bright Freedom points the way.
> Tho' the grape-shot thickly rattle,
> Onward, onward to the fray.

Excitement robbed Aaron of sleep most of the night but finally melted away before he was startled by the reveille bugle. After breakfast, the men formed ranks, stood at attention, and waited for the command to move forward. The officers rode at the front, followed by the regimental flag and the drummer boys, who looked hardly out of short pants.

"Forward at the half step, and one, two, one ..." The regiment stepped forward and began its march to the sound of beating drums and fifers tooting out "Yankee Doodle." It was not long before the music reduced to beats on the drum.

They stopped several times while marching through Winchester, where hundreds of women and children stood on their porches, waving to the soldiers and cheering them on. The men were in their glory as pretty girls gave them kisses and tucked flowers into their buttonholes. Aaron felt like a hero already. A fine bonus was being able to purchase hot bread from a street-side baker—the most delicious food he had tasted since he'd left home.

They marched another three miles, and then Colonel Elzey called a halt. He turned his bay gelding and faced the men, telling them again that the Yankees were threatening to move from the Union capital in Washington to the Confederate capital in Richmond. The troops of the Army of Northern Virginia were amassing at a small town called Manassas, the site of a major railroad junction. Colonel Elzey said that First Maryland would cross the Shenandoah River, march through Ashby's Gap in the Blue Ridge Mountains to Piedmont Station, ride a train to Manassas Junction, and "run the Yankees back to their mommies." Aaron shivered with excitement.

They marched two days and part of the nights. Eventually the weary men reached the railway station at Piedmont. Through the doorway, Aaron saw a large room with a few benches occupied by officers smoking cigars and drinking whiskey. The soldiers got dried beef with hardtack and coffee. Aaron tucked his pack under his head and tried to sleep. Then he got up and wrote a brief note to Helen.

My Dearest One,

Tomorrow we face the enemy. It's been almost two months since you and I were together just before I left for Harpers Ferry. Now I'm a soldier, ready to do my duty and get this thing over with. Now we'll fight. I'm ready.

He took the note into the railway station and gave a civilian three cents for postage. Then he returned to his place on the railway car.

His stomach churned with anticipation. *Tomorrow! Tomorrow we'll keep the Yankees from taking Richmond. We are David; tomorrow we'll kill Goliath. Tomorrow we'll win our Battle of Waterloo, our Thermopylae!* Nothing could be more exciting. He remembered his teacher, Mr. Arthur, telling about those battles. Now he was the warrior!

CHAPTER 5

Manassas Junction, July 21, 1861

The weary soldiers eventually boarded the train. Aaron thrilled at the power of the massive machine, this marvel of modern ingenuity. Although he had seen trains at Hagerstown and Harpers Ferry, he had never ridden in one. The black monster now stood before him, snorting like an angry bull. He watched as his comrades climbed aboard, half-wondering if the smoke-belching, land-roving leviathan would spit them out or swallow them up. When it was his turn, he climbed up and found a place to sit, cross-legged on the floor, his back against the paneled railing.

The locomotive soon lurched to a start. As it picked up speed, its whistle shrieking and wheels squealing, the power throbbed through Aaron's veins. Someone said the train could go more than twenty miles in a single hour, but Aaron didn't believe it.

"Look at those darkies," Steven Johnson mumbled.

"They look like they work a lot," Aaron said, noticing the muscled forms of the slaves as they bent at labor. "They really are magnificent beasts, the way they look with their black skins glowing in the sunlight."

"Look at the children." Youngsters, both white and black, dangled over a pond and dropped like overripe fruit with great splashes. "This way of life is why I'm here."

"Me too. People who want to be free will be free. Lincoln can't steal our slaves and force the states back into the Union."

Around noon, the train chugged to a halt near Manassas Junction. Aaron heard cannons in the distance and felt a shiver slither down his spine in spite of the scorching July heat. Colonel Elzey introduced a new officer.

"This is Brigadier General Kirby Smith."

Taking no time for pleasantries, the general barked instructions. "Lay down your knapsacks and musical instruments if you have them. We'll get them to you later. The Federals are trying to win here and move on to Richmond. You must stop them. You are brave fighting men. I'm sure each of you will do your duty for God and our new country."

Loud cheers rang from the men. The nation's capital would not fall to the barbarians from the North. They would save Richmond.

Elzey's horse shifted its weight with each cannon boom as the general continued. "Men, you will do wondrous things for the Confederacy today. You are here to stop the enemy hordes. Are you up to it?"

Again, loud cheers erupted. Some men threw their battered hats into the air and then scrambled to retrieve them. Aaron had never felt greater anticipation, yet the fearful uncertainty almost made him sick.

Then the troops were off to battle. The officers rode in front, their backs ramrod stiff as they guided their mounts. The foot soldiers followed, alternately marching and double-timing. The great army stirred mountains of dust—so much that Aaron could see less than ten feet ahead and could hardly breathe. July sweat poured down his face. At last, the general commanded a brief rest stop.

Aaron's canteen was empty, and he was desperately thirsty, so he joined others in scooping muddy rainwater from puddles beside the road. He slumped down next to Lawrence and Johnny Williams, sharply aware that he had had almost no sleep the previous two nights and nothing to eat that day.

Then, suddenly, he saw men running toward him. His hands clutched his rifle. With a blinding flash of relief, he realized they were not the enemy, but his fear exploded when he heard them yelling, "Go back! Go back! We're getting cut to pieces up there. Go back! Go back! You'll all die if you keep going. The battle's lost."

Aaron's knees trembled. His mouth was so dry that he could barely breathe the dusty air. His feet struggled as General Smith barked, "Forward! Forward! Move!" Just then, several wagons loaded with wounded and dead Rebel soldiers came over the hill.

Aaron had never seen a more sickening sight. His mind called out, *Retreat ... Retreat ... Why march into certain death?*

With a growl of frustration, he shook his head, hoping to shake some sense into it. *What will people think if I'm a coward? What will all these Sharpsburg schoolmates tell the folks back home? What will Helen think of me?*

Aaron had no choice. He suppressed every urge to flee and straightened his shoulders, tightening his grip on his rifled musket. Once again he was a brave soldier, ready to do his duty.

A short distance ahead, General Smith cried out and fell from his horse. Aaron gasped, petrified. The unit halted, and Colonel Elzey finally ordered the men to "Get down! Hug dirt!" Aaron at first resisted, but as a ball whizzed by, he dropped into the grass.

His heart skipped as he saw a dozen soldiers approaching, this time carrying the enemy stars and stripes. From his position on the ground, he steadied his weapon beneath him, aimed it, and pulled the trigger. The gun roared; black smoke obscured his vision, and the smell of gunpowder burned his nostrils. Through the haze, he saw a man jerk and mutter a loud "Ohhh" as he fell to the ground and added his blood to the red on the flag.

Aaron felt a strange joy mixed with horror. For a moment, he looked dry-mouthed at his conquest; the dying soldier was only a boy. There was nothing he could do, as more enemies were coming. Because it was impossible to reload the weapon on the ground, he stood and fired, then reloaded, and then repeated the process, perhaps shooting as many as two balls a minute. Many blue and gray soldiers fell, but somehow Aaron was not hit. To his great relief, the enemy soon turned and retreated from the Rebels, who rose up and pursued them, screaming a high-pitched battle cry. He knew, though, that some of his friends were lying around him, never to rise again.

Colonel Elzey, in command since General Smith had fallen, waved the men forward into a wooded area and ordered them to halt as the enemy ran on ahead. When Aaron realized they had won the skirmish, the shaking returned, worse than before. He watched as his comrades wandered the hillside they had taken, and then he sank to his knees and gazed back down the way he had come. Bodies lay in the grass, some writhing in agony, others still as stones.

He needed to see the boy he had first shot. Was he dead or alive? He turned back down the hill. There, among many bodies, he saw the American flag flat on the ground, its stars and stripes punctured by a sharp rock it had landed on. Lying on the flag was the gut-shot boy, screaming in agony. The red, white, and blue—colors Aaron had adored until they became his enemy—now shared the darker red of the boy's blood.

Aaron stood there for a time, listening to the dying victim beg for a quick release, but he found it impossible to end the boy's life. *How strange. How strange! A little while ago, he wanted me dead, but I shot him first. He was my enemy. He wanted to live, but he deserved to die because he was my enemy. Now he wants to die, but I can't kill him. Now he no longer threatens me, and I can't cause his death, even though he begs for it. As my enemy, I could kill him in a second. Now he is just a helpless boy. Why should he die?*

Aaron was still standing transfixed, watching the boy fade from life, when another Rebel soldier ran up, plunged his bayonet deep into the boy's stomach, and then pulled it out and ran on ahead. Aaron felt a strange sense of horror as the boy coughed up a torrent of dark black blood and then lay unmoving on the American flag.

A few minutes later, Colonel Elzey ordered the men forward through the forest. Aaron and his comrades moved toward the enemy with a screeching yell, their Mississippi rifles spitting fire. The Yankees fled, leaving behind hundreds of dead and wounded, along with muskets, haversacks, supply wagons, and other battle gear. With his comrades, Aaron picked up food the Yankees had left, ignoring the officers' warnings that it might be poisoned, and delighted in his first meal of the day—crackers, beef, and a ground coffee and sugar mixture. He ate as he moved along, and enjoyed sucking the sugar from the coffee grounds.

The chase soon ended, with the Union soldiers in rapid retreat. As Colonel Elzey reviewed his jubilant troops, three men rode into view. Two wore gray double-breasted coats with gold Austrian knots on the sleeves and three stars encircled by wreaths on their shoulders. The third had stylish civilian clothes. "Who are they?" Aaron asked no one in particular. "Two of them look like generals. I think one is General Johnston."

"Yes," a nearby soldier said. "That's Johnston all right. I think the other officer is General Beauregard." Then he added, "Oh! Do you know who the other man is? He's the president!"

"What? The president?" Aaron was stunned. "That's President Davis? Are you sure?"

"Yes, I'm sure. I saw his picture in the paper."

Aaron was so close that he could see the great man's eyes. When he removed his hat, locks of dark hair descended over the majestic ears. Aaron felt as if he were in the presence of King Arthur, and he knew that centuries later, this man, Jefferson Davis, would be honored as the first president of the Confederate States of America. *And I got to see him.*

The commanders soon ordered the men to again pursue the retreating enemy, some firing captured weapons. *Great! Use their own weapons on them. Give the invaders a dose of their own medicine. Send them back to Washington, where they can hide behind that ugly gorilla, Lincoln!*

The pursuit continued until dark and moved across the bridge, toward a house in the distance. Aaron had seen a lot of death that day, but he stopped short when, upon passing the house, he saw men carrying out a woman's body. It lay heavily on a blanket between them, the face covered with a handkerchief.

"Who is that?" he quietly asked a nearby officer, swallowing acid.

"I heard her name was Mrs. Henry. She lived in that house. I guess she refused to leave, even though she knew there would be a battle on her farm."

How sad, Aaron thought. *She paid a heavy price for her bravery, or maybe for her stubborn foolishness.* Which it was, Aaron would never know. Nor would he know whether she had died from a Yankee or a Rebel bullet. *I guess it doesn't really matter.*

The soldiers followed the Yankees much of that night until it was clear the battle had been won. As they sat around the campfire, someone asked, "What happened to Thomas Thomas? I never saw him at all after the battle began." Some speculated that he had been killed, but no one knew.

Around the campfire, the soldiers spun yarns about their military prowess, comparing themselves with the great armies of yesteryear. "One hundred years from now," one man said, "people will still honor the two great generals: General Washington, who won independence for the United States, and General Elzey, who won independence for the Confederate States!" The men bragged on and on and kept themselves warm with the sentiments of immortality.

Aaron retrieved his guitar, which had been brought with his knapsack. He sang of the great colonial victory in the American Revolution and thought of the Founding Fathers' dream, now fulfilled in the independence of the Confederacy. He had first learned and sung the American Revolution song as a pupil in the Sharpsburg school:

> The foe comes on with haughty stride,
> Our troops advance with martial noise;
> Their vet'rans flee before our youth,
> And gen'rals yield to beardless boys.
>
> When God inspired us for the fight,
> Their ranks were broke, their lines were forced.

Their ships were shatter'd in our sight
Or swiftly driven from our coast.

Aaron's excitement at seeing the president remained. He knew his president was proud of him and his fellow soldiers. Now the war had been won. The Yanks had failed to take Richmond. Soon he would be going home. He could hardly wait to tell Helen about his heroism and let her see his uniform.

CHAPTER 6

Sharpsburg, August 1861

Joel Haskins rode down the turnpike, his straw hat fighting the merciless sun as sweat trickled down his body. He dashed a sleeve across his eyes as he reined Buck toward a small house with whitewashed walls and a low picket fence.

Robert Arthur, Joel's teacher from his school days, was a well-read man who seemed capable of answering any question a student could pose. Joel was full of questions. Amid the barking dogs and cackling chickens, he tied Buck to the hitching post. Mr. Arthur came down the porch steps to meet his former pupil in the yard. Joel had always admired this man of great knowledge.

"What a pleasant surprise!" Mr. Arthur smiled, shaking Joel's hand. Mr. Arthur gestured to the two rocking chairs by the larger window and then went inside and returned with two glasses and a pitcher of delicious apple cider. The teacher remembered Joel clearly—always eager, inquisitive, and alive with the love of learning.

"So you're a married man now, Joel. How do you like the new life?"

"Amy's a wonderful wife. She's the best thing that ever happened to me."

"And how is Aaron?"

"He's in the Rebel army."

"I heard he had joined the South, along with at least eight more of my former pupils."

"Yes. We haven't heard from him since the big battle. But his name wasn't on the casualty list on the courthouse door."

"Oh, I'm so thankful."

"It seems like just about everybody in town was crowding around, looking at the lists. My heart hammered, afraid I might see Aaron's name. I looked several times, and I'm sure it wasn't there. But not everyone was so lucky. A lady I don't know gasped and cried, seeing the name of her husband, or son maybe. It was terrible."

Mr. Arthur refilled Joel's glass and waited.

"I have some questions about this war, Mr. Arthur. I know you've lived in the North and South both."

"Yes," the teacher answered. "I was born right here in Sharpsburg—in this house, in fact. I went to school here and lived with my family until I went to New Jersey for a university education. Then I came south and taught history and philosophy at a college in Virginia, but my father was injured, so I came home and replaced Hillis Mackey, who had been my teacher."

Joel grinned as Mr. Arthur's large gray cat, Socrates, sauntered past his chair.

"Mr. Arthur, I'm wondering about this war. Who's right? I wonder if I should have gone with Aaron to fight the Yankees."

"I'll try to help you understand, Joel. It's important that we know the entire picture." Joel remembered Mr. Arthur telling students not to decide on any important issue until they could debate it from both sides.

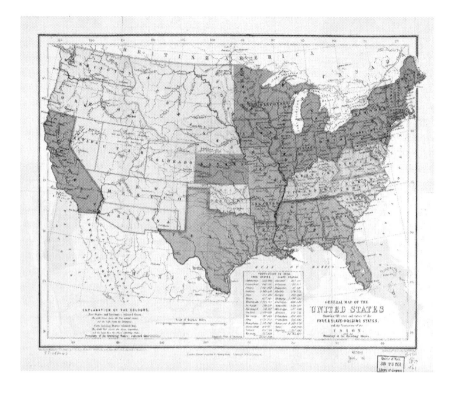

The teacher went to his desk and brought a large map to the table. "Look at the seven states that seceded originally." His fingers touched South Carolina. "Here. It was first—only about six weeks after the election of Lincoln. Then, in January, came Mississippi, Florida, Alabama, Georgia, and Louisiana. Then, on February first, Texas." Mr. Arthur's fingers moved across each state.

"So by February, seven states were out, and Lincoln didn't even take office until March. By Lincoln's inauguration, the seven seceded states had formed themselves into a nation."

"Yes, but I suppose Lincoln thought he had a real advantage, with most of the country backing him."

"True. Counting a couple out west, there were thirty-three states in the Union. Of course, by his inauguration, there were only twenty-six."

Mr. Arthur then became the teacher Joel remembered from school. "Joel, your name is Abraham Lincoln. Since you were elected president, seven states have seceded. It is now March 4, 1861, your first day in office. You're in charge. What are you going to do?"

"Wow, that's a tough question. I guess the choices are to just let them go or try to force them back into the Union."

Robert Arthur responded, "Mr. President, can you just let them go? What if a few other states have a dispute with your government? Should they have the right to just walk out too? How would you feel if the thirty-three states became thirty-three little nations? President Lincoln, history will remember you as the president of division, of splintering. The great United States of America will become the untied states of America. We will never be a nation with any power, and Mexico or Canada or any European nation can just take us over. And, President Lincoln, you caused all that."

"Yeah, big problem, Mr. Teacher. But think of the alternative. Suppose I take my nation to war. Thousands of graves! Billions of tears! And here we will be, just as divided as we were when I tried to force them back into the Union against their will. Why shouldn't they have the right to do what they think is best for themselves and their people?"

Joel paused and then added, "Well, it's your turn. Jefferson Davis is president of the Confederacy. President Davis, why did your states secede from this great union?"

Mr. Arthur chuckled and then played the game. "It's very clear. There was one reason. We Southerners feel very sure your election, President Lincoln, means Northern interests will overpower those of the South in Congress. Of course, this includes the most important: I think you, Mr. Lincoln, and those who support you are determined to destroy slavery. If you destroy slavery, you will destroy the Southern economy. We just can't let that happen. It would be a disaster."

"But, President Davis, I promised that if the Southern states came back into the Union, they could keep their slaves."

"Ah, yes—but who can trust you? As a Southerner, I fear that down deep you are against slavery and will try to do whatever you can to destroy it and thereby destroy the Southern way of life. Actually, whether or not you're for or against slavery, you want the North to rule over the South in Congress. President Lincoln, I see right through you. Getting rid of slavery will accomplish this objective."

Then Mr. Arthur added a crucial point: "President Lincoln, you made one very important mistake. You thought that if you amassed a sizeable army, the twenty-six states could easily beat the seven. So you called for troops to go to war against the seven Rebel states. Mr. President, what did you think Virginia would do?"

Joel answered clearly. "Yes, that was the key. I assumed Virginia would be loyal. Before I was inaugurated, they had voted to stay in the Union. How was I to know they would change their minds?"

Joel paused for several seconds and then said, "Mr. Arthur, I wonder about the Southern states. Do the big plantation owners really have all the power? Don't the poorer people have anything to say about it?"

Arthur shrugged. "Well, the plantation owners do pretty much as they please. But it's interesting that even though the poor whites don't own slaves, they want slavery too and are fearful when it's threatened."

"Yeah," Joel said. "Even though they're poor, they're white."

"Exactly. White skin is worth a lot in this country, South or North."

"Mr. Arthur, I think Northern whites are a lot like the poor Southerners. I think they're just as anxious to make sure Negroes don't challenge them." As he uttered those words, Joel's mind strayed to Gabe and Nattie, who were hard at work at home. They were like family to him, but of course they would never have any authority.

"I agree. You know that the big issue up north was the spread of slavery into the western territories. A lot of people didn't want slavery there, because that would mean there might be a lot of free Negroes too." Mr. Arthur continued, arguing that whites feared "uppity" Negroes who would compete for the menial jobs and degrade the neighborhoods. "And it goes a big step further. I think most Northerners are just as afraid of miscegenation as Southerners are."

"Mis—what?" Joel tried to curl his tongue around the word but failed.

"Intermarriage. Most Northerners would be devastated if their children married colored people."

Joel jerked in disgust. "Can you believe how we would feel if my little brother married our slaves' girl? The little kids play together all the time, but to marry would be ridiculous!" Joel's mind conjured up the small faces of Stephen and Sunny, one light and one dark.

Mr. Arthur said, "Before the election, I read a Lincoln campaign paper called the *Rail Splitter*, which was published up North. It accused Stephen Douglas, Lincoln's opponent, of being a Catholic and even said he visited the pope, along with other lies of that ilk—like that the Democrats wanted 'everlasting nigger equality.' Of course, its main point was that Lincoln and the Republicans would save the western territories for white men. I think this is the sentiment of a lot of people in the North, and it won Lincoln a lot of votes."

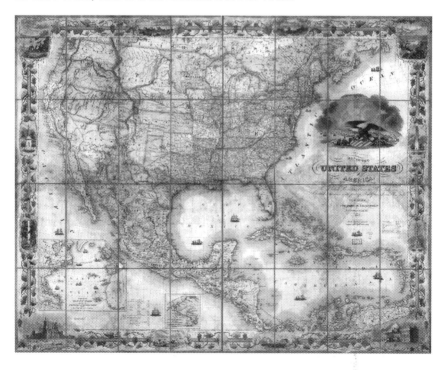

Mr. Arthur went to the United States map, touched Oregon, and then asked, "Did you know that Oregon, way out on the West Coast, voted to become a state a couple of years ago?"

"Yeah, I heard that." Joel looked at the map and tried to imagine what it was like in the wildness to the west. He had heard of the huge forests and the wild people who lived there. He decided he might like to visit the Far West someday and see the Pacific Ocean.

"The Oregon constitution prohibits slavery, but it also won't let free Negroes live in the state."

Joel's brow rose upon this revelation. He thought for a moment. "So you're saying that some Northerners are trying to abolish slavery down south but that most want to keep Negroes out of their neighborhoods up north and out west?"

"Yes, exactly. In some ways, I think Northerners are just as prejudiced as slave owners down south." Mr. Arthur pointed to Illinois on the map.

"That's why Illinois won't let free Negroes move into their state. Of course, there are several thousand living there, but since 1853, no more can come."

Gradually the conversation slowed and turned to happier subjects. The two men went outside and did the chores; then they enjoyed an hour in the shade, recalling old classes and fondly remembering the students.

Yet, as he rode home, the war hovered in Joel's mind like a hawk over a field, always circling, circling, casting its shadow across the world below. As Joel rode, the sky danced with reds and yellows from the setting sun, and the crickets began their loud chirping. He thought it strange that such pleasant music could come from a world in such turmoil. For a moment, he experienced a sense of peace as the crickets' song pulled his worried mind into a place of timeless order. *The crickets don't even know there's a war. How lucky they are!*

Joel reined Buck to the Sharpsburg post office and, to his great joy, found that the family had received a letter from Aaron. He galloped home and gave it to Aaron's mother. Amid tears, she read it and shared it with Robert and Grandma. That evening, the entire family gathered at the bridge to hear of Aaron's adventures, and Robert read the long-awaited good news:

Dear loved ones,

I have just been through a terrible battle, the greatest in the history of the world. We turned the Yankees back and kept them from Richmond. The South is saved! I feel just like Great-Grandpa in America's war for independence.

Did you hear that President Davis has named today, July 28, 1861, as a day of national thanksgiving for the great victory? We must all praise God and be thankful to Him for giving us this win. I have never been so proud of anything in my life, because I helped make it happen. I miss all of you. I will be glad when the North gives up and leaves the Confederacy alone. I expect it will happen in a few days, and then I'll come home.

You should have seen those Yankees run. A lot of Northerners came down from Washington to watch the battle, many in fancy carriages with gold pinstripes on the side, even including some women in fine clothes. We showed them who could fight. Those Union people were on a hill and got a good view of the Yankees running for their lives. One of our regiments caught a Yankee congressman and took him captive. How about that?

Maybe I'll get home before this letter does. I sure hope so. I'll tell you all about it.

Aaron Michael Haskins

The Haskins family rejoiced that evening. Aaron's letter was so proud and lighthearted; it seemed as if he would come marching up the lane, whistling a jaunty tune.

Robert and Abigail tarried a little longer by the bridge. Robert folded the letter carefully again and tucked it into his pocket. It would go into a special box in their bedroom.

Placing her hand over his breast pocket, Abigail shed a few silent tears. She was glad President Davis had declared a special thanksgiving day, a time to thank God for the victory, but she knew that in spite of Aaron's optimism, he might face other battles. She prayed that God would continue to spare him and that he would soon be home.

CHAPTER 7

Bolivar Heights, May 24, 1862

Aaron climbed Bolivar Heights like a man possessed. He longed to reach the top of this hill above Harpers Ferry, because it was just across the river from Maryland. He scrambled up, pulling at rocks and scraggly weeds to purchase a hold on the ground as he climbed.

Maryland! What a wonderful sound. *Maryland! Home!* It was his twenty-second birthday, and he had been gone a year and a day. His need to see home was an obsession. Birthdays were especially important to the Haskins family. He could hardly bear to miss the celebration he knew Joel and the rest of the family would have.

"Sarge, could you loan me a scope?" he had asked. "I want to go to the top and see if I can see the Antietam—and my home."

"Sure, go ahead. We have the afternoon off."

Aaron ran up the hill, through thickets, and around evergreens until he reached the clearing at the top. His hands trembled in anticipation as he steadied the scope, squeezed his left eye shut, and peered through the narrow glass channel.

He looked across the Potomac. Disappointment hit him like a cannonball in the gut. Elk Ridge stood in the way. He could not see Sharpsburg, Helen's house, or the family farm—only a wooded hill that blocked his view.

He traced Antietam Creek's probable course and squinted at a point beyond, certain that was where the farm lay, just out of sight. Could he not win this one small victory? And on his birthday! He wished he could just pick up Elk Ridge and dump it into the Potomac. *Isn't there a Bible verse that says if I have enough faith I can move mountains? O me of little faith!*

He lowered the glass and gazed into the hazy distance, envisioning family members. He knew they missed him almost as much as he missed them. He hoped Joel was enjoying their birthday. He wondered how the family would feel if they knew he was so close to home.

He looked toward the sun. *It's about one o'clock now. They'll be finishing dinner. Let's see,* he mused, lightly tapping the glass against his thigh. *Maybe Joel is already back in the field, or maybe he's in his cabin, snuggling with his wife.* Without Joel there to rib, though, the mental teasing sat unappreciated. It didn't seem funny that Joel was at home with his wife while Aaron wasn't even able to see his home, let alone the girl he hoped would be his wife. This evening they would have a birthday party, and he was so near—and yet so far! And the family would celebrate his birthday without knowing he was only 15 miles away.

Drifting into dark thoughts, he again experienced the year of frustration. All their lives, they had been so close; it was hard to believe Joel hadn't mustered in with him. Now, after a year, Aaron felt some resentment. The war he'd thought would end in a summer had taken all year, with little progress and no end in sight. He was amazed that it had gone on so long with so few battles.

He often wished he had courted Helen before he'd left—but would that have been fair, to court her and then leave her for so long? Yet, in his waking dreams, she appeared before him, her blue eyes flashing, offering words of love and comfort. The vision seemed so real at times. Often he wondered if someday she would meet him at the train station and welcome him home as her hero.

Again Aaron's mind saw Joel, wearing blue overalls caked with spring mud and a grin as real as ever. He raised his fists to his mouth. "Whoeee. Whooeee-ooeee-ooeee. Whooeee." The call was absorbed in the dense woods. Only his memory answered.

He retrieved a small stone from his knapsack. How well he remembered the day before he'd left his home. He had carried that stone for a year now and remembered his father's words about Bethel, the house of God. As loud as his voice would allow, he sang, "Then with my waking thoughts, bright with Thy praise, out of my stony griefs, Bethel I'll raise."

He pulled a well-worn letter from his knapsack. If he couldn't see his home, he needed to see the familiar words of the letter. Joel had told of Amy, of the family, and of Christmas. Aaron felt a wistful sadness when Joel mentioned that Christmas had lacked its usual music and joy due to his absence. Today's birthday party would be the same.

He smiled as he reread the part of Joel's letter that told of an advertisement in *Leslie's Weekly* about a book called *Psychomancy*. According to the ad, the book said that both sexes could fascinate and instantly gain the love, confidence, and affection of any person they chose. "It also has a guide to the unmarried of both genders," Joel had added. "Not bad for twenty-five cents, eh? I told you because I figured you might need it sometime, when you finally get up the nerve to propose to Helen." Aaron chuckled.

His eyes scanned Joel's letter again, falling on words that turned his stomach in disgust. The Maryland legislature had passed a law saying that anyone making war against the state or cooperating with the Confederacy would be sentenced to jail or death. For displaying a Confederate flag, a person would be fined fifty to one hundred dollars or imprisoned thirty to sixty days.

Those traitors, thought Aaron. *How could they threaten loyal Confederates who only wanted to serve their state and protect their families?* His fingers curled around the edges of the papers as his hands tightened into impotent fists. At that moment, Aaron hated Abraham Lincoln for forcing Maryland to remain a part of this corrupt Union.

Any letter from home helped Aaron get though the day, but that day he remained downhearted. *I wish I could just cross the Potomac and follow the creek to my family and to Helen. Lots of soldiers take off when they are close to home. I wonder …* Then he remembered two men from another regiment who had been shot before his eyes for desertion. Since Lincoln had forced Maryland to stay in the Union, he would be a fugitive in his own state. *How bizarre. If Confederate officers caught me, I could be shot for desertion, and if Maryland officers caught me, I could be shot for being a traitor.*

Aaron remained alone in the grass until late afternoon, hardly aware of the mosquitoes and insects that endlessly sampled his blood. He pondered his home and family, which were just below the clouds. He saw little Julia running around the barn barefoot, stepping in cow manure. He imagined the last time he had worked with his father shoeing a horse—the way they'd talked and laughed and shared the work. He remembered his twenty-first birthday party the day before he mustered in.

"Ah, Joel," he whispered, "I miss you the most—maybe even more than Helen." Then he reconsidered. "Well, maybe I miss you equally. I miss you for what we have had together, and I miss Helen for what we will have together. I'm sure you understand."

After a year of endless, painful marching, tedious drills, stale food, filth of all kinds, hoards of insects, and infrequent battles, he didn't know if he'd still want Joel there. Army life no longer inspired a glow of youthful enthusiasm. Still, Aaron lived for the moments when they distinguished themselves in battle, where they had accomplished the essential task of keeping the enemy from Richmond. He couldn't resist bringing his hands to his mouth and giving the twin cousins' call again. "Whoeee. Whooeee-ooeee-ooeee. Whooeee." A couple of hawks wheeled lazily in the evening sky before soaring over the Potomac toward his home. He hoped they would somehow carry his call to his cousin. In his mind's ear, he heard Joel's response: "Whoeee. Whooeee-ooeee-ooeee. Whooeee."

He allowed his thoughts to wander and imagine what he would tell Joel if he could. *I can't say life has been all good since I left home, but it hasn't been all bad either. I've seen places we used to dream about or read about in books or the newspaper. I even met Stonewall Jackson, the very officer who helped turn the tide at Manassas. I've been almost to Richmond and far up the Shenandoah Valley. Oh, and the battle a few days ago at Front Royal.* He laughed out loud in proud satisfaction. *We, the First Maryland Regiment of the CSA, captured the First Maryland Regiment of the USA!*

Aaron thought proudly of the church that had given $400 for "the glorious cause of Southern independence." He thought again of his mother as he pulled a tract from his knapsack, written for a Rebel soldier. On Mother's Day, the chaplain had handed out the message, written by some other Rebel soldier's mother. It bore the title "A Mother's Parting Words to Her Soldier Boy."

```
I gave up my son ... with joy, to enter the
army of his country. The war ... has been
forced upon us. We have asked for nothing
but to be let alone. We are contending for
the great fundamental principle of the
American Revolution: that all authority
is derived from the consent of the
governed ...

To the South, nothing remains but absolute
subjugation and debasement, or victory ...
I cheerfully offer my son, the cherished
jewel of my heart, on my country's altar;
and if I had ten sons, I would resign them
all with equal pleasure.

Let me urge you then, my son, to be what
I am sure you will be, a good soldier.

Mother
```

Aaron reverently opened his *Soldier's Pocket Bible*, knowing that two hundred years earlier, Oliver Cromwell's British army had carried the original copies into similar glorious battles. He scanned some of the subject headings that had directed many soldiers for so many years:

A soldier must not do wickedly
A soldier must be valiant for God's cause
A soldier must put his confidence in God's wisdom and strength
A soldier must pray before he goes to fight
A soldier must consider and believe God's gracious promises
A soldier must not fear his enemies
A soldier must love his enemies as they are his enemies, and hate them as they are God's enemies

He breathed deeply, his eyes closed. He pondered the final sentence. *Yes, Jesus said, "Love your enemies." But Union soldiers are God's enemies, and I must hate their wicked attempt to control the South. I did right at Manassas; I was God's servant, killing His enemies, even that boy carrying the American flag.* He felt a deep satisfaction in doing his duty for God, his country, and his family, now so near. He looked again toward the low clouds shadowing his hidden home and rejoiced in knowing that someday, when this war ended, he would return. In the meantime, he had a duty to fulfill.

As the evening clouds darkened, he knew his loved ones only fifteen miles away were beginning their birthday party for the twin cousins. He longed to be with his beloved family.

Yet, as his memory observed his birthday party, an ominous shadow obscured his reverie. *Will I get home, or will I fall and be left in an unmarked grave? Will a day come when a chasm far greater than these fifteen miles divides me from those I love? Dear God, please let me live. I want to go home.*

CHAPTER 8

Virginia, Summer 1862

Aaron's stomach knotted and erupted all over the grass as he witnessed the most horrible sight of his life. Scores of dead and dying lay on their backs with their mouths partly open, flies crawling over them. One man was on his hands and knees with his head blown off.

The 1862 battle at Malvern Hill had been a success, ending a week of battle. Once again, the Confederates had blocked a Union attempt to move to Richmond. This time, the fight had been east of the nation's capital. Union forces had moved in from the coast and up the Virginia Peninsula but had failed as miserably as a year earlier at Bull Run. Although delighted at the result of the Seven Days' Battle, Aaron would never forget the screaming and moaning. Down deep, he was glad First Maryland hadn't arrived in time to be in the battle. However, just seeing the results gave him bad dreams.

That night, he slept fitfully on a mountain of death, his dream-self returning to the stories he had read as a schoolboy. He saw men with hideous ax and sword wounds through plated armor as horses screamed and a castle burned. The smell of acrid smoke and the metallic tang of blood surrounded him as the specter of Thomas Thomas, his friend from a year earlier, slipped into the dream. Thomas was shouting, desperate to be heard—something about war and blood and death, but Aaron couldn't hear. Looking down at his hands, he saw that he held both ax and burning torch.

After First Maryland's near involvement in the Seven Days' Battle that ended at Malvern Hill, Aaron's unit moved west across Virginia. A few days later, Lawrence came down with the shakes. Johnny and Aaron took him to a field hospital. "We don't know why some get it and others don't," the doctor said, adding that there were many such cases in the army and that it was a "simple intermittent fever." Simple or not, Lawrence seemed in great discomfort, too tired to ward off the myriad mosquitoes, lice, and flies that were a soldier's constant companions. He was weak and short of breath, his complexion a waxy gray. The doctor described his illness as "Chickahominy fever, a strange disease that has afflicted hundreds of men in this battle, leaving them with constant diarrhea and fever."

Johnny sighed and gripped his brother's shoulder. "Is there a cure?"

"Oh yes," the doctor said, wiping his grimy hands on a towel. "It's called quinine, and some should be here soon. Those Union blockades make it hard to get the stuff. But I put in for some, and they said it should get here with the next shipment. Don't worry, boys; he'll be fine."

The quinine soon arrived, and Lawrence improved, but he hadn't recovered when the regiment boarded a train headed west. They stopped for a few days in Charlottesville, Virginia, where Aaron and Johnny got permission to visit Monticello, Thomas Jefferson's "little mountain." Years earlier, their teacher, Mr. Arthur, had required his pupils to memorize the first part of the Declaration of Independence. Aaron now stood at Jefferson's grave in the late afternoon sunshine and recited inwardly, *"When in the course of human events, it becomes necessary for one people to dissolve the political bands which have connected them with one another ..."*

He couldn't remember what came next but knew the document said that a people should break their ties with a government that destroys freedom. He recalled that the declaration said something about it being necessary to form a new government to replace an old tyranny. *Jefferson would be sad if he was alive today. He'd have to see how corrupt his government has become. He wouldn't believe that it's fallen so low as to threaten the right of a man to own slave property and that his beloved government has invaded the South and started a war. It's unbelievable.* Aaron could barely imagine Lincoln trying to take away Jefferson's slaves.

He looked down at the grave marker, which displayed the following inscription:

Here was buried

THOMAS JEFFERSON

Author of the Declaration of American Independence
Of the Statute of Virginia for Religious Freedom
And Father of the University of Virginia

The next day, they visited the University of Virginia, and Aaron longed to have Joel with him. They had always talked of books as boys, though it was Joel who was the student in the family. Aaron was content to listen to his theories and ideas—and disagree when Joel was wrong.

Lawrence soon got worse. Johnny sat beside the bed, his arms crossed and his face filled with hopeless resignation. "The chaplain came by," he reported in a toneless voice. "He prayed over him. The doctor told me it's only a matter of time." Aaron watched in horror.

"Well, maybe the doctor's wrong. You know how men live even when doctors think they won't. I'll bet Lawrence just needs to sleep some more." Aaron struggled for more words, anything to touch Johnny's despair. The two sat with Lawrence for the rest of the afternoon. Toward evening, his breathing slowed and grew more labored. Johnny and Aaron watched his chest heave and then collapse.

"No!" Johnny whispered. Lawrence struggled to breathe, and then his whole body seemed to shudder. It was almost as if Lawrence's soul was beating against the bars of marrow that confined it in his chest, like a bird escaping into heaven. Then nothing.

Johnny broke the silence, jumping to his feet and yelling, "Come on, Lawrence. Breathe! Breathe! You can't die. Please breathe!" But Lawrence had breathed his last breath. "No, no, Lawrence, you said you wouldn't die. I talked you into coming with me, and I wrote and promised Ma I would keep you safe." Tears etched dirty trails down Johnny's cheeks as he buried his face in his younger brother's motionless chest.

Aaron put his arms around Johnny, and the two sobbed together. After a few minutes, Johnny sat heavily on the cot and buried his face in his hands. Then he looked up at Aaron and said, "I'm all right now. You go on and get something to eat. I want to stay here with Lawrence for a little while." Aaron nodded and left the brothers alone together. He walked through the camp to the very edge and sat under a tree in silent mourning.

On August 17, Colonel Bradley Johnson told the First Maryland men that their regiment was disbanding. Aaron had heard a rumor that some Confederate politicians in Maryland wanted to lead the regiment and become famous, but he had no idea if there was more to the story. The only way the politicians could carry out such a plan, it was said, was to persuade the secretary of war to disband the regiment and start their own, to be called Second Maryland Infantry Regiment, CSA.

Aaron watched as the state flag, which had flown so bravely in the face of the enemy, was taken out of service. This was the flag they had followed in the heat of battle, the flag brave men had died for, the flag that devoted women had sewn in gratitude to the men who fought for freedom from Union tyranny. The new officers hoped that most First Maryland men would sign on with the new unit, but many refused to stay and fight for politically appointed officers. Instead, most went to join other regiments, and a few sneaked home.

While still debating his own future, Aaron got a letter saying that Joel was soon to be a father. The newest member of the Haskins family would arrive a few weeks after Christmas. For the first time in over a year, Aaron felt real regret for mustering in. *I have to get home. I want see Joel. I want to marry Helen. I want to see her round with our child.*

But Aaron could not run away from the cause for which he had already sacrificed so much. After some deliberation, he and his buddies decided not to join Second Maryland. They considered going home, but most agreed with Aaron. They wanted to fight, but in a different regiment. For several days, they retreated into the Blue Ridge Mountains, camped out, talked of their future, and mourned for Lawrence, who had been buried at Charlottesville.

Johnny almost went home to visit his grieving family but decided against it. He told Aaron and the other three that if he were imprisoned or executed by either the Confederacy or the Union, it would only make it worse for his father and mother. Then, late in August, the five headed north to Winchester and joined a unit named Fifty-Sixth Virginia.

Almost immediately, they learned that that General Lee was going to move the troops across the Potomac to free Maryland from Union control and allow it to be a part of the Confederacy. They bought a newspaper and read General Lee's message:

```
To the People of Maryland:

The people of the Confederate States have
long watched with the deepest sympathy the
wrongs and outrages that have been inflicted
upon you. They have seen with profound
indignation their sister State deprived of
every right and reduced to the position of
a conquered province. Under the pretense
of supporting the Constitution, but in
violation of its most valuable provisions,
your citizens have been arrested and
imprisoned upon no charge and contrary to
all forms of law.
```

Believing that the people of Maryland possessed a spirit too lofty to submit to such a government, the people of the South have long wished to aid you in throwing off the foreign yoke, to enable you again to enjoy the inalienable rights of freemen and restore independence and sovereignty to your State.

In obedience to this wish, our army has come among you, and is prepared to assist you with the power of its arms, in regaining the rights, of which you have been despoiled.

R. E. Lee, General Commanding

Aaron was thrilled to the core. "Now we'll free Maryland and run Lincoln out of Washington. The Confederate States of America will be an independent nation!"

The newspaper printed Maryland's state song—a new, patriotic version. Aaron stood at attention, and his clear baritone rang with purpose:

> The despot's heel is on thy shore,
> His torch is at the temple door,
> Avenge the patriotic gore
> That flecked the streets of Baltimore,
> Maryland! My Maryland!

> Dear mother! Burst thy tyrant's chain,
> Virginia should not call in vain,
> She meets her sisters on the plain—
> "Sic semper!" 'tis the proud refrain
> That baffles minions back again,
> Maryland! My Maryland!

I hear the distant thunder-hum,
The old line's bugle, fife, and drum,
She is not dead, nor deaf, nor dumb—
Huzza! She spurns the Northern scum!
She breathes! She burns! She'll come! She'll come!
Maryland! My Maryland!

At home, fear had come in full force. Everyone knew General Lee had crossed the Potomac and that Union troops were amassing to drive out the enemy. A major battle was brewing.

On Saturday evening, Fannie made an unusual request. "Glen, could we go to the Dunker Church tomorrow? I know this may seem strange, but with the war threatening so close, I would just feel comforted to be there."

Glen made no argument. A perceptive man, he admired his wife's sensitivity. He knew that she would gain comfort from visiting a church that stood for many of her Quaker values, including the love of God's creation, and the disdain for destroying sacred human lives—even enemies.'

The family dressed simply and walked to the little white church. As the sun filtered through the windows, they tried to settle into the spirit of the meeting and worship the Prince of Peace, whom the world had made into a god of war. She remembered that as a child, she had squirmed on the wooden benches but managed to sit silently with the special First Day dolls they carried to Quaker meeting. The dolls were soft and made no sound as they brushed the pews or floor. As she grew up, she had always loved sitting quietly, waiting to hear the inward voice of Jesus.

Although the Dunker manner of worship was different, she loved the Mumma family and the other brothers and sisters who shared her peaceable convictions. Yet whenever she tried to hear Jesus, the artillery on South Mountain intervened. It thundered like a distant storm about to erupt, one that might tear their whole world apart.

She prayed that the battle would not come near their home and that God would send his angels to protect Aaron. Yet she felt ashamed, knowing that if the battle did not come here, it would come near someone else's home. Why would God protect her family while another mother's house was destroyed and her loved ones killed?

Fannie could not know how close the battle was. She would have been shocked had she realized that Aaron was a part of it. That very evening, his Fifty-Sixth Virginia unit lost half its eighty men in a battle at Boonsboro, only seven miles away.

CHAPTER 9

Sharpsburg, September 15, 1862

A layer of mist covered the Haskins farm, and the light of dawn turned the vapor to a bright white that shrouded the barn. Joel hesitated, taking in the beauty of sunrise. He then went to milk the cows and once again enjoyed his little sister Kylie's kitten, Fuzzy, who stood on her hind legs and feasted on the warm milk he squirted into her mouth.

In those quiet moments, Joel sensed the unease and guilt that had become a part of his life. Many times, he had felt detested by neighbor parents whose sons were risking their lives. Some had given theirs. Hardest of all was to see his own father's reaction when their neighbors bragged about their heroic sons.

Joel leaned his head against Bessy. The fighting had been fierce, and now Robert E. Lee was on the march again, this time in Maryland, right in his own backyard. Where was his twin cousin? Joel heard the rumble of cannons in the distance. The fighting was drawing nearer and nearer, and each day he had to struggle with what he should do.

Can the Rebels force the Union to let Maryland secede? Or are the federal troops strong enough to keep Maryland in the Union even though it is a slave state?

He knew that Union troops had driven the Confederates off South Mountain, toward Sharpsburg. Several ragged Rebel soldiers had stopped by his home, begging for food, and the women had taken pity.

The Haskins men had discussed the frightening problem the day before. They heard that many Sharpsburg farmers were going to evacuate, so they sent Joel to cousin Obadiah's farm fifteen miles away to see if the family could stay there until the threat of battle passed. He returned with the assurance that Obadiah would welcome them.

Family members gathered their most valued belongings and loaded the wagon. Chelsea shushed her sister Kylie, who begged to take her kitten, Fuzzy, and told her to sit in the wagon with her twin brother, Kylan. With a sigh, their sister Grayce packed the last of the fine china and then hid it in the darkest recesses of the cellar. She handled it carefully, knowing it had been brought from England by Grandma's grandma.

Joel helped Grandma onto the wagon. She settled herself, straightened her bonnet, and gave Joel a wrinkled smile as he climbed to the buckboard. Everyone was soon ready, and with a "Geddup" and a flick of the reins, Joel started Babe and Butch, the two heavy draft horses.

As the wagon pulled away, Amy and Fannie waved good-bye before returning to their work. Along with Glen, Robert, and the slaves, they were staying behind to finish securing things as much as possible. Joel would come back for them after settling the rest of the family at Obadiah's. Robert and Glen stood and waved as the wagon passed them in a clearing. They were burying the family's money in small parcels throughout the farm. Robert dug the small holes, and Glen marked their placement on a crude map.

The wagon reached its destination before noon. Joel had dreaded seeing Obadiah, knowing the war hero considered him a coward for not mustering in. Now his fears were confirmed as the old man met him with a floppy handshake and a pointed "It's nice to see you here, Joel, with all the other womenfolk." Joel forced a pained smile and a mild "Hello."

Joel took Grandma's hand and slowly assisted her from the wagon. She winced but smiled when she touched the ground. For a moment, she stood before Joel, looking up into his eyes, and then she lifted a gnarled hand to his cheek and murmured, "You're a good man, Joel. I know it. Don't you worry about him." Then she turned and walked into the house with the elegance of a queen.

Joel touched his face, caught unaware by the tender moment from someone he loved dearly. After unloading the wagon, he joined Obadiah's son, Daniel.

"We're glad to put you up, but we're sorry that it looks like the battle will be around Sharpsburg," Daniel said, his dark eyes gazing off into the distance.

"Well, I'd better get on my way," Joel said. "I need to get the other load back here before sundown." As Joel was leaving, Obadiah hobbled out and handed him an article from a church journal. "Read this, young man. It might cure what ails you."

He scanned the title: "Piety and Patriotism: The Demand of the Times, Sanctioned and Enjoined by Christ." A Baptist minister in New Jersey had delivered the sermon. Joel assured Obadiah that he would read it on his way home and tucked it into his pocket. About halfway, he eyed a grove of trees and decided to rest his team for a few minutes. He picked a plum, sat down, and scanned the sermon from the Union minister.

We are called to a high and holy patriotism. God summons us to it …

Remember that to be at a bayonet's point is as nothing, compared with being brought into collision with the mighty volleys of God's hot wrath, and that this righteous indignation shall surely fall upon the disobedient.

Joel understood the message but wondered whether failure to join the Union army would really bring God's wrath.

Christ is our example in citizenship … He, then, who said unto his disciple, "Put up again thy sword into his place," now bids the South to submit unconditionally. And when he adds, "All they that take the sword shall perish with the sword," he but foretells the doom of that same South.

Joel thought this verse was a call for peace, not war. Still, he wondered, *Is it really true that the South, which this pastor thinks started the war, was disobeying God's command and that Southerners will perish because they used the sword?* The sermon ended with a hymn—a call to submit completely to God's will in defense of the United States of America:

O, what a joy, with God to fight, His holy truth defending, assured that we are in the right, that wrong's dread power is ending.

Joel climbed onto the buckboard and continued toward home. As he turned into the barnyard, he wondered why the chickens were making such a racket.

He stopped in front of the wide barn door, perplexed. It was cracked open several inches. He approached warily. Was it possible that some soldiers had sneaked inside to steal a horse or gear? Then he chuckled to himself. *How silly of me. It must be Gabe and Nattie's boy; he's been scurrying around in here the past week, chasing that litter of kittens around the stalls.* He smiled, pleased that he had ambushed poor Carl. He slipped through the door and called, "Carl, where are you, you little rascal?" He heard rustling from the direction of the third stall and tiptoed toward it, ready to act scared when the slave boy burst out at him.

His eyes slowly adjusted to the shadows, and his ears picked up the slight sound of scuffling. As he approached the stall, he made out a curious shape leaning against the wall. It was a rifle! The blood in his veins turned to ice as he grabbed the weapon. Peering anxiously into the dim light, he saw a large, gray-uniformed man holding something against the wall.

As the intruder turned, Joel felt cold terror. It was Amy! The burly, bearded man was holding Amy inside the dark stall, pushing her against the wall, clasping her mouth shut with his large hand.

Joel saw Amy's fear-struck eyes and screamed in rage. The Rebel let her drop and raised trembling hands as he took a step away. Joel was seized by a blinding rage; his muscles shook as he raised and cocked the rifle and then aimed it at the intruder's heaving gray chest. His finger squeezed the metal trigger. The roar echoed in the silence of the barn. Joel felt the gun kick against his shoulder, and he saw panic in the man's evil eyes as a scarlet rose blossomed on his chest and spattered over the barn wall behind him.

The assailant fell, screaming, squirming, and clutching at his chest. Then he jerked violently, gasped, and lay still. Blood stained the fresh straw, pooling red on the floor around him.

Amy sat hunched in the corner, her hands covering her face. A mournful sound emerged from her throat. Joel ran to her and knelt down; he wrapped his arms around her and pressed her close, their baby nestled safely between them. She clung to him like a lost child. "Joel, he had his hands on me. I fought him off the best as I could, but he … he …"

"It's all right, Amy. It's all right." Amy only sobbed harder as he picked her up from the ground. He gave the dead monster one last glance, headed for the door, and carried her outside. She clung to him and wept on his shoulder. Before he had gone far, Fannie, who had heard the shot, came running across the bridge.

"What is it, Joel? What happened?" Fannie scurried along beside Joel, throwing glances between his face and his sobbing wife.

With a small shake of his head, he mumbled, "It'll be all right."

Joel carried the sobbing Amy into the living room, placed her on the couch, and then knelt by her side. Fannie gently stroked her back while Joel related the basics in a deadened voice.

Fannie grew pale. After glancing at Amy, who rocked forward and backward with her arms clasped around her knees, she suggested that Joel heat bathwater and get fresh clothes from their cabin. Soon back, he put the clothes in Fannie's hands, placed the kettle on the hook over the fire, and then strode out the door.

Amy sat staring at her bloodied skirt. Fannie understood the need for the young woman to distance herself from the terror she had just experienced. She quickly removed Amy's clothes.

"Burn them," Amy said softly. Fannie obeyed. The clothing caught quickly, causing the fire to rise up and consume the rapist's blood forever. Fannie grabbed a quilt that hung over the couch and wrapped it around the young woman's trembling shoulders.

Outside, Joel trembled as well. He paced the porch, his mouth jerking. He then stood, gripping the railing with all his strength, still feeling faint. He sank down on the steps and covered his face.

Later, Amy came out of the house in clothes that looked new and clean. Joel drew her close, and with his arms supporting her, they walked slowly to the wagon. Robert was already seated on the buckboard, and Glen stood nearby, waiting to help his wife. He caught Fannie's eye as she trailed behind the couple. Before climbing into the wagon, Fannie leaned against her husband. He put his arms around her and kissed the top of her head.

Joel placed Amy on the wagon seat and sat next to her. She nestled into his shoulder and closed her eyes as he drove the team. Gabe and Nattie watched silently from their positions in the back. For most of the trip, the clopping of horses' hooves and the ominous thunder from cannon fire on South Mountain were the only sounds they heard.

Joel comforted Amy that night, stroking her hair until she fell asleep on a dampened pillow. He fidgeted for another hour. The day's horrors reached to his soul. His wife had almost been raped. He had killed a man.

He disentangled himself from Amy's arms, slipped to the door, and stepped outside. Looking up at the moon and stars, he shivered in the vastness of the clear, cool September night. He stumbled to the railing and vomited. He had done what he could to protect his wife, but now he was haunted by her fear and by the look in the dying man's eyes. Wiping his mouth with water from the pump, he took a deep breath, forced himself to shove his suffering soul deep inside, and returned to his wife.

What else could I have done? Any decent man would protect his wife. It was a long night that produced little sleep.

CHAPTER 10

Haskins Home, September 19

The buckboard bumped and clattered over the rutted road leading back to Sharpsburg, where Robert knew, based on information from horse riders, that a terrible fight had taken thousands of lives. News of the battle filled him with dread and concern for Aaron. Abigail had become as quiet as he'd ever seen her, and he knew better than to push her to reveal her emotions. Those would come in time. He looked over at Glen. "I don't think things will ever be the same," he said, exhaling slowly and shaking his head.

Glen nodded. "The man who stopped by Obadiah's made it sound like it's terrible all around Sharpsburg. Too bad he didn't know how it was down along the creek."

The Haskins men sat on the buckboard, with Obadiah following in his wagon. The women and children filled both, with the slave family sitting in the rear. Joel watchfully led the way, mounted on Buck, with Smokey and Obadiah's mount trailing on lead ropes.

"From what the man said," Robert said, "the Union pretty much ran the Rebels out. I'll bet they forced them back across the Potomac somewhere around Shepherdstown or Williamsport. But the river's high. It's possible that they couldn't cross and the Union captured them. Anyway, the area is still controlled by the Union, as I understand it. I suppose the cannons we hear are just mopping up."

As they approached Sharpsburg, Joel's stomach tightened. He saw people looting empty houses. *Oh my. Oh no. Have they been in ours?* Then he began to see bodies—dead human bodies. *Oh, how horrible. How horrible.* He saw hundreds of people hauling food, caring for wounded, and burying dead. Over the horses' hooves Julia's singsong voice asked, "Mama, what's that bad smell? It hurts my eyes and crinkles my nose."

"I know, I know," Abigail said, holding a handkerchief to her own nose and turning her daughter's head.

Willie piped up. "It smells like when that raccoon died under the house and we didn't find it for a week." Abigail was thankful that the temperature was only seventy degrees instead of ninety, as would have been likely if the battle had been in the summer.

Stifling the urge to spur his horse and run, Joel forced himself to look at the carnage. It was truly beyond his comprehension how people could kill one another like this, but the thought vanished quickly as he remembered the man who had tried to rape Amy.

Bibles, letters, playing cards, and haversacks littered the front yards of their Sharpsburg neighbors. Guns, caissons, and wagons were strewn haphazardly. Willie watched two mounds in the distance as they grew larger and finally called out, "Are those people?" Sure enough, the humps became piles of bodies with bloated bellies and blackened skins. Abigail wanted to put a dark curtain between the children and the slaughter, but she could not. She had no way to protect them from the harvest of war. Willie sank into silence.

"Mama, those men are all … dead, aren't they, Mama?" asked Julia in a hushed voice as she scooted closer to her mother.

"Yes, Julia. They were killed in the battle." Much as she wanted to, she couldn't keep from telling her daughter the truth.

"Mama, I want to go home," Julia pleaded, tucking herself into her mother's arm.

"Yes, we are going home. But it might look different. You're going to have to be a brave girl." She gently caressed the small head.

A wagonload of wounded men emerged from the woods. Amy gasped as she recognized her twelve-year-old friend driving. He sat up straight on the bench, clutching the reins of the two large workhorses.

"Levi, what are you doing?" she called, standing and bracing herself against the side of the wagon.

"I'm driving this wagon. I'm taking these men to Mr. Middlekauf's house. They've made it into a hospital."

Amy was horrified. Boys as young as Levi, and men as old as her father, lay in the wagon. Most looked near death.

As Levi drove away, the family entered the woods north of Sharpsburg and saw among the bodies a leg that had been blown off at the knee lying several feet from its owner. The cornstalks in the Millers' field had been shorn by bullets and artillery shells. The field was a virtual harvest of death.

The younger children now hid their eyes. Willie bit his tongue because he thought it might not be proper to talk of dead men. After three minutes, he could wait no longer.

"Are these men colored, like Gabe? I didn't know that they were who was fighting! And why are their tummies so fat?"

The adults exchanged helpless glances. Then Robert said, "No, they were white. But when a person dies, strange things happen to his body. After a while, the hot sun makes the dead man's skin look dark, and his belly gets all bloated." He tried to swat the flies that swarmed around the wagon. The flies preferred the defenseless targets on the ground but also pestered the living.

As they passed, Joel could see his mother was shocked by the changes in the Dunker Church since the family had attended only five days earlier. It had become a shell-littered makeshift hospital. So had the Lutheran church down the road. Moving onto Lower Bridge Road, they passed the Sherrick and Otto farms, noting that someone had torn down the fences, trampled the fields, and stripped the orchards.

Joel slowed the team as they passed the churches, thinking of the sermons he had heard urging him to fight. *Maybe I would have gone if I had known how terrible the Yankees are to do something like this!* Then, in revulsion, he thought of the Rebel who had attacked Amy.

As the family rounded the bend above the stone bridge, an audible gasp arose. Their farm was strewn with bodies and covered with refuse. The buildings had shell scars and blackened spots where fire had singed the wood.

The wagons halted. Grandma surveyed the scene with silent horror. The house William had built for her was now wracked with shell holes. Her beautiful maple table, the wedding gift her husband had fashioned over fifty years ago, was now on the lawn, serving as a bloody butcher's stand where man and limb were separated.

There was no hope of denying it—for the Haskins family, the war had come home. Try as she might, Abigail couldn't keep from wondering, *Was Aaron in the battle? Is he one of these bloated bodies?*

Joel guided Buck through the carnage to a man in a blood-smeared apron. "Excuse me, sir, this is our home." The surgeon, who had laid Robert and Abigail's front door across two barrels for an operating table, replied, "We regret having to use your house like this, but we had to make it into a hospital. We're serving all the wounded, both Union soldiers and Rebels. Can anyone in your family help us? Most of these men are in rough shape."

Joel said, "We'll do what we can. We can start burying men, if that'll suit you. The womenfolk will need to take care of the children and my grandma."

The doctor looked into Joel's twitching face and gave a brisk nod, his eyes saying, "Thank you."

Joel returned to the wagons. "We need to start burying these bodies. First, though, we have to find a safe place for the women and children. Both houses are full of wounded soldiers."

Fannie broke in. "Son, I'll help these doctors. I don't know much about gunshot wounds, but I've nursed sick babies and a sick husband, and I'd like to help."

Robert said, "Amy, I think that you two should take Grandma and the children to your cabin so they won't have to see any more of this. Children, maybe you can convince Uncle Obadiah to stay for a while and tell you about when he was your age."

The group went to the new cabin, now marred. Amy trembled as she looked into her house. Someone had ransacked her cupboards. The floors were strewn with glass and debris. Her beautiful rocking chair now had a splintered hole. She fingered it slowly and then climbed the ladder and peeked into the bedroom loft. Even the feather tick was missing.

She wanted to cry out in despair but kept control. Coming home filled her mind with the helplessness and fear she had experienced three days earlier. She couldn't keep from glancing across the creek to the barn and feeling panic well up inside her once again. Burrowing her face into her husband's comforting chest, she took a deep breath and whispered, "Please, God, help us! Is nowhere safe?"

"I love you, Amy," Joel said, caressing her cheek. "We can make it through this."

She clung to him and nodded. "I love you, Joel."

Joel found several kerchiefs to tie around each man's nose and mouth, and then the men returned to the surgeons for further instructions.

"Sir, we're ready to help now. I'm Robert Haskins."

"Much obliged, Mr. Haskins. I'm Dr. Jacob Schleichter, and this is Dr. Oliver Randolph. We're surgeons in the United States Army. If you would be so kind as to start by burying the bodies that are lying out on the piles of straw and then get to burying those limbs, we'd appreciate it."

Then the doctor added, "There are wounded still out there, and we need to get to them. While you men are doing those things, I'll reamputate some limbs of men we amputated yesterday. Some of the stumps have gotten gangrene and need to be cut off higher up."

The men went to work. They were surprised to find that many corpses weren't wearing shoes, and other valuables had been stolen too.

Seeing his father, Joel asked, "What's Ma doing?"

"She and Abigail are trying to put both houses in some sort of order. There are men wounded in almost every way imaginable, and they're in about every room of both houses and all over the floors."

"Are the children all right?"

"Yes, I think so, considering. Most of them are with Obadiah in our cabin. Thank God he's so good at telling stories to distract them. I hope he doesn't tell his war stories, though. What about Chelsea and Grayce?"

"We told them to get buckets of water from the creek and dipper it into men's mouths. They all seem very thirsty, and since the girls are a bit older, I think they'll be all right."

Robert was on the lawn, helping the doctors, when he heard his wife scream. "Robert, Robert! Oh Robert, come here!" He rushed inside.

Tears ran down Abigail's cheeks as she held high a piece of paper. "Oh Robert, Robert! This is from Aaron! He was here while we were gone." Trembling, Robert stood close to his wife as they read the note from their son.

Papa and Mama, I'm part of the army that is going to make Maryland free. It looks like the big battle will be right here, around Sharpsburg and maybe our farm. In fact, I went up to my room and looked out the window and across the creek, and there are bunches of Union soldiers getting ready to fight. I guess you thought so too and left to avoid it. I wish I could have seen you, but maybe it is better for you to be away if the battle is right here. I love you lots and look forward to finally getting this thing over and coming home to stay.

I have only been here a few minutes, but I did one other important thing. I know the little stone you gave me before I left came from the Antietam. Well, I took it down to the creek and held it underwater. Joel would laugh at me and think I was trying to baptize it. Well, maybe I was! I've carried it ever since you gave to me, and I just thought it would enjoy having a minute or

two in the creek again. Now it's back in my
pocket, and I'll carry it until I get home
again. I have to go now. With love,

Aaron

Robert and Abigail held each other close and then reread the letter.
They both felt great joy that their son had been home. Each felt great
fear about what might have happened to him in the battle. Was he one
of the bodies that were so prevalent on the farm and in the town?

The men set about to do their repulsive work. Joel and Gabe
dragged the bodies from the barn and lined them up. Glen and Robert
dug a long trench about six feet wide and eighteen inches deep. They
worked silently, preparing graves for young men they had never met and
would never know. They couldn't help but think of the boys' families,
wondering what it would be like to learn that Aaron had been buried in
some far-off place by men who didn't even know his name. Even worse,
suppose he was being buried someplace in Sharpsburg by neighbors
who didn't realize who he was? Or what if he was one of the bodies
they were burying right here on the farm where he grew up? Would
they ever know?

At first, the smell made the men retch and gag, but eventually their
minds grew numb to what their hands were forced to do. On and on
they buried. When they finished, they began searching for wounded
men to bring to the front yard for the doctors to attend when they had
time. Near the creek bank, they heard a low moan. Following the noise,
they found a boy who could not have been eighteen years old. Joel knelt
beside him and tried to give him a drink of water. The boy sputtered
as the cool liquid passed through his cracked lips and mumbled, "I'm
gonna die. Will you tell my father that I love him? My mama's dead.
I'm Hugh Harrison, Eleventh Connecticut."

Joel swallowed a lump in his throat and lied. "You're not gonna die,
Hugh. You just wait right here, and we'll get you some help." Every inch
of Joel's body yearned to start running and never stop, but he forced

himself to look calm. Joel laid a reassuring hand on the boy's lone arm and listened.

"We had to cross open ground with the Rebels shooting us. I followed Captain Griswold across this bridge." He sputtered a weak, wracking cough. "He was ordered to cross this creek. He was hit over and over, but he never gave up. Write his family too, please?" With this plea, Hugh Harrison followed Captain Griswold once more, this time into eternity. Joel jerked his hand from the young man's shoulder as if death were contagious.

Joel and Gabe completed their search and then went back to Robert and Glen. Joel asked permission to look for Aaron. He went through Sharpsburg and then to the sunken Hog Trough Road. A fire blazed, and the putrid smell intensified. He could see that it was a pile of dead horses and covered his nose with a second handkerchief.

At the farm, Fannie was directing Chelsea, Irene, and Devin, whose jobs were to fetch water for all who wanted it. She asked the girls to find some paper and pencils and write letters for the men who seemed to be nearest death's door—or, if not letters, at least their names and regiments for their grieving families.

Fannie carried a kettle of hot water in one hand and a pail of cool water in the other, with a rag in each container. She went to those in the most pain and washed their bodies with her warm cloth, removing caked blood and mud. Then she swabbed their faces with cool water. The men looked at her in gratitude. Those able to speak thanked her, and many called her Mother. She smiled, trying to give each young man the attention his own mother would give if she were there.

As they returned to Joel and Amy's cabin, Joel told them of his grisly discoveries, "There are bodies everywhere, especially near Hog Trough Road. It's awful. So many men are piled up that, in some places, they are two and three deep. A woman was praying for the 'dead of this bloody lane,' and I can't think of a better name for it—it's just a bloody lane."

The setting sun brought a crimson sky over the bloody land as Joel went to check the barn. He found it hard to go near where the Rebel had attacked Amy, but he felt he must.

When he entered the barn, his eyes immediately sought the place the Rebel had died choking on his own blood. He walked to the spot, stepped over the darkened patch of straw, and viewed a splintered hole in the wall. The memory came flooding back—the crushing discovery, the red rage, the gun's roar. He could still taste the gunpowder in his mouth.

Joel was so completely lost in the vivid horror that he almost didn't notice the sound. Shaking his head, he realized it was real—a whimper, a faint sobbing.

Warily, he went around to the back of the barn. There was little Kylie, seated on the ground, crying softly. In her lap, she held a small bundle. Her knees were drawn up tightly, her bare toes peeking from beneath the hem of her dress.

"What is it, Kylie? What happened?" He knelt beside the grieving child. With shaking hands, she pulled back the scrap of cloth. Beneath it was the bloody and lifeless body of her kitten, Fuzzy.

Joel could say nothing. He sat down in the dirt beside his little sister, put his arm around her, and shared her grief.

Kylie held the smallest victim of the war. When her eyes finally dried, Joel walked her to the family; then he came back and got his shovel. He had one more grave to dig before he slept.

CHAPTER 11

Decision Time for Joel, October 1862

Joel rode against the October wind, trying to ignore the mutilated landscape around him. It seemed as if the day the family had returned to the farm after the terrible battle had been only hours ago, so real was the carnage, but the reality was that the days had slipped into weeks.

His ears whistled with a faint sound, almost like Aaron's signal. His heart longed to hear it again. He stopped Buck, put his hands to his lips, and blasted out the cousins' call, even though he knew Aaron was hundreds of miles away. It was foolish, but it made him feel better.

As he rode along, Joel saw the wasteland around him—the mass graves, the devastated farmhouses, the desecrated churches. Once again, he felt sickness rising from the pit of his stomach.

When he approached Mr. Arthur's farm, a scruffy shepherd dog greeted him noisily. Its barking drew Joel's teacher from the barn. "Afternoon, Joel. Pleasure to see you."

"It seems you have a new dog," Joel said, eyeing the dubious canine. Mr. Arthur shrugged.

"He adopted me as lord and master and now presumes to encroach on my generosity. He has proven a decent guard, albeit one that barks at anything, whether it be friend or foe. Socrates is living in protest of his presence, but I believe they will come to terms in due time."

Joel laughed as he tied Buck to the hitching post. Finding something humorous was so unusual that he greatly enjoyed the moment.

Mr. Arthur led the way up the porch as a whirlwind of leaves swirled around their legs. The new dog followed close at their heels and managed to squeeze into the house. Mr. Arthur bustled over to the fire and added two more logs. The flames leaped happily.

"I know there was a lot of damage to your farm."

Joel's coffee hand clinched. His mind clouded again with the smell of dead men and horses. "It was terrible. I can hardly describe it."

"Do you know whether Aaron was in the battle?"

"Yes, he was, but he's all right. We got a note from him last week. It was short but said he was with his unit in Virginia."

Mr. Arthur noticed that Joel's eyes shone with relief.

"I helped bury a lot of the dead men. I was so scared. So many just lay there, and every time I turned one over, my stomach knotted, knowing the face could be Aaron's. Sometimes I thought for a second that it was Aaron. I can't explain it. Each time I looked at a face, I was tense, expecting a terrible kick in the belly. Then, each time, there was relief when I realized it wasn't him. So I moved on to another body that might be Aaron, and then another and another. I thought it would never end. I saw so many dead men. I tried to stop, but I just had to look at one more in case it was him."

"I'm so glad Aaron is all right. And how are *you* doing?"

"Well, Mr. Arthur, that's really why I came today. You know it's been hard—not going with Aaron, and being away from him. A lot of people think I'm a coward. It's really hard on my father."

Joel paused for several seconds, his finger twisting into his jacket. His teacher could see the deep emotion in this young man, one of the best students he had taught.

"I'm thinking about joining the Union army. I wonder if you can help me decide. I've been thinking about this proclamation of emancipation the government has announced. I have to admit that I kind of think slaves should be free, at least down south on the plantations. Yet a lot of people like Aaron say we should fight to keep our freedom to own slaves, and to protect them. But doesn't this proclamation mean that the Union is fighting for the freedom of the slaves? Are both sides fighting for freedom—one side to free Negroes from slavery, and the other side for freedom to own property without having it taken away by the government?"

Mr. Arthur filled Joel's coffee mug. The steam spiraled like the young man's despair. After a few moments, the teacher responded.

"I think it's basically true in every war—both sides are protecting their own rights and freedoms. It's a real problem, isn't it? If Negroes are fully human, then the North seems right, but if they are property, the South is right."

Mr. Arthur took the coffeepot to Joel and filled his cup again. "Look at our three wars. In the American Revolution, we were fighting to preserve freedoms the colonists had been given much earlier but which seemed threatened. Yet today, Canada has as many freedoms as we do, and it looks like they will soon become independent without fighting. The War of 1812 was said to be for free trade and sailors' rights, but those issues had been settled before we went to war. In that case, a lot of Americans wanted war because they thought it would give us a chance to get part of Canada, but that didn't work. The 1848 war was to take land from Mexico, so if anybody was fighting for freedom, it was our enemy, who lost half their country. And look at the wars with the Indians. Those battles weren't for our freedom. They were to take away the Indians' land and freedoms. I'm suspicious when people say we should fight for freedom."

Joel studied the dancing flames as Mr. Arthur stoked them again. The heat flared from the embers and caressed his face. "I wonder if President Lincoln thinks the slaves will find out and begin to fight for their own freedom."

"Ah, yes, Joel. I think that's his hope. It would devastate the Southern plantation owners if their labor just got up and walked away or actually rebelled against their masters."

Joel sat a few moments, lost in thought. Then, his face twitching, he said, "It seems to me that the proclamation will just encourage the slave owners to fight."

"Ah, yes, I agree. In fact, I read that the Confederate Congress has already responded, saying that if Lincoln doesn't back off emancipation, the South will imprison any US officers they capture, and if any of them are commanding Negro troops, the punishment will be death."

After a moment, Joel responded, "I think I see what Lincoln wants. He wants to make the war a holy cause about slavery, and he wants a big slave revolt. If Lincoln wins and forces the Southerners back into the Union without their slaves, the abolitionists will demand that the slave owners *never* get their property back—ever! Can you imagine?"

The two talked for a few more minutes, and then Mr. Arthur said, "I have to finish some chores. Would you like to come with me?" Joel nodded and followed the older man outside as Socrates and the new dog led the way. Arthur's small red barn housed two horses and a few cattle. Joel pitched some hay and then went to the chicken coop and delivered the mash and gathered the eggs.

The morning air refreshed him, but he still had many questions. He wasn't sure how he felt about the slaves being freed, about no longer having Gabe and Nattie to do a lot of the work. And where would they go if they were free? Joel knew they loved being with the Haskins family, but if the law said they were free, would they be pressured into leaving? If they left, who would take care of them?

Joel again addressed his teacher. "Mr. Arthur, what do you think about the future of slavery?"

"I don't think it'll last long. The war has really brought the issue to a head. But I think slavery would have ended soon anyway. England freed slaves for the entire empire almost thirty years ago. If the Southern states hadn't been pressured by their own fears and their exaggeration of the abolitionists, a compromise might have been worked out—something with gradual emancipation, with compensation to the slave owners.

There wouldn't have been a war, because there wouldn't have been a cause for one."

As their conversation about slavery died down, Joel asked the new dog's name. Mr. Arthur responded that it was Sophocles, eliciting the following response from Joel: "How fitting. With a cat named Socrates and a dog named Sophocles, you have a matched set—a Greek farmyard."

The teacher quickly responded, "My goats, Willie and Billie, just had a youngin'. Guess what they named him? Aristophanes. But he bleats to the name Stophanies."

Joel laughed. "Socrates, Sophocles, and Stophanies. You certainly have a philosophical farm."

Arthur smiled in return.

Joel returned to the central question. "I do think there will be a real problem when the war is over if the Union wins. Who will take care of the freed slaves? Gabe and Nattie depend on us."

Again Joel paced, piecing together the new ideas that were tumbling one upon the other. "Do you think slaves could take care of themselves? If Lincoln frees them, he will have to give them land or figure out a way to make jobs for them or something. There's plenty of land out west. Maybe the freed Negroes could have some sort of Homestead Act, like was just passed for white men."

Mr. Arthur enjoyed his student's logic. "Something will have to happen if the slaves are freed. They'll need help. You have some good ideas, but not many white people will want to do much for freed slaves if the Union wins the war. Most whites are willing to spend millions fighting this war, and some even rejoice that the purpose may become emancipation, but I would be surprised if many of those same people would be willing to give the Negroes a handout like whites are getting in the Homestead Act."

"Maybe," Joel said, "but I think that if Negroes were given land and taught to manage it, they could do it with some help and training." He paused a moment and then exclaimed, "You know, it wouldn't have to be land. Why not free the slaves and give them training for all kinds of jobs?" For Joel, this was a moment of delight, a pinnacle experience. The slaves should be freed—even Nattie and Gabe!

An hour later, Joel rode home, his mind racing and his belly sloshing coffee. As usual, he felt his teacher had provided some good answers and a feast of food for thought. The war now had a real purpose.

When he got home, Joel was delighted to learn that the family had received a long letter from Aaron—that is, until he read the last paragraph.

Joel, I still can't understand why you didn't join in the fight. We needed you. You've sat at home for a year and a half while I have been risking my life for you and Southern independence. I'm sorry if this sounds like I'm balling you out, but you should be balled out. You're being stupid and cowardly.

It had been a hard day for Joel. His conversation with Mr. Arthur had confirmed what was becoming a strong opinion: the war had a purpose, but its purpose was to free the slaves, not to keep them in bondage. Now his best friend had derided him for not fighting to keep slavery. Yes, it was a hard day. How he wished the United States had freed all the slaves in 1833, as the British Empire had.

The next morning, he went to see his mother, whose counsel he had not sought since he'd rescued Amy. He found her settled in a rocking chair by the fire.

"Look, Joel! I'm helping Amy get clothing ready for your baby." She held up her knitting needles, and he saw that a small boot was forming. Joel stepped closer to examine it with pleasure. He then turned to his mother, the anchor in his life, and said that he had been discussing Lincoln's Emancipation Proclamation with Mr. Arthur and was considering joining the Union army. He knew this was a terrible blow for his mother. She just sat and squeezed his hand in dismay.

Still, Joel knew that his mother's family was against slavery. He had heard harsh rumors that her Pennsylvania relatives had helped to hide slaves who were stolen from their owners and moved to Canada, but no one had confronted Fannie about it.

"Joel, I need to tell you something I've never told anyone—ever."

He was suddenly unsure whether he wanted to hear this revelation. It sounded as if some kind of confession was coming, and he could hardly imagine his mother having anything to confess.

"You know my family back home is Quaker, and I'm still a Quaker at heart, even though I chose to marry your father. At that time, he was going with me to Friends Meeting, but of course that all changed when Grandpa died and we moved here. But we Quakers believe Jesus wants us to do good for our fellow human beings, including Negroes. None of God's children should be reduced to slavery. My parents had a hard time accepting my marriage into a family that owned slaves. Of course, your father was hoping to stay in Pennsylvania and farm without slaves, but when Grandpa died and we had to move here, we just about had to accept being slave owners. It was hard for me, and I think it hurt your father too. At least, I could tell he felt bad for me. But he was part of a family that owned slaves, and I had become part of that family. I either had to accept slavery or leave my husband, and I couldn't possibly do that. We've had only two adult slaves, but it's still been hard for me. We are the kindliest masters, and we treat Nattie and Gabe almost as if they were free, but they aren't free."

Joel could see the distress on his mother's face. In their closeness all these years, she had hidden this secret in order to keep peace in the family, since there was nothing she could do about it. For the first time in his life, Joel became the parent, squeezing his mother's hand, leaning his head against her, helping to bear her deep burden. After relaxing in the arms of her son, she gulped the agony that filled her throat.

"Nattie and Gabe aren't treated like we treat white people, and I think that's a sin against God. But I can't do anything about it, because those choices aren't up to me. I accept Nattie as if she were white, at least as much as possible. I would even let her come in through the front door if I had my way."

Fannie had a still bigger secret to share. "Nattie and Gabe had never met until the day we bought them and moved them into the cabin together. You know that Quakers have no ordained clergy, and women are accepted equally with men as children of Jesus. Well, one day I asked Nattie and Gabe if they would like to be married. They said they would, so I went into their cabin and performed a marriage ceremony. Gabe said, 'In the presence of the Lord and this Friend, Fannie, I take thee, Nattie, to be my wife as long as we both shall live.' And Nattie repeated the same vows but of course said 'Gabe' and 'husband.' So in Jesus's eyes, they are legally married."

Joel was shocked, but he understood. He had long been aware that his mother was extra kind and loving to the slaves. He was about to respond, when she continued.

"I was glad when I read about the proclamation of emancipation. There's finally a reason for the Union's fighting. War is wrong, and I hope you never fight, but at least this war now has a purpose. If the Union wins, most of the slaves will be free."

Joel could see that for his mother, two issues collided. She would rather have him stay with his decision against war, but a war for freeing slaves might have some justification. He said, "I need to talk to Amy about it, of course, but I may go." No matter how much she had tried to prepare herself for this moment, Fannie shuddered quietly.

"Are you sure, Joel?" Before her courage deserted her, she added, "But do what you have to do. I'll always love you."

Then Fannie told Joel of some cousins named Conner, who lived in Pennsylvania.

"Yesterday we got a letter from the Conners. They mentioned that their son, Charles, is in the Union army and fought in the battle here. He is now stationed over at Harpers Ferry. I hope you don't join the army, but if you feel like you should, maybe you could get into the same regiment Charles is—Seventy-First Pennsylvania, it is called."

She caressed his cheek and said, "Let me pray with you, Joel." He bowed, as he often had, in his mother's love as she prayed that her son would follow Christ's leading, whatever the decision. She prayed, too, that Amy and their baby would be comforted and protected and would always walk with Jesus. She offered a sincere prayer for Nattie and Gabe and their children, including praise to God that they had personally accepted Jesus and were married in His eyes.

After Fannie finished, Joel prayed for God's blessing on his decision and on his life. Then he said, "Thank you, Mama. I know this is hard for you, just like it is for me, maybe even harder."

They stood for a long moment, silently holding one another. "Let God be your guide, Son. I will accept whatever decision you and Amy make."

As her son walked out the door, Fannie sat heavily in her chair. She gazed at the small boot that she had been knitting. How long had it been since she had knitted for her own first baby? Now he was grown, no longer a child she could protect. She knew she must give him to the horror of war if he and Amy felt it was justified. She clasped her hands and bowed her head, giving his safety into the Lord's keeping.

Joel spent time with his father too. Glen was pleased that his son was probably going to become a soldier, but he was dismayed that Joel was taking the Union side. He had been embarrassed for eighteen months that Joel wasn't going to fight. Now he was embarrassed because his son would be fighting on the wrong side. He gave Joel his opinion but again recognized aloud that the decision was not for him.

That evening, Joel and Amy ate barley soup and wheat bread in their cabin. As they chatted about the baby, Joel relished his wife's rosy glow. The firelight glinted off her hair as she sat in her prized rocking chair, which Joel had repaired to almost as good as new. Her hand rested on her growing stomach, and she took Joel's hand and placed it with hers. He grinned, feeling the baby kick.

After the dishes were washed and the bread dough set out to rise, Joel faced the hard moment. As Amy stood by the cabin's lone window, lost in her own thoughts, Joel walked up behind her and turned her into his arms. She snuggled into his broad chest with a contented sigh. "Amy, I need to tell you something."

Amy was no fool. The two had discussed the war several times in the last month, and she knew that when he went to see Mr. Arthur, the decision was imminent. They embraced for a long time, those two frightened souls surrounding the most important one in the world. Finally, Amy raised her head from his shoulder. "I love you, and I'll be here for you when you come home. Think of the baby and me when the war is hard. I'll wait till the day after forever for you to get back," she vowed.

Joel struggled to breathe. "Thank you, Amy. Your love will always be enough." His shaking hands lifted hers to his lips and kissed them gently. Mother, father, and unborn baby shared the bittersweet moment.

The following day, as Joel took his leave, Amy stood on the porch. She pulled her shawl tighter around her shoulders and wiped a tear with the back of her hand. "Here, Joel, I want you to have this." From her apron pocket, she took a picture of herself and a lock of her hair, tied with a green ribbon. Joel pulled out his pocket watch. His tears blurred her picture as, with trembling hands, he placed the hair inside. He snapped the watch shut and put it in his pocket, near his heart. Overwhelmed with tenderness and love for Amy, he caressed her check. *How I will miss her. And our little baby inside!*

Again he crushed her in his arms, easing his intensity only upon remembering the wonderful, fragile treasure that nestled in her body. Then he knelt before her on the porch and placed a gentle kiss on her stomach as a blessing on their child.

After Joel swung into his saddle, Amy laid a hand on his leg as he bent down to kiss her again. She touched his face gently and said but one word: "Forever." Joel straightened in his saddle, "I'll love you forever too. With God's help, I'll come back to you soon, Amy Harris Haskins." With a finger to his hat brim and a nod of the head, he urged Buck toward the bridge. Alongside rode Devin, who would return Buck. Family members waved good-bye.

Amy raised a hand in farewell as her husband rode away. She tried to console her lurching heart with thoughts of the hundreds—no, thousands—of women in both the North and the South who had said good-bye to their men. Down deep, she felt some relief because she no longer would be embarrassed when she was with the many wives whose husbands had gone to war. Yet she knew most of them had husbands fighting on the Rebel side and would shame her anyway. She shivered as the October wind chilled her skin, while grief chilled her heart.

Fannie invited her to her house, but Amy wanted to be alone. Sitting before the fire, she began to sew more clothes for the baby. If anything could fill the awful void left by Joel's absence, it would be their child. "Yes," she mumbled, almost as a prayer, "everything will be all right. I just have to let my husband go for a time."

At that moment, their baby gave a powerful kick, as if vowing to love Daddy forever.

CHAPTER 12

Joel, Seventy-First Pennsylvania, Late 1862

As a new soldier at Harpers Ferry, Joel was delighted to meet his cousin Charles Conner.

"Charles, I'm so glad your family wrote and told us you were in the battle on our farm and that you are stationed in Harpers Ferry. Now that I've joined up, it's great to be with my cousin."

"I'm glad you joined us, Joel. It's good to be with family."

Joel enjoyed his newly discovered cousin as Charles told of his life. His family had moved to Philadelphia from their Pennsylvania farm when he was a toddler, shortly after Joel's parents went to Sharpsburg. The two talked about their common great-grandparents, William and Mary Haskins. Then Charles fascinated Joel with his story of the war.

"When Lincoln called for volunteers, I helped start a militia called the Blue Reserves. We had a fife and drum corps and marched around Philadelphia, rousing men to protect the Constitution of the United States. I will never forget seeing women waving their handkerchiefs, and children throwing their hats into the air. So this regiment, Seventy-First Pennsylvania, had a good beginning."

Several more men emerged from the darkness, drawn by the warmth and conversation. They found spots around the fire, sitting or leaning against the logs, as Charles made the introductions. Joel was delighted to meet his new comrades.

A private named Sam Larkin told about the day he'd mustered in, firelight glinting off his spectacles as he spoke. "I joined right at the time things first started heating up down here—just after the Rebels attacked Fort Sumter. I was a college student when Lincoln called for volunteers to put down the rebellion. It seemed like everybody rallied to the good cause. I'd never seen such excitement, such patriotism—not just on campus but in the whole town, even the whole country. That is, the right-thinking part of the country."

Joel was fascinated as Sam gestured broadly, his voice building. "We held a community meeting in the college chapel. There weren't enough seats, so men stood in the aisles and open doors. You could feel the energy—if someone had struck a match, the air would have caught on fire!" With that, he threw a pinecone into the fire. It popped loudly, and the men laughed.

"One student argued that we should finish school before mustering in. He got hooted down for thinking we should miss the chance to fight for our country and for God. If the room hadn't been so packed, we might have ridden him out of town on a rail."

Sam turned toward the man who sat hunched next to him whittling on a pine branch. "Jim, do you remember a year and a half ago when everyone thought the Rebels would give up and this would be done with before summer was over?" Joel's mind skipped to Aaron.

"Yeah, I thought so too. Pretty stupid, weren't we?"

Sam rubbed the bridge of his nose under his spectacles and said, "Remember how every rich guy in town pitched in a hundred dollars to form our company? All the ladies got together and made gifts for the men who volunteered. They made these white flannel havelocks too, and they gave us little pocketbooks full of needles and thread."

He chuckled. "If we could have caught the Rebs asleep, we would have sewn them up so tight they couldn't have raised their arms to fire a gun." Sam held his arms tightly to his side and struggled to pull them free. "Then again, we might have bled more trying to work those little needles than if the Rebs were shooting at us."

A man named Humphrey began to recall the battles. "The worst was just a couple of months ago at Antietam Creek, over across the Potomac." Joel winced as Humphrey continued. "I heard it was the bloodiest day this country has ever seen. But we stopped the Rebs and sent them back across the Potomac where they belong."

Sam interrupted Joel's thoughts, admitting, "I've been in a half dozen battles, and that was the worst one. But in every battle, I feel this thrill and nausea, both at the same time." He looked around at his friends and asked, "You know what I mean? Has the same thing happened to you? It's like I can't stand it, but I want it. I go into battle, and everything is uncertain. Anything's possible. I could kill a secesh, or I could die at any moment."

Joel didn't know the word *secesh* but then realized it referred to a traitor who had seceded from the Union. He listened nervously as the talkative man said, "The first time I killed a man, I thought I'd never be able to hold a gun in my hands again. But I learned discipline. It's kill or be killed; it's kill a stranger or lose a friend."

The fire died down as, one by one, the men left for the night. Charles's tent mate had recently deserted, providing space for Joel. Charles explained that each man had been issued a shelter half—a piece of canvas about five and a half feet square, with buttons on one side and eyelet holes lining the other. Each pair had made tents by buttoning their pieces together and draping the combined canvas over a ridgepole supported by two rifles that had been thrust, bayonet down, into the ground.

On October 30, the men broke camp. The next evening, Joel and his friends sat around the campfire, where Sam Larkin was spewing his anger. "The whole thing makes me sick! You know what I heard? The colonel said that over fifty men have deserted since the Antietam battle. Fifty cowards! That leaves less than four hundred in Seventy-First Pennsylvania."

"Why did they leave?" Joel asked.

"Some probably left 'cause they're just sick of fightin'. They don't want to go through another Antietam. But most are just chicken and want to go home to their mommies," Nettleton said. "Course, I understand how lonely it can get and how they worry 'bout folks at home. My wife had a baby, and it died 'cause no one was there to help her."

Joel gulped, thinking of Amy and their baby, as Nettleton continued. "I wish I could have been with her, but I'm a soldier. I know my duty, and I'm not leaving like these chicken-hearts." Joel could hear the bitterness in the voice of this grieving man.

"Well, I know why most of them left." Joseph Woods's face flamed like his red hair. "They just weren't going to risk getting killed so Lincoln could turn the niggers loose. But when I entered this army, I took a vow of obedience." Woods raised his right hand, exposing two missing fingers. "I'm not going to break that promise. My country is most important, even if it does some stupid things like freeing niggers."

"Still," Jim Nettleton said as he paused with his whittling, "I think it's a great way to punish the Southerners for all the mess they caused. They started this war. Serves 'em right to lose their property. That'll show 'em!"

A few days later, the soldiers marched south, camping near Falmouth on the Rappahannock River. After bivouacking, they received a welcome mail call. Joel delighted in a long letter from Amy and shorter ones from other family members. In spite of the terrible problems from the September battle, the folks at home seemed well.

He enjoyed his family for two hours and then penciled a reply, detailing three weeks of camp life and the rigors of the long march. He wrote of the uncaring officers who rode ahead, unmindful of the marching men's need for rest, of men who fell behind while carrying heavy loads of winter clothing, and of the many curses he had heard heaped upon generals, the war, the United States, and certainly the Rebels. Then he reread his letter and threw it into the fire. His family didn't want to hear his complaints. Instead, he composed a letter focused on the family at home and on the positive side of army life.

The men spent most of their time talking and reading newspapers purchased from the subtler. The *London Post* said that President Lincoln had lost all control over what happened. It called the Emancipation Proclamation "a joke, the laughing stock of Europe."

Joel hardened in anger. The proclamation was the reason he was here, the reason he'd had the strength and courage to leave Amy and to miss their baby's birth. *What do the British know about what is happening here, anyway? If they're so smart, why did they lose the American Revolution?*

The soldiers shared newspaper advertisements. Because many soldiers kept Charles awake with their coughing, he read a *New York Times* advertisement for Dr. Tobias's Venetian Liniment, which would cure rheumatism, colic, croup, sore throat, and pains in the limbs, back, and chest. "Nothing has ever been discovered that stops pain like it," he read.

A *Times* advertisement for Dr. G. W. Scollay's Air-Tight Deodorizing Burial Case caught Joel's attention. According to the ad, "a human body may be withheld from internment some sixty to ninety days, or more, without the emission of the usual offensive odor." The secret was a self-adjusting valve that allowed gases to escape, in addition to a chemical compound "that renders the escaping gases inoffensive and disinfecting." *We needed about a million of them at Sharpsburg,* he thought. *And they should make them big enough for horses.*

As the men shared around the campfire, John Humphrey said, "Did you know that thirteen men in our regiment deserted since we arrived here at Falmouth? With all those who took off when we left Harpers Ferry, and the ones who dropped out along the way, it leaves us pretty shorthanded. It's a good thing you came in, Haskins. You have to replace about a hundred men."

Joel laughed with the crowd and said, "I'll do my best." Then he added, "But doesn't that mean I should get their rations?" Humph punched him lightly on the shoulder.

The regiment soon moved again, this time to woods where they felled trees and cleared the area for winter huts. They dug holes, made walls from four or five logs laid horizontally, and then filled the gaps with mud and roofed the huts with shelter halves. The structures included makeshift fireplaces and chimneys. *It's not quite like home, but it does beat the tents in the winter weather. Actually, it's about like Gabe and Nattie's slave shack. But I guess I should be glad for what I have and not complain about what I don't have.*

A few days later, Joel and his comrades marched to Stafford Heights, about a half mile north of the Rappahannock, across from Fredericksburg. Through the fog, Joel could see engineers laying pontoon bridges across the four-hundred-foot river. By midafternoon, the pontoons were completed, and Seventy-First Pennsylvania followed several regiments across the water. Confederate batteries firing from the west caused some casualties, but for the most part, the evacuated town was easily occupied.

Then Joel experienced a shock. Union soldiers were looting the empty buildings, taking jewelry, foodstuffs, clothing, and even pictures. By dawn, the marauders had ravaged the most precious personal treasures the Rebel population possessed.

Although Joel was embarrassed and frustrated by what some soldiers were doing, his army's objective was clear: move south to Richmond, take the capital, and force the Rebels back into the Union. This would require defeating the Confederate army on a hill called Marye's Heights. *Okay. Drive through the Rebel army on this hill and then on to Richmond!*

Joel was delighted that General Burnside was the commander. He had led Union forces across the Stone Bridge on the Haskinses' property. Now Joel had a chance to see this great man up close. When he first saw the general, he laughed gleefully: the general had a mass of facial hair. *His name is Burnside, and look at his sideburns! I think he ought to be called General Sideburn.*

Burnside's army had one objective: capture Richmond, return the Confederacy to the Union, and end the war. Aaron and his Confederate comrades had defeated similar plans at Bull Run and in battles to the east. *I wonder if Aaron is part of the Confederate army here!*

The battle soon raged, but Joel's inexperience caused his commander to assign him to the ambulance corps, where he helped tend to hundreds of Union soldiers who had been wounded by enemy bullets. Many died, one in his arms. For Joel, it was a horrible experience.

Joel was deeply disappointed that the Union plan didn't work. In fact, the army didn't even get to the top of Marye's Heights, let alone move on to Richmond. He brought many wounded soldiers to the rear for treatment and was glad he hadn't been shot, but he was deeply disappointed in the outcome of the battle.

That night, unable to sleep, he wandered out into the nearby field. Many piles of bodies awaited burial, lying where they had been dumped after being carried back across the river. Some produced the repulsive odor his mind had borne since the battle at home.

Then a strange noise caught his attention. It sounded like hogs rooting and squealing. Sure enough, the moonlight revealed dozens of pigs in the open field, feasting on the corpses. He stared in fascinated horror as the swine snorted, grunted, pushed the bodies, and bit into them. The dead had become a marvelous feast, a delightful hog trough loaded with the finest banquet any pig had ever enjoyed.

He remembered a similar sight at Sharpsburg. It made no difference whether the bodies were Yankees or Rebels, good men or bad. The pigs didn't care.

Joel's stomach twisted into a knot as he thought about these young men. All had had hopes and dreams for the future. All had families they had loved and who loved them. None had expected to end up as nothing but hog fodder.

CHAPTER 13

Joel, Christmas Day 1862

Joel awakened on Christmas morning as a frigid wind howled. He shivered in the darkness of despair, wondering if he would ever be warm again.

He was mourning a man he had known less than two months, a good man he would never really know. Charles's life had filled a void; his death left Joel's heart with a gaping hole. Charles had been a veteran soldier, a man Joel had enjoyed and trusted. *Who will get me through this hell now?* He went to the river and filled his canteen and then took a cold drink. Raw loneliness snaked through his chest as a flurry of snowflakes descended from the dreary sky. How he wished he could be home with his family this Christmas Day. How he longed for a peaceful birthday celebration for the Prince of Peace and the warmth of the family fireplace with beloved kinsfolk all around.

I have to visit Charles's grave today. I have to write his family. I've waited too long, but what can I tell them? Your son is dead. He was a good man, but someone killed him anyway. He won't come home again, and you will probably never see where he is buried. And we lost the battle that killed him. As he slung the canteen over his shoulder, his knuckles brushed against the precious pocket watch in his vest pocket. He pulled it out and gazed at Amy's picture, longing for the warmth of her arms and body. He ran his fingers across Amy's lovely lock of hair. He imagined how she looked now, eight months with child.

We didn't accomplish a thing in the battle, he raged again. *All we did was lose a lot of good men, like Charles. If God is on our side, why did the Rebels beat us?* The rage ran its course, and Joel's head drooped. He snapped his watch shut, no longer able to enjoy Amy's loving smile.

The winter sun fought through the thick clouds. It was the first Christmas he had been away from his family. He knew they missed him as much as he had missed Aaron last year. Again his mind went to Amy. He knew she was thinking of him too. Every night, he went to sleep trying to imagine what she looked like, wondering when their baby would be born, wondering whether it would be a boy or a girl. Sometimes he woke in the night with the sound of a child's laughter ringing in his ears—a sound he secretly cherished and jealously guarded. He wondered how Mary had felt, having to travel to Bethlehem that first Christmas Day. He was glad Amy didn't have to ride a donkey.

That morning, the very real sound of men talking and singing Christmas carols reached him. Others played cards or marbles, and some got up a ball game. A few had stolen some whiskey and cigars from Rebel homes. Thanks to a flock of chickens from a nearby farm, one group made eggnog and augmented it with a flask of rum lifted off a Rebel body.

Joel knew he had to do it; he must go visit Charles's grave. He hiked the mile to Falmouth, where he and his friends had buried the body. He sat down alone on a nearby log, preparing to write the letter he had avoided for nearly a week. He stared at the blank page before him, angry that he didn't even know what had happened. All he knew was that Charles had been injured and died in a makeshift hospital in Falmouth. Joel couldn't say if Charles had suffered or died quickly, nor could he even offer some valiant last words.

When they'd first met, Charles had told Joel of his hometown and the family he loved. Now, on this dreary Christmas Day, the lonely survivor finally finished the task and put pencil to paper.

December 25, 1862

Dear Conner family,

My name is Joel Haskins, and I am Glen and Fannie Nutting Haskins' son. By now, you probably have heard about Charles's death. I am so sorry. He was a good man—a brave soldier.

Thanks for writing to my family after he fought in the battle on our farm. When I decided to muster in, I chose Seventy-First Pennsylvania so I could be with him. We met at Harpers Ferry and were together until the battle that took his life. We had become good friends.

Right now, I am sitting on a little bank near a hospital in Falmouth, Virginia. Charles died in this hospital, and we buried him right beside the place where I am now sitting. When the war is over, I hope you can come to visit Charles's grave. Maybe I can come with you and show you exactly where it is. You can be proud of him. He died in the service of his country. I enjoyed being with him and am now very lonely.

Joel paused in his writing; he knew he had to continue but felt unable to do so. He sat gazing at the place they had buried the body. He had seen Charles's dead face just before they had covered him, and now his mind saw it again. It was an image he feared he could never release. He had seen many dead faces after the Sharpsburg battle, but he hadn't known any of them personally. The tears welled up from deep inside and watered Charles's grave. Finally, he gathered himself, set his resolve, and finished the letter.

```
I don't know how Charles was hurt, but I
know he suffered a wound in the torso. He
died a few days later, on December 20, I
think.

I am glad to assure you that he is in a
better land. He spoke to me of his faith
in God, and I know he is in heaven right
now. I know he loved you. He did God's will
by fighting for the United States in its
hour of peril, and he is a genuine hero. I
am proud to be his cousin. I know you are
proud of him too.

I hope to come see you after the war.

Joel Charles Haskins
```

Joel returned to camp, glad the sun had spent most of Christmas Day smiling and warming his dreary mood. After a nap, he wandered down to the river as day yielded to night and a pale yellow moon beamed in the cloudless sky. Although not on picket duty, he joined a small group from his regiment who had that assignment. Leaning against a tree, he watched the moon's reflection in the icy current of the river below.

He brightened at the sound of a violin being tuned. Some of his company had gotten together for Christmas music around a campfire by the river. He settled back and closed his eyes and then opened them again as Sam Larkin began to play the flute and Jim Nettleton picked up the harmony on his violin. Soon other men began to sing. Most had voices no better than Joel's, but that didn't matter, and he was caught up in the emotion of their songs. The carols continued several minutes, with the group growing as other soldiers came to the river. Now in a lighter mood, he joined in on "Silent Night."

As the song ended—"sleep in heavenly peace, sleep in heavenly peace"—Joel imagined he heard faint strains of music from across the river. Could it be real? He ambled to the bank and sat down on a fallen tree trunk, held his breath, and listened. *It must be the Rebs. The Rebs are singing "Silent Night" just across the river!* It was eerie and wonderful, almost dreamlike. He hummed along until another carol from his own men sounded loudly behind him. Jumping to his feet, he ran back to the campfire and asked the others to come. They assembled at the river's edge, where Sam and Jim started playing "Silent Night" again. The rippling waters caressed Joel's boots while he stared across to the southern shore, perhaps four hundred feet away. In a moment, he saw a light emerging from the trees on the other side.

In the still darkness, male voices echoed across the ebony expanse. The men in Joel's company looked at each other in amazement. Their enemies stood on the opposite shore, extending their voices and music as fellow worshippers. Then Jim raised his violin and matched the notes reaching him from the Southern fiddler's bow, and at once they lifted their voices in unison with the enemy. "Silent night, holy night, all is calm, all is bright." Those words, so full of hope, caught the wind and were carried up to the brightest heavens. "Holy infant so tender and mild, sleep in heavenly peace." *Even in war, God sends us peace, if only for a moment. I wish we would spend more time singing and less time killing.*

After several more carols, the Rebel fiddler led out. Then a trumpet joined him. Its bright tone rang across the river. It sounded so much like home that Joel imagined he was with his family, with Aaron playing and singing.

He sat down again and leaned against a tree. Once again, it was Christmas at Robert and Abigail's, and he was drinking deeply of the joy of family. He thought of Amy and their unborn child. He imagined his kin singing these same familiar songs, as they probably were doing at this very moment. His mind saw Aunt Abigail's nimble fingers dancing across the piano keys. Joel's fingers twitched on his knee in time to the music, his thoughts completely given over to the joy of home.

Then a Rebel started one of Joel's favorite songs. He remembered learning Longfellow's splendid words in school and singing them with Aaron at home. The song was part of the family Christmas tradition.

> I heard the bells on Christmas Day
> Their old familiar carols play,
> And wild and sweet the words repeat
> Of peace on earth, goodwill to men.

Most of the singers didn't know the next verse, but a few carried on. One Rebel led out above the others, his clear baritone echoing across the waters. Joel sang along quietly, deep in the memory of Christmas at home.

> I thought how as the days had come,
> The belfries of all Christendom
> Had rolled along the unbroken song
> Of peace on earth, goodwill to men.

Joel felt so much at home that he imagined the Rebel sounded like Aaron. He even pictured Aaron singing the melody.

> Then in despair, I bowed my head;
> "There is no peace on earth," I said,
> "For hate is strong …"

Joel was suddenly wide awake. It did sound like Aaron! It sounded *just* like Aaron! Could it be? Could Aaron be across the river?

Joel's legs followed his galloping heart into the darkness and to the water's edge, where he miraculously found a small rowboat. Thanking his luck and hoping against hope, he recklessly shoved it into the water, rowed to the enemy shore, and secured it in the bushes.

Moving quietly up the bank, he positioned himself below a crest to make sure the Rebel guards didn't see him. Once sure of his hiding place, he brought his shaking hands to his mouth and tried to blow the boyhood signal. At first, nothing came—he was too excited. He took a deep breath and then another, and then he relaxed and blew.

"Whooeee. Whooeee-ooeee-ooeee. Whooeee."

Joel's call rang out, and he could only wait, wondering if Aaron would hear it, or if he would recognize it after more than a year and a half apart, or if Aaron was there at all. After waiting a few seconds, he signaled again. "Whooeee. Whooeee-ooeee-ooeee. Whooeee." His whole body strained to hear the returned call above the sounds of water and men.

He tried a third time. "Whooeee. Whooeee-ooeee-ooeee. Whooeee."

Then, wonder of wonders, a majestic reply echoed from the Rebel camp: "Whooeee. Whooeee-ooeee-ooeee. Whooeee."

Joel was so intent on hoping that he almost didn't believe it when it came. He shook his head as the call came again. He calmed his trembling fingers and blew the signal in response, and he soon heard Aaron's hushed but excited voice calling softly, "Joel! Joel! Is that you? Come out, Cousin. Oh, please! Where are you?"

Joel laughed as he rasped out, "Aaron! Aaron, I'm over here!"

Almost immediately, a bearded stranger emerged from the shadows in front of him, crying out, "Joel! It's you!"

Joel sucked in a harsh breath. Aaron looked so frail in the moonlight, so thin and haggard, and a beard covered his face and neck. But his eyes were as kind as they had ever been, and his voice told Joel that, yes, it was indeed his cousin. They vaulted to each other and embraced, laughing. Aaron asked, "How in the world did you get here? How did you know I was here?"

"I heard you singing. I just knew it was you. You sounded just like you." The two were so excited that their voices carried. They heard others nearby and hunkered down to conceal themselves.

"I'm so glad you came," Aaron whispered.

"Well, if you were just across the river, nothing could have kept me from trying to see you."

Aaron suddenly paused. "Across the river?" Aaron leaned back slightly to look closely at Joel in the moonlight. His eyes narrowed as he realized that Joel was in uniform—an enemy uniform. "You joined them?"

Joel nodded. He couldn't deny the harsh truth, but he wanted so badly for Aaron not to be angry. "Aaron, I love you. But I had to make my choice. I really believe the Union is right. But when I heard you across the water, I didn't care whether it was the Antietam or the Red Sea. I was going to cross it and see you tonight."

Aaron was in shock. Gradually, though, his mind cleared.

"Aaron." Joel breathed the word in a stream of thick mist. He extended his arms to embrace his cousin. Willing him to accept the offer, he put all his love into his hope that past joy would overcome present despair.

With a bowed head, Aaron moved to fill the space. He gripped his cousin's shoulders and hugged him as if he were taking a piece of home into himself. War choices would matter, but not tonight.

Aaron whispered, "Joel, you took a terrible chance in coming. If they catch you, they might shoot you or put you in prison. Let's go into my tent. My tent mate was killed in the battle, so I'm alone for now."

The twin cousins went into the tent, where they sat and talked softly of home. Every few minutes, Aaron stared at Joel's face and then down at his disgusting uniform, wondering how his closest friend had gone wrong. He felt overwhelmed with his disappointment, but his pain and resentment were smothered in love.

The two talked softly of home, but the war soon stole into their conversation, tugging at their minds so incessantly that the present horrors couldn't be avoided. Aaron explained what it was like to be a soldier.

"When I'm facing an enemy, I know my buddies will do everything they can to protect me. They risk their lives all the time to save mine, and I do the same for them. They're a part of me. We're a family. It's fantastic to know that your friend is putting his life on the line for you."

Joel didn't want to argue. He wanted to delve further into his best friend's soul. The two had always been so close that he could ask anything.

"Have you killed any men?"

Aaron looked at Joel with the fatherly air of a man enlightening his son about the real world. "I've killed several, yes. I don't know how many, really. You don't have time to count. It's probably better that you don't count." Joel watched Aaron shrug his bony shoulders.

After a long pause, Aaron opened his soul to the only one on earth with whom he could share his deepest secrets.

"I was scared to death the first couple of times. The world feels different when you go into battle. My heart pounded, and I felt faint, knowing that at any moment a bullet might send me out of this life."

Joel didn't know what to say. He only managed to mumble a few incoherent syllables, so Aaron went on. "The first man I killed was only a boy. Since then, I've killed a lot more, but after a while, you just do what you have to do and don't think about it anymore. It's like another day slaughtering chickens or something."

"Slaughtering chickens? How can you say that killing people is like slaughtering chickens? Aaron, that's stupid." The men glared at each other in the moonlight.

"Well, the Union is a bunch of wild animals down here ravaging the South. They deserve to be slaughtered. Besides, if we don't get them, they'll get us."

Joel couldn't resist. "That's idiotic! The Union isn't ravaging the South. I'm a soldier in that army you call wild animals, and I haven't been ravaging anything. We're just getting back at the South for tearing this great nation apart. All we asked was that the South come back into the Union."

Aaron didn't feel like arguing with his best friend. "I guess the most important thing is that we're all part of a team, each one risking his life to protect the lives of his fellow soldiers, and all of us fighting for a good cause. I know that each of the men I killed might have killed one of my friends if I hadn't gotten him first. So, you see, I probably saved several lives. Besides, I'm doing God's will. It's important that I kill bad people in order to save good ones. It's like Israel in the Bible."

As Joel bit his tongue, his mother's image swept softly over the river's waves and into his heart. How sad she would be if she knew her son and her nephew were likening God's children to savage animals—and on Christmas Day as the world honored the Prince of Peace. There seemed little honor among the thieves of human lives.

The two men sat in forced relaxation, each aware of their lifetime of love and trust. By this time, Joel was Aaron's best friend again, not a disappointing enemy. It was Aaron's first chance to really let go, to tell his loved one his innermost thoughts.

"The worst thing, though, is seeing your buddies die. Several of our schoolmates from Sharpsburg who mustered in with me are now dead—like Lawrence Williams, Joseph Grant, and Philip Jordan. You're walking beside a friend, and the next thing you know, he's dead! It's hard to believe. One minute he's alive and fighting; the next minute he's dead. One second he's a human being, talking, thinking; the next second he's still and can't be reached by any sound. It just overwhelms me how quick it is, from life to death."

After a pause, Aaron continued. "A war like this really causes some strange things to happen. I've heard stories about soldiers running into relatives on the other side. In one battle, two brothers were killed—one fighting for the North, the other for the South. I heard another story about a Confederate being captured, and lo and behold, he was sent to a Union officer who turned out to be his own father. Isn't that bizarre?"

Aaron soon said he was afraid for Joel's safety—that Joel probably should get back across the river. The two walked silently to the rowboat. The twin cousins shared a long embrace on the muddy bank. Each knew that he might never see his best friend again.

Joel rowed across the river, pulled the boat upstream, and tied it where he had found it. He raised his hands and, as loud as possible, gave the call: "Whooeee! Whooeee-ooeee-ooeee! Whooeee." From across the waters, he heard the reply: "Whooeee! Whooeee-ooeee-ooeee! Whooeee."

Shivering, he slipped into his tent. He had enjoyed his time with his best friend, even though he was his enemy.

CHAPTER 14

Christmas at Home, 1862

At the Haskins farm, Christmas dawned gray and misty. The farm was now a graveyard; unmarked mounds were sad reminders of the final resting places for hundreds of soldiers who would never again enjoy Christmas with their families. Fannie looked out at the graves and saw scores of vacant chairs in homes throughout the North and the South.

Before the war, Christmas had been the greatest family day of the year, celebrated with joy, laughter, gifts, and wonderful music. They had missed Aaron and his music a year ago; now, with both boys away and the farm a graveyard, Christmas joy was palpably absent. How could a Christian family celebrate the Prince of Peace when their children made war against each other?

The family members gathered as usual, and they did their best to celebrate the day by sharing a delicious meal, visiting, and exchanging simple gifts. As the cheerless sky darkened, Fannie leaned over a basin of tepid water and stared dully at the pile of unwashed dishes. Her daughters Grayce and Julia, armed with dish towels, waited beside her. Nattie came up behind Fannie. "Miss Fannie, you just go on. I can do those dishes up real quick before I leave."

Fannie roused herself, her melancholy eyes turning to her servant. "That's all right, Nattie. You go home now. The girls and I can do it. It's time for you to have Christmas with your family."

Nattie paused a moment and looked at her mistress's face. Fannie gave her a weak but sincere smile. While Nattie gathered her shawl around her shoulders, Chelsea and Irene put together a generous bowl of leftover turkey, potatoes, and greens for the slaves.

As Nattie shut the back door, Abigail came into the kitchen with another armload of dishes. She set them on the counter with a clatter and bustled back into the dining room.

Since Joel had joined the Union army two months ago, Abigail had been distant. Prior to that, she had talked with Fannie about her grief and worry over Aaron's danger in the war. They had grown even closer during those months, but now Abigail could not seek solace from the mother of her son's enemy. It seemed that, despite their quarter century of loving, cooperative family living, a curtain had dropped between them as divisive as any battlefield. Abigail and Fannie never talked about those things, but each knew.

Tears coursed Fannie's cheeks as she thought painfully of how far she had slipped from the teachings she had once enjoyed and shared with Glen. She truly loved him—just as much as ever—but life had dealt a deadly turn from her values of peace and love. When Grandpa William died, it had been appropriate for them to move home to Glen's family, but Fannie had never adjusted to owning slaves. Now her family was at war—outside and inside. For her son to be a warrior broke her heart, and to be distanced from her sister-in-law was a horror she had never imagined. She longed to be back in her Friends Meeting, silently listening as the inward voice of Jesus spoke to her and sometimes spoke to others through her.

Glen and Robert sat by the fireplace, drinking steaming coffee. Glen propped a foot on the bullet-shattered porch railing. "How many of those boys out in our fields do you suppose have parents hoping for their next letter, not knowing they died here?" His brother didn't respond, so Glen added, "I can't quit thinking about it. I wish we could have taken the time to find out who each of them was, so we could let their kin know. It'd be horrible not knowing." His voice faded and then finished sadly, "But I guess if they haven't heard from their sons since September, they must assume they're dead. What a lonely Christmas."

Robert grimaced. "But, Glen," he said, not wanting to relive the memories of gathering the dead and separating them from the still-living, "the smell … and the heat … We couldn't take all that time sorting through those boys' things. It would have taken hours more than we had."

"I know, I know. You're right. Of course we couldn't. I just hate that it had to be that way."

The brothers began to eat some warm applesauce. Then Robert asked, "What do you think Lincoln's up to now, saying he'll free all the slaves in the Confederate states come the first of the year?"

"I'm not sure," Glen replied thoughtfully. "Except it means he's going back on his word. He promised he wouldn't touch slavery except to prevent it from spreading into the West."

Robert's voice was thick with anger. "That's exactly right! Here you've got the South seceding because the government threatens to take away its slaves, so Lincoln promises he won't. Now he says he *will* take them away if the states don't unsecede."

The issue was difficult for Glen, who had grown up in a slave-owning family, then moved to Pennsylvania and almost become a Quaker, then defended secession when the war broke out, and now had a son fighting against it. Yet he refused to let it become a breach between him and his brother.

Without rancor, he countered, "I guess he figures his promise doesn't have to hold, since the Confederates seceded anyway."

Robert ladled two more spoonfuls of warm applesauce into his mouth. "You know why I think he's doing it?" he asked, tapping two fingers against the table. "I think he's trying to start a slave rebellion, that's what. He gets the idea into the slaves' heads that they can be free—and pretty soon they start disobeying you on little things. Then, after a while, they decide to run away—or maybe kill you. Even Nattie and Gabe seem a little uppity these days. I could swear Gabe doesn't respect me like he used to—he takes his time now following orders. I wouldn't be surprised if he flat-out defied me someday. He was never any trouble before—he was always happy and never questioned our authority. He was the best nigger anyone ever worked—slave or free. Never once did we have to beat him."

Glen thought a minute. "You know, at first I thought Lincoln's proclamation wouldn't affect us here in Maryland, but I've heard that slaves all over have gotten uppity because of it."

Robert sat back in his chair and then inched forward. "I was talking with George Barnhart the other day. He said his boy, Jesse, took a little moonlight stroll without even asking for permission. George said he tied that nigger's hands and got ready to flail him, but he cried and said he'd never do it again. He said he didn't know what got into him and that he'd pray God would help him to be more obedient. Can you imagine? George has owned that boy for more than forty years."

"What did George do?"

"Oh, he let him by. You know he can't stand firm on anything. He was always too easy with his niggers. He may find out what his loose reins will earn him when they up and run off to Canada some night while he sleeps. It'd serve George right if his boy got hooked up with those cowardly, nigger-stealing Quakers and Mennonites on the Underground Railroad."

Glen's nostrils flared, the applesauce suddenly tasting flavorless in his mouth. The positive influence of Fannie's Quaker Meeting had never left him. Sometimes he wished he and Fannie could still live that godly reality. He wondered how their lives might have been different had his father not died. But he had never been sorry that he had come home to be with his mother after the tragedy.

Glen picked up the two empty wooden bowls and placed them on the side table for Nattie to wash in the morning. Upon returning to the fire, he said, "I think the worst thing about this whole Emancipation Proclamation business is that it might make this war last longer. If the Confederates ever had thoughts of laying down their arms, they vanished the moment Lincoln signed a decree that said the slaves would be free January first."

Robert stopped sipping his coffee and looked at Glen. He knew it was true. The war everyone had thought would be over in one summer had already gone two, and it would no doubt continue to drag on.

In deep silence, the brothers stared at the fire as the flames crackled in the hearth. The largest log shattered into a hundred tiny embers, sending fiery sparks flying up the chimney. The log seemed like the world—popping, burning, and exploding before their very eyes.

Abigail came into the room and told Robert, "If you don't mind, I'm going to bed now. I'm really tired."

A few minutes later, Fannie bundled her sleepy children and crossed the bridge to their own home. Glen soon followed. He was exhausted, not from a hard day but from a woefully discouraged spirit. He found his wife sitting before the looking glass. Her long auburn hair hung loose down her back, and her white gown obscured her small feet. She smiled up at him with a gentle sadness.

Glen bent down behind his wife and studied their mirrored images. Fannie turned to him and gently touched his cheek. Her fingers trembled. As she looked at him, her eyes filled with tears. Glen helped her to her feet. She gasped, the tears flowing freely now. "We've been through so much, Glen. I don't know if I can live if Joel dies. I miss him so much."

Glen pulled his wife close and rocked her in his arms. It was her first admission that their son might not come back. He wanted to say everything would be all right, that the war would end soon, that their prayers would be answered and Joel would be unharmed, but he could not. He said nothing and only held her closer to him as she shook with her grief.

They looked deep into each other's eyes. Husband and wife, they had been together through many hardships in the past quarter century, but nothing like this. Once they had worried about early frost or a colicky horse, but now they feared the death of their beloved son.

Only two years ago, the family had enjoyed a normal, fun-filled day of love and peace. Last year's Christmas hadn't been the same with Aaron gone. This year, Joel was gone too, and the land—even their land—was littered with the bones of thousands of dead sons, each as precious to his parents as Joel was to his.

What would next year bring? Would Christmas of 1863 be a time of peace, a time for family rejoicing? Or might it be something worse, something they could not dare imagine? Each held the other close, not knowing what lay ahead but comforted by the fact that whatever the future held, they would live it together.

CHAPTER 15

Joel, January–April 1863

Joel clung to memories of his Christmas night with Aaron like precious jewels. He often gazed across the river, wondering if his cousin was still there, wishing he could go find out, but no one answered his whistle calls.

On December 31, the Philadelphia Brigade officers held their final muster of 1862. Officially, they reported 388 present and 281 absent. The enlisted men rolled their eyes at the numbers, believing there to be even more runaways than the official count suggested. Every night, more men disappeared like swamp ghosts.

The Emancipation Proclamation, freeing all slaves in seceded states, took effect New Year's Day. A giant of a soldier named Joseph Woods said, "Well, today Virginia's niggers are all free. I wonder where they are. I don't see a lot of them running around here."

"Think what would happen if they really were free," said John Humphrey. "I don't like it one bit. That's why so many men have deserted. They don't want to fight a nigger war. I don't blame them. I mustered in to fight the Rebels, not to free the niggers." Humph absently scratched at the stubble on his chin with his mangled left hand and spit into the fire.

Joel felt his pulse quicken. "Well, I think the Emancipation Proclamation is a good thing. I think the Negroes should be free and that they should be treated as equal as anybody else."

"Yeah, and free to marry your daughter, I suppose. I can just imagine seeing you get your first look at your mongrel grandson. It'd serve you right."

Later Joel went to his shelter, where he huddled in his blankets, lit a lantern, and began writing a letter home. After telling of Charles Conner's death and thanking the family for sending *Great Expectations*, he wrote,

```
We live in shelters we made of logs, with
mud pushed into the cracks. They're a lot
like Gabe and Nattie's cabin. We cut down
the trees and laid them on their sides,
then sawed them into pieces, piled them
up, and put our tent shelters over the
top. One Massachusetts regiment decorated
their streets, setting out lines of trees
and enclosing their hospital building and
headquarters with all sorts of decorations,
made mostly with twigs and branches.

It has rained a lot. One of the men wrote
this poem:

Now I lay me down to sleep
In mud that's many fathoms deep;
If I'm not here when you awake,
Just hunt me up with an oyster rake.

Kiss our child for me when you deliver,
and know that I am with you—forever.

Joel Charles Haskins
```

Not long after Joel posted his letter, General Burnside gave the order to attack Fredericksburg again, but the whole offensive disappeared into the Virginia muck. Mud was king. The "mud march," as the men called it, would live forever in their bitterest memories, especially when Rebel soldiers across the river raised placards reading "Burnside's Army Stuck in the Mud."

One night, the weather cleared, and the men sat around the campfire, engaging in their favorite pastime of complaining. They weren't short of ammunition. Lincoln shouldn't have fired the soldiers' favorite, General "Little Mac" McClellan; the army paymasters gambled with the men's pay, and it didn't get to those who had earned it; and the officers got furloughs, but the men's requests were turned down with military efficiency. The complaints were as long as the winter and as dark as the pools of murky water around them.

As Joel listened, he knew many of the opinions voiced belonged to only a minority of soldiers, but he realized that some were rooted in truth. His schoolteacher, Mr. Arthur, had taught him to never accept one side of an argument without evaluating the other. Some of the complaints seemed contradictory. The soldiers applauded Little Mac because he refused to spend their lives, but they lambasted his failure to take the offensive. Joel did wonder about the pay, though. Most of the men got their September and October money in January, but none had received his thirteen dollars for November, nor December. He found relief from the repetitive, dragging days when he received the most wonderful letter of his life.

My dear husband,

I'm happy to tell you that we have a son! I was delivered of our baby three days ago, on February 1. He is very sweet, and I am overjoyed to be his mama. Both our mothers were with me, and Grandma too. It took about six hours, and, Joel, I thought it would never end. It felt like I was being torn apart inside. But then he was in my mama's arms, and he started to cry. I suddenly didn't feel anything else except this desperate need to hold him and soothe him. Everything about him is perfect.

We named him Braden Joel, like you and I talked about. My mother is going to go home and bring my grandmother to see him as soon as the rain stops. He has dark hair. I can't quit looking at him. He is a greedy little eater, but I seem to have enough.

I think of you every time I look at Braden, so you never leave my thoughts. I miss you, my dearest. Please hurry back to your family. We long to see you.

Your affectionate wife, Amy, and your wonderful little son, Braden Joel Haskins. I'll love you forever!

Tears rolled down Joel's cheeks as he read the letter four more times. He folded it carefully and slid it into his bundle of treasured letters, tied with a brown satin ribbon. Then he took out his watch and feasted on Amy's picture and the lock of her hair.

The desire to slip off into the night like so many others was stronger than ever, and he could almost feel his body turning toward home and his family. It seemed like such a simple matter to walk away, go see Amy and Braden, and then get back to camp. *No one would blame me. Other men have done it, lots of them. Of course, those who were caught were punished.* He remembered seeing a man tied up by his thumbs, standing on tiptoe for hours. Others were forced to march carrying knapsacks full of bricks. Then, too, he might get caught by the Rebels and put in prison—or even shot.

In the chapel service the next Sunday, Reverend Doogal warned that army life invited "low standards of behavior." Joel had seen many young men in the company of the girls who followed the armies and visited the camps. Some soldiers paid dearly in money and disease. Syphilis and gonorrhea were almost as common as typhoid and dysentery. Joel had also been shocked at the amount of alcohol some soldiers consumed—a subject that also caught Reverend Doogal's attention. A drunken brawl between Seventy-First and Seventy-Second Pennsylvania drew a stern rebuke.

Reverend Doogal ended the sermon, as he always did, by saying that the United States was a Christian nation and that George Washington had been a providential man given to the nation at a providential time. He compared President Abraham Lincoln with the Abraham who had begun the nation of Israel.

"God has a purpose as regards this war. A sublime conquest is to be made. Liberty is to triumph. America will continue to be a free nation."

The next day, Sam Larkin raised a thorny issue. "I got a letter from home last mail call. Do you know what they're doing? They're putting Negroes into the army!"

"Oh, they tried that a year ago," John Humphrey said with a shrug. "It didn't work. When the Union captured Southern land, they took the slaves and made soldiers of them. It turned out that the niggers weren't very good soldiers. For one thing, some of them thought they should be free to do whatever they wanted."

"Well," Sam said, "this is different. These are Northern niggers. I guess that, since the Emancipation Proclamation, a lot of them want to free their families and other darkies down south, so Lincoln is trying to get them trained to help out. They will even be paid, but not as much as the white soldiers, of course."

"They shouldn't get paid," Joseph Woods chimed in. "Problem is, the free niggers in the North already are uppity. If you go into the nigger part of the town I come from, they'll hardly step out of the way to let a white man walk by."

Joel took a breath, remembering the emotion that had sparked the last time they'd talked about slavery with Woods, but he said it anyway. "I think it's okay for Negroes to be in the Union army, and I wonder why it wouldn't be all right to pay them the same as we get."

Some of the men stared in disbelief, blinking at him like

dumbfounded owls, but Joel barreled on. "I think the reason we look down on Negroes is because they've been slaves for so long. We took them out of their own country and made them less than whites. They never had a choice."

"There's never going to be a time when a black man is as equal as a white man," Woods cut in. "You mark my words! A hundred years from today, they still won't be. God won't allow it. No, sir."

As the weather cleared, the men spent time at the water's edge, trading with the Confederates across the Rappahannock. Soldiers on both sides built makeshift wooden boats a foot or two long and then positioned themselves upstream and let the current carry the boats near the opposite shore, where enemy soldiers fished them out with long, limber poles. Then they went upstream and sent their responses back. In this way, the soldiers sent and received messages, tobacco, cards, foodstuffs, newspapers, and other items. Those who had built the boats collected a little from each shipment and enjoyed a lucrative business.

A few weeks later, Amy wrote that the family had gotten a letter from Aaron, saying that his regiment was somewhere in North Carolina. That night, Joel filled the lonely hours writing by candlelight.

```
Dear Amy, Braden Joel, and the rest of the
family,

We had a great game of Base Ball today.
Our 71st PA regiment beat the 72nd PA
regiment. Aaron and I used to play it at
school a little, but I didn't know much
about the sport until after I mustered
in. I think it's fun. Didn't Walt Whitman
write that the game of ball is glorious,
or something like that? I think he was
right. Anyway, you take a large stick in
your hands and hit a little round ball
when a man called the pitcher throws it
toward you. Then you run to base and are
not "put out" unless someone on the other
team throws the ball and hits you with
it. They call this "soaking." I made four
```

scores today because I can hit the ball quite far and am fairly fast and can avoid getting hit by the throws.

Sometimes we play Foot Ball, which is done with a lot of kicking and running with a big oblong ball, and we have fun running foot races, playing cricket, doing leapfrog, and broad jumping. One time they let us go and watch the cavalry race their horses.

Well, I will soon be twenty-three years old, and here is all I have with me: a knapsack, a haversack, a canteen, one shelter half, a rubber blanket, a rifle, a bayonet, and sixty cartridges. Most important, I carry a wonderful watch with a beautiful picture and lock of hair in it. Of course, most of the important things I have are at home, and they are people. I love all of you and am anxious to see you. Give our little Braden Joel a special kiss for me.

Joel Charles Haskins

When Joel finished his letter, he lovingly folded and sealed it and then emerged from his tent to join a conversation around the fire, where not all the heat was coming from the flames.

"What does the government think it's doing?" Humph was shouting, his voice harsh and loud. "I thought men who mustered in were being treated as slaves, but how about *this*?"

Joel asked, "What happened?"

"Lincoln is going to *force* white men into the army! *White* men. Can you imagine? They call it *conscription*. Just a fancy word for slavery, and on white men."

"Why are they doing that?"

"Because they need a *bigger army*. Lincoln needs more men because so many are skippin' out and headin' home. So they're gonna *force* men to fight. And I thought this was a free country."

Joel was reminded of the version of the Lord's Prayer that he had heard several times in a joking sense.

> Our father, who art in Washington,
> Uncle Abraham be thy name,
> Thy will be done at the South as at the North.
> Give us this day our daily rations
> Of crackers, salt horse, and pork.
> Forgive us our shortcomings,
> As we forgive our quartermaster,
> For thine is the power,
> The soldiers, and the niggers
> For the space of three years.
> Amen.

A few days later, the officers instructed the men to prepare themselves for a very special occasion. The president of the United States was coming! The next week, Joel wrote a special letter home.

My dear wife, Amy; Braden Joel; and all the folks at home,

Well, I got to see President Lincoln! And I got to see his young son, Tad. It was easy to recognize the president. He is tall and thin, much taller than me. He looked very tired.

The more I looked at President Lincoln, the more I felt sorry for him. He looked discouraged, probably because the war hasn't gone well. He looked right at me. I think our troops made him feel good. We cheered real loud when he came by.

Kiss little Braden for me.

```
Your loving husband,
Joel Charles Haskins
```

President Lincoln had proclaimed the last day of April a day of national humiliation, fasting, and prayer. Joel smiled impishly. *This army can use all the prayers we can get, but we've lived with humiliation for a long time already. And I wouldn't like fasting, but I guess I could give up hardtack for a while.* Still, he felt a sense of pride that his president was asking the nation to pray that God would bless the war effort. *That will be a lot of prayers.*

Joel knew they would attack the Rebel army soon and found himself thinking, *I know President Davis has set aside days for thanksgiving and prayer too. I just hope God pays attention to Lincoln and not Davis.*

CHAPTER 16

Aaron, January–July 1863

Aaron's second winter at war was a cold and damp version of hell. In this place, there were no horned fiends with pitchforks tormenting the souls of the damned; his particular demons were extreme discomfort and a relentless tedium that drove men to the brink of madness.

He thanked God and congratulated himself as well as Mother Nature for protecting Richmond. He had helped do it three times—at Manassas, on the Virginia Peninsula, and now at Fredericksburg. The Confederates laughed as the winter rains pelted their shelters, knowing that the same rains kept the Northern barbarians from doing more damage.

Not ready to miss an opportunity for mischief, Garnett's brigade, to which Aaron belonged, organized a snowball ambush against Kemper's brigade, a nearby Confederate camp. Members of Garnett's brigade, including a few officers, sneaked into position just outside the Kemper camp. They raised the Confederate flag and let out a shrieking Rebel yell, pummeling their unsuspecting comrades with hundreds of carefully stockpiled snowballs. It was a valiant charge, well timed. The battle was soon won.

Everyone laughed as Hiram Lott told of chasing one enemy away from the slit trench latrine where he was squatting. "I sneaked up on him by creeping between trees and then nailed him with my snowball. It hit his arm and went everywhere, even inside the drawers that were around his ankles. He ran out of there so fast he forgot to pull up his trousers! You should have seen it; he fell flat on his face!"

"Sounds like he fell about as flat as the Yanks did at Fredericksburg," Johnny Williams said, crossing his arms in smug satisfaction.

"Sure did," Hiram said. "It is fun to beat another Rebel regiment at snowballing, but the real fun is to beat the Yankees."

Most evenings, the men sang around their campfires. One night, Aaron led the familiar favorite, "Hard Tack Come Again No More," a song derived from the prairie tune "Hard Times Come Again No More."

> 'Tis the song, the sigh of the hungry:
> Hard tack, hard tack, come again no more.
> Many days you have lingered upon our stomachs sore.
> O hard tack, come again no more!

While the men sang, Hiram Lott hurried to his tent and soon returned with a piece of paper. "My uncle wrote that somebody invented new words to that song. I think they fit, considering this stuff they're feeding us now."

Aaron scanned the letter with a chuckle. Strumming on his guitar, he sang,

> But to all these cries and murmurs,
> There comes a sudden hush
> As frail forms are fainting by the door,
> For they feed us now on horse feed,
> That the cooks call mush!
> O hard tack, come again once more!

'Tis the dying wail of the starving:
O hard tack, hard tack, come again once more!
You were old and very wormy,
But we pass your failings o'er.
O hard tack, come again once more!

This new version of the old song became an instant favorite.

When each new shipment of hardtack arrived, however, the new lyrics lost their early appeal.

Several Negroes served their masters as personal attendants, cleaning the campgrounds, foraging for food, and looking after their masters' clothing. These servants passed through the camp like dark, silent ghosts.

Exhausted from a four-week march, Aaron's brigade finally reached the outskirts of Washington, North Carolina, a town held by the Yankees. Ladies in muffs and bonnets cheered and waved handkerchiefs and flags with patriotic pride.

Aaron asked Hiram Lott, "Do you think George Washington would support the South if he were alive today?"

"He'd be on our side, no question. He fought to keep the British from taking American freedoms. Now *we're* fighting for freedom, and Washington would be leading *us*. We're defending the same freedoms he did."

"One thing for sure," a local North Carolinian said, "Washington would be against Lincoln's abolition administration. General Washington understood that everybody is better off if the darkies are in their place. Suppose Lincoln tried to take Washington's slaves away!"

"Same with Thomas Jefferson's slaves," said Johnny. "America has gone way downhill since those two Virginians led it. It started out as such a moral nation, but look at it now. They'd be ashamed about what has happened, with the government they set up to make men free now trying to deny freedom to the South."

The attempt to dislodge Union troops failed, and Fifty-Sixth Virginia moved toward home. One night, Lewis Shook asked Aaron, "Have you heard the news?"

"What news?" Aaron asked, returning to his haunches and piling more damp wood onto the struggling flames.

"Up at Chancellorsville, over by Fredericksburg, the Rebs won another great victory!"

Cheering men gathered around. "Those Yankees tried to cross the Rappahannock and march to Richmond again. You'd think they'd learn."

A few minutes later, another man approached. "Have you boys heard what happened?"

"Yeah, we won at Chancellorsville. Ain't it great?" Lewis Shook said, his eyes glowing.

"Yeah, we won, but Stonewall Jackson got shot in that battle. He's dead." The men all gasped. Ashen silence descended.

"Are you sure?"

"He was shot by one of his own men by mistake!"

"What? His own men? How?"

"They don't know exactly what happened. Just that somebody shot him by mistake."

Aaron couldn't believe his ears. *Stonewall Jackson, the hero of Manassas, dead?* Yet he knew how easily it could happen. Like an errant gust of wind that tugged at the struggling flames of their fire, men's lives were snuffed out so quickly. In the wild emotion of battle, they died all around, sometimes tragically by their own men. Occasionally, an officer was shot intentionally, but Aaron knew that couldn't have been true with Stonewall Jackson.

That night, he couldn't sleep. Again and again he drifted off, only to awaken with a start, disoriented and confused. At long last, he entered a dream world. He vaguely saw General Jackson mounted on his horse, his long black beard flowing in the breeze, standing like a stone wall, stopping the enemy hoards.

Into this dream a tall man came striding mystically across a clearing, and Aaron suddenly realized it was his friend Thomas Thomas. He stopped in front of Aaron, smiling, pointing to the ground. Aaron watched in fascination as a red puddle began to build. It flowed in a small trickle and then a stream, a creek, and, finally, a gushing river. Its red waters forced the two men apart. Thomas shouted something about it lasting longer and reaching farther than anyone had expected.

Aaron's dream-self touched a finger to the thick, warm liquid. As he tasted it, the metallic tang of blood greeted him, and the river began to recede. Thomas could move closer once more, and he stepped over the stained ground to reach the dreamer. Aaron collapsed into the older man's arms, sobbing about the general's loss and his own fears.

"War is never what we expect," said Thomas. "It's like that river, dividing friends and families. And it always leaves a red stain." When Aaron awakened, he knew his friend was right.

June brought a long-anticipated surge of excitement, as Fifty-Sixth Virginia waded the Potomac River into Maryland. *The South is invading the North! This time it won't fail like when they stopped us at my home. That battle was to help Maryland become a part of the Confederacy. This one is even bigger. It looks like we're going to go into Pennsylvania and on to Washington. When we capture the Union capital, we'll have won! The Confederate States of America will finally be a free nation!*

Aaron shivered with excitement as he crossed into Maryland. *Maryland! Home! Helen!* His mind caressed each word, speaking it as sweetly and reverently as a prayer. He was thrilled when they arrived in Williamsport.

Williamsport! I'm not much more than ten miles from home! Only ten miles!

Except for a few minutes before the Sharpsburg battle the preceding September, he hadn't been home for more than two years. It would be easy to sneak away and see Helen. He knew it could be done. He could just drop out of the line at a farmer's house along the road and borrow a horse.

The thrill overwhelmed him; his stomach knotted as excitement jammed his throat. Every impulse said to take the chance. *Why not? All my life I've been adventuresome. Why not now? Won't Helen be shocked! Then I'll stop by my own home for a few minutes and gallop to Hagerstown and catch the brigade this evening.*

His heart hammered in his chest, and his hands twitched as he considered the possibilities. *So close, so close,* his mind urged. *Helen can see me in uniform! I can go to battle knowing she still waits for me.*

Torn between his duty and the siren's call, he felt he would rip in two. *I haven't seen the girl I love in over two years, and it might be two more before I get to see her again! Ten miles!* Yet his head slowly waged a counterattack on his wildly beating heart. *Would it work? How would I return the horse? What if someone sees me? Should I tell Johnny Williams? He'd like to go too. What if Helen isn't home today?*

Hard though it was, he could feel the tide of battle shift as his mind continued its onslaught. Desertion? The true and terrible word invaded his romantic daydreams. *There's no way I can go. I'm a soldier on a mission. It'd be better for me to return to Helen later as a hero than to surprise her now like a boy sneaking from his duty. It's better that way. She'll love me more when I return to her for good after we have won independence.* Still, the battle raged deep inside.

Aaron's decision was confirmed a thousand times over that very evening, when the soldiers witnessed a sickening sight—the execution of a disobedient Southern soldier. The officers formed the entire brigade into a *U* shape in an open field. The men all had to watch, since this was an example of military justice. It was a warning to them all, they were told. The guards tied the struggling man with his back against a stake in the ground, beside his coffin. He made a desperate effort to free himself, his cries echoing across the field. A guard cuffed him in the head, lashed him to the stake, and blindfolded him. Twelve riflemen marched to the front of the troops and aimed their guns at the man's bare chest. Aaron couldn't breathe.

Everything was silent except for the man's sobbing. Then "Ready …

Aim ... Fire!" Aaron jerked as the miscreant's body collapsed. The scene was messy and brief. The wretch hung limp. Someone cut him loose, and he fell into his coffin. Aaron felt numb, light-headed, and faint. Any remaining thoughts of sneaking away to Helen were carried into the wind with the gun smoke.

The infantry was soon on the move again, marching through Hagerstown and into Pennsylvania. *Maybe we'll go right on to Washington. Maybe we'll capture Lincoln himself, or at least run him so far away he can't do any more harm. Surely the war will be over then.*

General Lee had forbidden scavenging, but an abnormal amount of chicken, pork, and beef did much to relieve Aaron's stomach. In times like these, he told himself, it was better to fill up than to ask questions. He consoled his conscience with what the Yankees had done to Fredericksburg. *They ransacked the houses there. It's about time they pay for causing this war.*

The troops moved toward their ultimate goals of Harrisburg and Washington until it became clear that the Union army was going to try to stop them at a little town called Gettysburg. The battle had been going for two days when Fifty-Sixth Virginia arrived. It was the afternoon of July 3 when commanding General Pickett ordered his division into an open field beyond the woods, telling them to lie in tall grass behind the artillery caisson.

The earth trembled as the Confederate cannons boomed against the enemy ahead. Union artillery rained down its fiery response. The big guns bucked and roared as, for two hours, the men wilted in the sultry sun, breathing hot dirt and stifling smoke. Canteens soon emptied, but the officers denied all requests to go for refills.

After what seemed like forever, the artillery guns stilled, followed by an ominous silence. At General Pickett's order, the men clambered from their hiding places. Colonel Stuart shouted, "Fix bayonets." As the soldiers attached the deadly barbs, he appointed file closers in each company, ordering them to march behind and shoot any comrade who lagged or retreated. If a file closer refused to shoot the straggler, he was to be shot dead by the other file closers.

The colonel barked out, "Advance slowly with arms at will. No cheering. No firing. No breaking from common to quickstep. Dress on the center. Forward. March!"

As the infantry passed them, the artillery cannoneers lifted their red-trimmed kepi caps in salute. Colonel Stuart gestured across the valley, shouting, "See that wall? It's full of Yankees! I want you to help take it!"

"God pity those Yankees hiding behind that little wall," Aaron muttered to Johnny beside him, adding, "Before the sun sets, most of them will be dead." *Most of us too*, he feared silently. Aaron knew Johnny wondered if his parents could endure another letter of horror.

Aaron looked straight ahead at that miserable little wall. He pulled his cap down, checked his ammunition, and steeled himself for the march into the mouth of hell.

CHAPTER 17

Joel, Summer 1863

While Aaron moved with his Rebel unit into Maryland and Pennsylvania, Joel's Seventy-First Pennsylvania was stationed at Bull Run Creek in northern Virginia. He sat on the creek bank, recalling Aaron's assumption that the battle there two years earlier would end the war.

Joel viewed that battle's grisly harvest. Before him lay half-buried, decaying bodies. His gaze drifted to a nicely rounded bit of white in the dried grass, glowing in the twilight.

There used to be a brain inside that skull. Maggots long since took it. Now nothing is left—nothing.

Joel kept staring at the skull, so white and empty, so forlorn in its final resting place. *I wonder what kind of dreams raced around inside that skull. Maybe a wife and children? Certainly parents. That brain probably had as many hopes as mine does. Yet all those dreams ended up in maggots'*

131

bellies. I wonder if that skull was a Yankee or a Rebel. I guess the maggots didn't care.

Joel wasn't alone in his somber mood. Private Richard Anderson, sitting next to him, spoke up. "What a mess! Here we sit, right where the Army of the Potomac was *two years ago*, and what have we gained? We'll never take Richmond. I say we should all just go home. Who cares if the South is in the Union or not? They're scum anyway and sure not worth fighting over."

As Joel mused, Lieutenant William Bounty spoke harshly. "Let me tell you, young man, that you have no business saying things like that. You sound as if this war has no meaning. It's chickens like you that encourage the Rebs to try to splinter the best nation on God's earth."

Lieutenant Bounty continued harshly. "After Antietam, I couldn't sleep, thinking of my comrades who had shared my blankets the night before—men who were now lying cold and stiff on the ground. I saw their dead faces, and I wept for those lives that had been stolen. That night at Antietam, I asked God the question that plagued my mind. 'Why can't the fighting end? Surely you, God, hate this unbearable slaughter.'

"I said everything you've said, young man, and much more—and God answered me that night. It came in a tearful voice from that dark battlefield, a voice that cried to me like Abel's blood from the ground where Cain slew him. And it asked me, 'Compromise what? Can righteousness be compromised? Can we allow traitors to destroy the greatest nation on God's earth?'"

Joel watched, mesmerized by the officer's magnetism.

Bounty went on. "I had no answer. I only knew that this is a war of righteousness such as the world has never seen. I must not quit fighting until God's will is accomplished. God is with President Lincoln and our cause. God made this great Union. Now the Satan of the South is trying to tear it apart." Bounty's hands curled into fists, but slowly he relaxed as his gaze began to roam around the circle that had gathered, holding each man's gaze and finally falling on the shamed Private Anderson.

Richard was speechless. Joel could see that he was mortified, that he wanted to retreat to his tent. Bounty only reached out and squeezed

Richard's shoulder, his large hand resting lightly on the younger man. His warm gesture brought a subtle change. Through moist eyes, Richard looked up at the lieutenant again, this time with gratitude, thanking him and swearing to never criticize the Union cause again.

The next day, the soldiers bought newspapers from a subtler, with headlines announcing that the Rebels had invaded the Union and now occupied Williamsport and Hagerstown. President Lincoln had issued a proclamation saying that because Southern troops were threatening the North, one hundred thousand additional militiamen were to be mustered from Maryland, Pennsylvania, Ohio, and West Virginia for six months of service. In addition, the president had asked New York for twenty thousand militiamen, and the governor of Pennsylvania had called for volunteers.

In late June, Seventy-First Pennsylvania, reduced to 366 men and 27 officers, crossed the Potomac into central Maryland on a pontoon bridge built on boats placed together sideways, each drifting from upstream anchors. Now commanded by General Webb, they marched through Maryland and into Pennsylvania. The new general called his troops "yellow-bellied sorry excuses for soldiers" and warned that he would "shoot stragglers like dogs."

No one was going to see if Webb would carry out his promises, especially the one involving disembowelment for cowardice. The Pennsylvania regiments flew their flags and cheered as they entered their home state. It had been a long walk for Joel. His feet ached, and so did his back and legs.

That evening, as Seventy-First Pennsylvania camped on a conical hill named Cemetery Ridge, Richard Anderson told Joel of the area. "I used to live near here, Joel. Up ahead is a town named Gettysburg. I was born there and lived there until about five years ago, when we moved to Philadelphia."

Private Anderson sketched on the ground with a stick. "On up ahead is a cemetery, and then the road leads to Gettysburg. It's kind of like the spokes of a wheel, with roads coming in from Taneytown and Emmitsburg, and from Chambersburg and other towns."

Although Joel was very tired, sleep didn't come easily. He knew this might be his last night alive. He tossed and turned; his aching body cried for rest, but his mind reeled from Amy to his mother and then to the recognition that tomorrow night he might sleep in the nearby cemetery.

The next morning, July 2, General Webb addressed the brigade. "We face an important battle, men—a very important battle. The Rebels want to march into Washington and destroy the greatest nation on earth, and they have us outnumbered. But we are going to stop them, and stop them right here! We have the high ground. I expect you to defend it with your lives. Anyone who does not do his duty in even the smallest way will be dealt with severely, and any man I see retreating, I will shoot personally. And I am not one to miss when I shoot to kill." He waved his sidearm wildly in the air to prove his point. "This is Pennsylvania. Defend our state and our country with all you've got."

The reminder that they were to defend their home state struck deep into the hearts of the Pennsylvania men and reminded Joel that his mother had been born in this state. Earlier, the war had been an unsuccessful attempt to take Richmond, the Confederate capital. Now, for Seventy-First Pennsylvania troops, it had become a war to defend their own homes and their nation's capital. Each man stood a little taller and took extra care in checking his weapon.

The officers stationed the Philadelphia Brigade behind a two-foot stone wall near the cemetery. Other brigades manned the barrier in a solid blue line to the south. The ground had been chosen. The Confederates would try to break through and move to Harrisburg or Washington. The Yankees knew they must stop them.

Patriotic music blared from the regimental bands behind. "Mine Eyes Have Seen the Glory of the Coming of the Lord," with its promise of victory for the Union troops, gave Joel a thrill and bolstered his spirits, but had to turn away from his comrades as the Union band played "Just Before the Battle, Mother, I Am Thinking Most of You." He wondered what his mother would think if she knew what her son would soon be facing. The horrid words raced through his mind: "while upon the field we're watching, with the enemy in view. Comrades brave are 'round me lying, filled with thoughts of home and God; for well they know that on the morrow, some will sleep beneath the sod."

As the sun set on July 2, Joel could see the battle developing to the south as enemy soldiers marched across the valley. Eventually, some of the enemy came directly toward Seventy-First Pennsylvania. Joel's heart pounded like a hammer on an anvil; his fingers trembled, and his legs shook. He needed a latrine. As the enemy neared, the order to fire rang out. His heart jumped as he aimed at a man in gray and pulled the trigger. The victim jerked and crumpled. Immediately, another gray uniform leaped forward to take the fallen man's place. It took Joel at least a half minute to reload. He raised his musket, sighted an enemy along the barrel, shot—and missed.

Again he reloaded and shot; he had no time to think of anything else as the sounds of battle surged around and below him. *Hit the closest. Don't let them get to you.* The enemy was at the wall; Joel rammed the butt of his rifle into the jaw of a Rebel soldier. With the sickening sound of shattering bone and a gasp of horror, the man crumpled in a heavy pile as Joel spun the weapon to place the bayonet blade into the next man who appeared before him.

Miraculously, the Rebels began to retreat, and the Philadelphia Brigade chased them back across the road at the valley floor. Joel was exhilarated. It was life or death, and he still had life. He had helped stop the enemy from moving to Washington. Joy and relief coursed through him and filled him so full that he shouted in celebration. On the way back to their high-ground position at the stone wall, Joel and his comrades seized weapons from the dead and those thrown down during the retreat. They loaded these arms and stacked them along the outer angle of the stone wall, just in case the Rebels attacked again.

We won the battle! We stopped the Rebs! That wasn't so bad after all. Sure, I was scared, but so was everybody else. I proved that I'm a good soldier! That wasn't so bad.

Early the next morning, Joel rose from his bedroll and viewed the previous evening's battlefield. Hundreds of bodies lay across the shallow valley to the west. Although hc had seen the ravages of war at home, the sight hit again with horror. The air was thick with flies and the oppressive odor of death.

The commanders again ordered Seventy-First Pennsylvania to defend Cemetery Ridge against another expected attack. Joel was again stationed at the angle where the stone wall made a ninety-degree turn.

Early in the afternoon, he saw something that stole his breath away. Thousands of Rebels rose up from the grass in battle formation and began to march the three-fourths mile across the valley. Other Rebel soldiers surged out from the woods behind them. There seemed to be far more than the day before, and they all came at once. *Are they all going to march over here? How will we ever live? But they'll never make it—I hope.*

Mounting desperation built in Joel, squeezing his lungs and guts. They could do nothing except wait for the massive tide of enemy soldiers to come into range. They marched shoulder to shoulder, closely followed by another line. It was the most horrible sight Joel had ever seen. The Union cannons took a heavy toll, but the enemy surged on, with new Rebels replacing those who fell.

The horror inched across Emmitsburg Road, by the smoldering embers of the Bliss buildings, and up the hill, screeching out the terrifying Rebel yell. Some of his comrades began to retreat. Joel had heard no order, so he stood his ground behind the little stone wall. Out in front, the Rebel general on horseback called, "Boys, give 'em the cold steel!"

Suddenly, the general slumped in his saddle and fell to the ground. The horse reeled backward. The stunned Rebels faltered for a moment. The general's body had not yet been thrown clear, so the horse reared up, trying to dislodge the dead weight. The Rebel soldiers scattered to avoid the lethal hooves; they stood in confusion and then regrouped and moved closer.

Joel heard the order: "Fire!" He quickly aimed at the closest enemy, fired, and saw a body drop. He reloaded and fired again without hitting anyone. The enemy was too close for him to reload, so he picked up one of the guns he had collected and loaded the previous evening, fired at an oncoming soldier, and then picked up another rifle and fired again and then again.

Somewhere in his deepest recesses, the term "slaughtering chickens" rose up and hovered strangely. He slaughtered another and another. Sweat and flecks of blood mingled on his brow as he struggled to see clearly, barely having time to sweep a sleeve across his eyes before firing again. His mission now was to kill until killed.

The Rebel line advanced, shoulder to shoulder. Through the dense battlefield smoke, a dim figure rushed forward. Joel's finger curled for the kill.

Just as he began to squeeze the trigger, a terrible sense of recognition jolted him. In that instant, his enemy hesitated. Joel tried to stop, tried to release the pressure on the trigger—but it was too late. His wretched scream joined his gun's deadly roar. In a moment that seemed like an eternity, the Rebel jerked violently and sank to the ground.

Joel screamed, "No!" and lurched forward. Everything swirled around him in blurred confusion. His knees buckled, and he fell unconscious onto Aaron's bleeding body.

CHAPTER 18

After Gettysburg

Oh my dear God. I killed Aaron. Oh no, oh no. Oh my dear God. It can't be. Joel pleaded, rocking himself and trembling. *Aaron won't forgive me, my family won't forgive me, and God won't forgive me. My best friend ...*

Tears rolled into his dirty beard. *I couldn't have! I just couldn't have!* But he could not deny the final frozen image: Aaron screaming in agony as blood drenched his body. Over and over he saw the bearded man burst through the haze and then freeze in a horrible instant of recognition. He saw Aaron lower his rifle a fraction. Joel had a split second to see his enemy's face before he shot. It happened so fast—but somehow Aaron had recognized him and stayed his own shot.

That moment cost Aaron his life. Everything after that disappeared, lost in the battle smoke. *I'm alive because Aaron is dead. Why couldn't he have killed me instead? His last great adventure, and I sent him off alone again. I can't go with Aaron this time either.*

Maybe it wasn't Aaron, his soul cried out, hoping against reason.

Maybe that man just looked like him. So many have the same build and hair color … But he stopped himself, shaking his head, knowing it was hopeless. He had seen his best friend's eyes and black beard, and he could never forget. *The last thing Aaron ever knew was that I shot him.*

Joel buried his face in his grimy hands. *I want to die. Oh, please, let me die and be with Aaron so he'll know I'm sorry. Why didn't he shoot me too? Why didn't he shoot me instead?*

Another truth invaded his mind. *I am a prisoner. Somehow the Rebels captured me. I didn't know what I was doing, and they captured me. It looks like they got some other Union soldiers too.*

The night passed slowly. As dawn eased the darkness, a Confederate officer barked, "Prisoners, line up over there." Joel came shakily to his feet. They were being organized to march, not in a military manner but like sheep, with the Rebel guards flanking them and prodding them forward with sharp kicks and threats.

Joel had no idea where they were going. It didn't matter. He had to follow, and he didn't care where. Anywhere on earth was hell to him now, so who cared what part of hell he was in?

The men walked all day and then stopped as the last riotous colors of the sunset mocked the ugliness to which Joel had condemned himself. He heard a guard say, "Well, this is Williamsport."

Joel sucked in a breath. *Williamsport? That's practically home.*

In spite of Joel's haunted fear of condemnation, a spark fluttered briefly in his heart as his thoughts turned to his family, who were little more than ten miles away. How he would love to escape and be in Amy's arms. How he wished he could awaken from this terrible nightmare and be home.

How wonderful it would be to see my little Braden. But his heart faltered. Did he want to go home and face the guilt? Any happiness he found would be poisoned. No, this nightmare was real. He could not wake up—ever. *No, I don't want to go home, even if I could, even to see Amy and Braden. I couldn't face my family after I've killed Aaron. What would I say to Abigail and Robert? And to Helen? I killed her future. I couldn't even look her in the eye.*

A small grunt escaped his chapped lips as a very real possibility assaulted him: Aaron's body might never be found. His final resting place could be in an unidentified grave next to strangers, like those buried on their farm. It was too much. He remembered fearing he would find Aaron's body on their farm ten months ago and how happy he had been to discover his beloved cousin had not been killed in that battle. Now Joel wished he had been. Dying at home from a stranger's bullet was much better than being killed far from home by your best friend.

He wished he could cup his fingers and blow the signal, but there were no ears to hear it. He remembered their dreams as boys together. War had been a great adventure, and men were noble. They had peered at the world through a magical looking glass; but with Aaron's death, the glass was shattered, the magic gone. Joel was trapped in this awful kingdom of disease and death. War had promised adventure but produced drudgery; it had promised honor but delivered disgrace. It had promised glory but brought the greatest suffering one could ever know.

The prisoners crossed the Potomac on pontoon bridges and then plodded south for several days before finally reaching Staunton, Virginia, where they were loaded into boxcars and shuttled east to Richmond. After many hours, the train passed through a town, crossed a river bridge, and came to a halt. The wooden door clattered open, and a Rebel soldier ordered them outside. Several Confederates stood around the car with rifles slung casually over their shoulders.

"Welcome to Belle Isle, Yankees. This prison camp will be your home until the South wins its independence—unless your government thinks you're worth exchanging. We will treat you fairly. We'll give you the same rations that are issued to our own boys in the field. They are enough to live on, and I expect to hear no complaints. Rations are dispensed at nine in the morning and three in the afternoon."

Joel shuddered as he heard the lieutenant warn, "If you try to escape, you will be shot. If you approach the ditch just inside the prison walls, you will be shot. If you attempt a large-scale escape, those cannons up on the hill will shoot you if you aren't already drowned in the river." The commander concluded with a sneer, "Enjoy your stay."

The days dragged slowly by. *How I had hoped to get to Richmond so the Rebel capital would be captured and the war would end. I didn't expect to get to Richmond this way.*

He constantly wondered about the folks at home. *How would Amy feel if she knew where I am and what I've done?* Soon, Aaron's parents would receive a letter telling them of their son's death. They would read it as a family and weep for the loss, and then they would wait to hear from Joel, keeping the hope alive that he still lived. Joel toyed with the idea of never going home—just letting his family think he had been killed too. He felt branded by his crime, and his heart carried a scarlet letter *K* for killing his cousin.

A guard announced that mail would be sent and received the next day. *I should write a letter to my family,* Joel thought. *They deserve to know where I am.* He fished inside his coat pockets and found a short, blunt pencil and his black leather-bound journal.

Where to begin? He couldn't imagine. How do you tell about a nightmare to people who are still dreaming? He wrote about how much he missed his family. By the second page, he knew he'd soon have to tell them about the battle. He stared at the empty sheet. After a few minutes, he folded it and put it back into his pocket. The rest could wait.

That night, he lay awake in the dark, hearing the incessant whine of insects near his ear, along with the usual snoring. He knew now that he wanted to go home someday, but how could he face his family? He couldn't even write what he had done.

He rolled to his side, reached into his pocket, and retrieved the half-written letter. He inched his way to a patch of bright moonlight shining through the flap of the tent. Gazing at the ghostly white paper in the pale moonbeams, he penciled the second page, unable to tell the full, horrible truth.

```
I must thank you all for your prayers.
Gettysburg was as bad as you must have
heard by now, but God carried me to safety.
I am in Belle Isle prison in Richmond now.
I love you dearly, Amy. Please take care of
```

our sweet little boy. I love him so much,
even though I've never even seen him. But
someday I'll come home and won't have to
miss any of you anymore.

Joel Charles Haskins

Joel reread the letter carefully and then scratched out the line "God carried me to safety." *How can I boast that God carried me to safety but let Aaron to go his grave?* Then he scratched out the part about coming home. *Aaron isn't coming home.*

Finally, Joel wadded up the second page and threw it away. He then wrote in the margin of the first page, "I am a prisoner at Belle Isle in Richmond." With a sigh, he folded the letter and tucked it away. The next day it was in the mail.

A few weeks later, he received a reply in his mother's hand, dated September 7, 1863. He shook helplessly as he opened it; his breath slowed in his lungs. He was suddenly terrified, trembling. He knew the words within would damn him—and in his mother's own hand! His guilt roared to life, stronger than ever, but he had to see, had to know.

Dearest Joel,

We praise God every moment that He has
brought you to safety. When we got your
letter, it soothed our worried souls. We
waited more than two months after the big
battle in Pennsylvania and prayed that
you were alive. I hate to imagine you in
prison, but I know God has done what is
best to keep you for your son. He is so
sweet—angelic even. God sent him straight
from heaven above to give us joy. It's hard
to believe he's nearly seven months old
now. We wish you could be here and hold
him. You will be a wonderful father and
will love raising Braden Joel to be the
kind of man you are. But we know you wish
that too. Soon you will come back to us. I

know it. Maybe you will be exchanged for
a Confederate prisoner.

Joel, I hate to tell you this, but there
is some bad news. Your aunt and uncle
got a letter a few days ago. It was from
the Confederate army. Aaron was shot in
the battle in Pennsylvania and is in a
hospital in Richmond. He lost his arm,
Joel. A Union soldier fired at him up close,
hitting him just above his left elbow. They
amputated it, and he's getting better now.
The important thing is that he's alive,
and he's going to be all right.

Joel sank to his knees, crying. He threw his head back and spread
his arms out, shouting, "Aaron's alive! He's alive! Oh, thank God!"
Tears flowed as he clasped his hands in thanksgiving. *Aaron was dead
but is alive again. Thank God! Oh, thank God! I didn't kill Aaron! Oh,
thank you, Jesus!*

Aaron heard the crows before he saw them; they circled Gettysburg
like black jesters joking at the macabre parade that sat still as death. He
lay in one of hundreds of ambulance wagons, his cheek pressed into the
rough grain of the damp, smelly floorboards. Squeezing his eyes shut,
he prayed that when they opened, he would be at home and this would
all be a terrible dream. But he knew better; there was evil in the very
air around him. Home could never be like this.

Opening his eyes, he looked at his left arm and saw why it burned
like fire. All he could see was a bloody sleeve; all he could feel was
terrible pain. Never had he felt so alone and helpless. He tried to grasp
a memory untainted by pain and fear, but reality narrowed to one vivid
horror: Joel's face sighting down the barrel of a gun.

In that millisecond, he had recognized his beloved cousin and somehow refused to fire. Through the bluish haze, he had seen Joel's eyes, perhaps even the glint of recognition in them. Then Joel's gun roared, and the world exploded into the worst pain he had ever known—then nothing. When he awakened, it was clear that the charge across the valley had failed. He heard shouts, and a fleeing comrade tugged him to his feet. All he knew was that he had to get away from the enemy side and to his own lines. Men around him ran, limped, and dragged themselves back. He stumbled to his feet, vaguely wondering whether Joel was dead.

Somehow he made it through the bodies and staggered the mile to Seminary Ridge, where he joined others as they bathed their wounds in a little creek. The parched men drank bloody water. General Pickett looked haggard and somewhat dazed, as if he knew already that of the entire body of twelve thousand, more than half were dead.

Aaron's eyes opened wide with horror as he gazed at the sea of ruined men. He saw, too, that a few men wore Union uniforms. Somehow they had been captured by the retreating Rebel army.

That night, Aaron lay sleepless in an orchard outside a Confederate field hospital. The stench was awful, and the men moaned or lay still as stones, never to moan again. Eventually the horrible night turned to morning, and Aaron was helped onto one of the many hundreds of wagons designated as ambulances. Day sank into another night with neither food nor medication. Aaron found himself in another battle, with hundreds of enemy soldiers about to shoot him. He awakened, shaking, nearly sobbing.

Later—much later, it seemed—the ground lurched as the springless wagon began to move. It made occasional stops, and once a soldier from another wagon asked Aaron to help him get water. Aaron winced when he saw that the bloody man was missing a hand and an ear. Together they drew water from a farm well, each pulling with his good arm. They drank deeply and took turns dousing their wounds in the cool water bucket.

The wagon train moved on and then, much later, stopped again. "Where are we?" Aaron asked anyone who would listen.

"We're in Maryland, at a town called Williamsport," the driver responded over his shoulder.

"Williamsport? That's only a few miles from my home!" Aaron could hardly believe it had been just two weeks since he had been here as they marched toward Gettysburg. He recalled how he had longed to go see Helen. *What has happened to me in just two weeks?*

After another horrible night, someone helped Aaron onto a door that was stretched across two barrels. A tall, tired-looking man in a blood-smeared apron passed his hand across his dripping face and rubbed the sweat into his bloody apparel.

The surgeon checked Aaron's arm and quietly picked up his saw. "Son, your arm's shattered. It will never be useful again, and with the bone damaged as much as it is, you'll die if we don't amputate."

Aaron tried to argue, but the words stuck in his throat, and the surgeon said, "This could save your life, and it can still be a good one."

Aaron didn't see the surgeon wipe the bloody saw against his dirty apron, but he screamed as it bit into his flesh and bone. His arm soon fell to the ground. The doctor clamped the artery and tied it off and then tossed the lifeless limb into a heap of mangled arms and legs. Scores of flies rose and then returned to their bloody banquet, feasting once more on man's folly.

As the surgeon moved away to remove another soldier's leg, the bearded assistant covered Aaron's open stump with wet lint and wrapped it with damp cotton dressings; then he moved Aaron onto another pile of straw to wait for the chloroform to wear off. As he departed, Aaron heard him say, "Haskins is your name, right? Aaron Haskins? I'm sorry you lost your arm." Then he added, "The wages of war is death—and arms and legs and broken families." Through the pain, Aaron realized the man was his friend Thomas Thomas.

As he began to awaken, Aaron's gaze fell on the oozing pile of discarded limbs. He thought his arm lay near the top—pale and gray against the blackening limbs beneath. He desperately wanted to retrieve it and clutch it to himself, to tie it back into its rightful place. He wanted to believe in a miracle—that one day he might be whole again—as he finally drifted into pain-filled sleep, escorted to that happier state by images of arms and legs rising from the pile to find their rightful owners.

The days passed, and as Aaron's mind gradually cleared, he learned that the retreating Confederate army had joined the wounded at Williamsport. Although there had been some fighting, they eventually crossed the Potomac and into the Confederacy. Soldiers put Aaron on a train to a hospital in Richmond, where the surgeons performed a higher amputation, very near his shoulder.

Aaron's Richmond ward held about sixty wounded men. Some convalescing soldiers acted as nurses, aiding those who moaned most desperately. He often looked at his arm. It wasn't there. He was haunted by ghostly sensations; he could feel himself clenching his fist or flexing a muscle, but there was nothing now but rotted flesh and a discarded bone in Williamsport.

Over the next few weeks, Aaron enjoyed the nurse who cared for him, who was about his mother's age. She smiled at him, humming as she fastened the bandage, and then softly sang, "Lavender's blue, dilly dilly, lavender's green."

The words made him think of Helen and soothed his depression as he sang with her, "When I am king, dilly dilly, you shall be queen." She laughed and stood up to leave, still singing quietly.

"Please wait, ma'am. Could I know your name and call you by it? My name's Aaron."

She paused a moment and then said, "Tanya. Really, in my native Russian language, it is Tatiana. And, yes, you may call me Tanya or Tatiana if you want to."

Tatiana. He watched her walk away, playing it over and over in his mind. *Tanya ... Tanya ... Tatiana ... What a beautiful name. My mother would enjoy her.* He propped himself up against the wall behind his bed and was rewarded with a sharp reminder in his shoulder. The reality of why he was there thundered back; his life would never be the same.

A few weeks later, the surgeon removed Aaron's stitches, bandaged his shoulder, and told him he could go home. He had never heard a word that was its equal—*home.* After more than two years in the war, followed by nearly four months in the hospital, he was finally free to go home. Tatiana helped him with his clothes and told him that her father had paid for a train ticket that would get him all the way to Sharpsburg.

"Thank you, Tanya. I appreciate you so much! Thank you for helping me. Now I am going home!"

CHAPTER 19

Home, November 1863

When Aaron first glimpsed Antietam Creek, he was overwhelmingly drawn to the banks that welcomed him home. *Home!* As he gazed down and drew in the comforting sounds of the water's passage, he was suddenly overcome. Tears welled, and a song entered his mind: *'Mid pleasures and palaces though we may roam, be it ever so humble, there's no place like home. A charm from the skies seems to hallow us there, which, seek through the world, is ne'er met with elsewhere. Home! Home! Sweet, sweet home. There is no place like home; there is no place like home.*

He gazed toward the home he had longed to see for nearly thirty months, yet he was rooted to the spot, a mere hundred yards away. He descended to the creek, knelt, washed the tears from his eyes, and wiped them with his dangling sleeve. He wanted to run into the house like the carefree child he had been, but that boy was long forgotten, buried forever at Manassas and Fredericksburg and Gettysburg, and in the bone pile at Williamsport.

After a few minutes, he approached the door and knocked. It soon opened. His mother stood before him, haloed by the lamplight in the entryway. Each day of waiting, she had envisioned the arrival of her strong, handsome son—not this haggard, bearded stranger. But in an instant, she knew. Here stood her beloved boy. Her face transformed into an expression of relief and every ounce of love and happiness that she felt for him.

"Mama," he whispered.

The word was like a magic incantation, binding mother and son together. With her own words stuck in her throat, Abigail stepped into an embrace, sobs of joy shaking her as she clung to him. He wrapped his arm around her, trying not to wince as she unwittingly struck his stump. Abigail clung so tightly it was as if she wished to mold him back into her body and make him whole.

"Oh Mama … I've missed you so," he murmured into her silvery hair.

"Thank you, God. Thank you, Jesus. Aaron …" she said between gasps and sobs.

As they stood there, neither willing to release the other, Robert came to the door and pulled it open. Soft light from the house spilled out across Aaron and his mother. "Aaron? Aaron. It's you! Oh Aaron."

Aaron released his mother and wrapped his arm around his father's neck. Robert held the malnourished, bearded body in a strong embrace. "I'm so glad you're home safe. I've missed you so much." Aaron buried his head in the curve of his father's neck and sobbed like a child.

"You must be cold," said Abigail, clasping her hands. "Let's get you inside and warmed up. You must be famished! I'll heat some supper for you. You look starved." Standing on her toes, she kissed his hairy cheek and then pulled him inside.

Aaron's five-year-old sister, Julia, stepped timidly down the stairs, dragging her doll by its cloth hand. She stopped near the bottom and eyed the strange man warily, her bare toes curling beneath her in suspicion. He walked toward her, and she inched back. She narrowed her eyes and looked at him. He stepped up and reached out to take her hand, but she retreated farther and looked to her mother. Abigail stood beside her son and laid a comforting hand on his right shoulder.

"Julia, this is your brother Aaron. Don't you remember him?"

The little girl studied Aaron's face for several seconds but hung back.

Abigail turned to Aaron. "It's the beard, honey. She doesn't recognize you with the beard. And she was only three when you left."

Aaron sat on the stair beside Julia. "I know what you'll remember." He began singing her favorite song: "Jesus loves me this I know, for the Bible tells me so." Her eyes widened with delight, and she cried out, "Aaron! Aaron!" as she scooted closer. He lifted her from the stairs and carried her to the living room, her arms wound around his neck. He looked into her face and almost laughed out loud as she wrinkled her nose and said, "You smell funny."

"Well, I guess I do smell bad, my dear. I'm sorry, but some Yank stole my best bar of soap last week, so I couldn't make myself smell good for this dance." Julia giggled as Aaron set her down and then gave her a mock bow with a shamefaced look while rubbing his beard against her cheek.

LaVonne appeared from upstairs, asking, "Did I hear Aaron, or am I dreaming?" As her eyes met those of her brother, the nineteen-year-old squealed and flung herself at him. A few moments later, Grandma came down to investigate the uproar. After rounds of embraces, everyone moved into the dining room. Aaron asked Grandma to sit next to him. He looked at his family, drinking in each face. Nearly thirty months--a long time.

Abigail asked, "Robert, will you get your brother's family? They must see Aaron—they'll be so happy he's home."

Robert rose and walked to Aaron. He placed his right hand carefully on his son's left shoulder, just above the stub, and said, "I'm so proud of you, Son. You're a hero. A real hero." As he crossed the bridge toward Glen's house, he heard the crickets happily welcoming his son home.

Abigail sat across the table from Aaron, pleased to see him enjoying the home-cooked meal. He shoveled food into his mouth as if he were afraid it would disappear. It did, bite after delicious bite. A perceptive mother, Abigail had already opened and buttered his biscuits, making them easy to eat with one hand. She was aghast at how thin and frail he had become, and she quickly refilled his bowl. As Aaron gulped down his second helping, Robert returned and flung the front door wide open. Glen and Fannie rushed inside, along with their children.

Fannie looked past her nephew's gaunt features and into his eyes. "You've come back to us. It's wonderful." Aaron stood as she hugged him.

She moved aside, and Glen shook his hand, trying not to look at the hollow sleeve. "It's so great to have you home," he said, his voice husky.

The entire family crowded around Aaron and watched as he finished his third bowl of soup. Julia slipped around his chair and climbed onto his knee. "Aaron! Where's your arm?" she asked, thinking he might be playing a trick on her. "Where'd you put it? Let me see it."

Abigail sucked in a breath, visibly shocked by the candidness of her littlest child. Aaron made an almost imperceptible shake of the head, signaling for everyone to stay silent as he pressed his little sister close to him and gently asked, "No one ever told you I lost my arm in the war?"

He felt Julia's head shaking against his chest and heard her ask, "Where did you lose it? Can't you find it?"

Aaron didn't laugh at his littlest sister. "No, what I mean is that I was wounded. My arm was shot by a gun, and the doctors had to take it off. It's gone now, and I won't ever be able to get it back. But I still have one good arm."

Julia's brow twisted in concern. "But, Aaron, if you only have one arm, how will you milk the cows?"

Aaron spoke softly to her. "I don't know yet. I'll have to find a way." Then he repeated, "I still have one strong arm to hug you with and push you on the tree swing. And maybe you can help me with the things I can't do alone. Maybe we can milk the cows together!"

Julia beamed her pleasure at being deputized as her brother's left arm and said, "You can sit on one side and milk with one hand, and I'll sit on the other and milk with both of mine."

Aaron rested his chin in her soft hair and whispered, "Thank you, Julia." His eyes passed over the children to the adults, finding it difficult to hold anyone's gaze.

Julia's five-year-old cousin Kylie moved close. "I'll help too."

"So will I," said Kylan.

Aaron squeezed the twins. "Thank you, Kylie and Kylan. I'd like that."

Out of the corner of his eye, Aaron noticed Amy quietly lingering by the doorway as she held the sleeping Braden against her shoulder. He couldn't imagine the emptiness she must feel with Joel locked away in prison. He held eye contact with her, and in that exchange, he saw pain and confusion. Above all, though, he saw quiet strength, telling him that she could bear anything for the sake of her husband and child.

Pulled from Amy's gaze by a persistent tug on his shirtsleeve, he looked back at Julia, who asked, "Does it hurt, Aaron?"

"It hurts some but not nearly as much as it used to. It's strange. Sometimes I feel like my arm is still there, like I feel my fingers wriggling."

Julia's eyes grew wider as she asked, "How did it happen? How did you get shot?"

Aaron's mouth went dry. He glanced at the silent Amy and wondered if she knew. "Well, Julie, a Yankee shot me—just above my elbow." He held Julia's arm and rubbed the tender spot.

Fannie sat on the sofa, fingering a hole in her apron, envisioning her own son there next to her nephew—the way it used to be, the way it should be. Abigail was mostly happy now; she had her son—most of him, anyway. Fannie still feared that she would lose all of hers.

Aaron broke the brief silence and asked Glen, "Joel's still in prison, isn't he?"

"Yes."

"Where is he being held, do you know? Is he still at Belle Isle in Richmond?" He knew more about the prisons than he wished, and he worried for Joel's welfare.

"Yes, he's still at Belle Isle. It's been a long time—close to four months."

"I think about Joel a lot. You know I was in Richmond too—Belle Isle is in the middle of the James River, not far from where I was."

As Abigail and Robert's grandfather clock struck eight, Amy announced that she had to get home to get Braden to bed. She put on her wrapper and bundled the baby, happy that Aaron had come home. Yet the walk across the creek to her empty cabin seemed very long. Holding Braden close, she stumbled forward, tears stinging her eyes. Although she was truly glad for Aaron's safety, she ached for her husband. Never had she imagined that Aaron's return would increase her pain over Joel's absence. She realized anew how much she missed the sound of his boots on the back porch, his body filling the other side of the bed, and, most of all, his love and care. She entered the cabin and laid the sleeping Braden in his crib. Then, sinking to her knees, she sobbed.

After the crowd left, Abigail said to Aaron, "I almost forgot! I made a new quilt for you, with your favorite colors." She clapped her hands together. "I'm so excited to finally be able to give it to you. But I should tell you—some of your things were destroyed when our house was used as a hospital in the battle here a year ago. But we've restored your room as much as we could. Oh, Devin took your bed when you left, but when you wrote that you were coming home, the boys agreed to sleep together again."

She took his hand and pulled him up the stairs behind her. Many of Aaron's schoolbooks still sat on his desk with those of his brothers. A beautiful quilt with a log cabin design covered the cot.

"Ma, this is beautiful." He passed his fingers over the perfect stitches and geometric designs. "Thank you so much for making it for me." Then Aaron asked, "How is Helen?"

His mother moved toward him and placed one hand on his. "Her mother says she's waiting just for you."

Aaron wanted to believe her. "Ma," he said. He stepped into the hallway and lightly closed the door to the bedroom, "It's been so long, and so much has changed. I'm a different person. Sometimes I can't sleep—I lie awake thinking about the battles. Sometimes I dream terrible dreams. I'm afraid she won't want me."

"Nothing's really changed, Aaron. Nothing at all. She still wants you."

Abigail wrapped her arms around her son, intentionally placing her hand lightly on his stub. For the first time in many months, she was happy. As she left, she said, "The water should be hot for your bath now."

Aaron partially undressed and stood in front of the looking glass, which now had a long spiderweb of cracks. His eyes stared back at him from behind a scruffy beard. He let his gaze drop to his bared body and almost reeled in horror. He had never seen the amputation in a looking glass. His head seemed too large for his body, his remaining arm spindly, and every part of him looked dissected by the cracks in the glass. *I am a monster*, he thought.

He recalled the last time he had looked into this mirror, imagining himself proudly wearing a uniform. He was still proud to have been a soldier fighting for a noble cause, but he hadn't expected such a heavy price.

He spent the next hour bathing and trying to shave. Then, exhausted, he fell into bed. He blew out the kerosene lamp and lay there, staring up at the dark ceiling, thinking about Helen. *I hope Ma is right, that Helen still wants me.*

His body finally relaxed beneath the warm quilt. Then, sometime later, he saw a Yankee soldier pointing his gun! He dove for cover and found himself on the floor. Devin was by his side.

"Aaron, Aaron, it's okay. It's okay. You don't need to scream. You're home. Aaron, please calm down."

Aaron gradually awakened and looked at his bleeding, inflamed stub. He felt ashamed, but Devin seemed to understand. The two were able to wash it and stop the bloodshed.

Aaron climbed back into bed. He realized that although his body was home, his brain was still at war.

CHAPTER 20

Aaron at Home, November 1863

Aaron roused to an aroma that had drifted through his dreams all the time he had been at war. He stretched, expecting to hear reveille soon, still halfway dreaming of home, with its smells of freshly brewed coffee, fried sausage, and his mother's baked cinnamon rolls—what a wonderful memory.

Then he realized the smells were real. *Oh, thank you, God.* Gratitude washed over him as he bolted from bed, dressed as quickly as he could, and hurried downstairs. The family was already seated and praying. He tiptoed toward them and waited just outside the dining room until his father said, "Amen."

"Oooh," he said, "I haven't smelled such a great thing in years. I'll eat five of those cinnamon rolls." He snatched one without ceremony and stuffed it into his mouth; sugary frosting trickled down his chin. His sisters giggled as he munched the warm delight.

"We didn't want to wake you," Abigail said, beaming at her son's changed appearance—semi–clean shaven and dabbled with frosting. "We waited awhile but decided to go ahead."

"That's all right, Ma. Just as long as you left me some cinnamon rolls."

Julia kept sliding glances at her brother and said, "Aaron, you look like Mr. Perkins's old hound dog, Patches, when we dressed him up one time. He had those funny black patches all over his face. Just like you." She giggled and poked at the coarse, irregular stubble.

Aaron roared with laughter, straddled the chair near Julia, and spoke through another mouthful, "Well, Julie, you can just call me Patches the Second."

Within a half hour, he downed four eggs, two helpings of sausage, three cinnamon rolls, and three cups of the best coffee he had had in years. His mother looked both delighted and mortified. His missing left arm didn't slow him much from savagely scooping the food into his mouth. Aaron caught a few surprised looks at his wolfish eating and shrugged. In the army, there had been no ceremony, and the manners expected in the real world would be slow to return.

When he finished breakfast, LaVonne offered to help him finish shaving. She had always appreciated her big brother, and now, at nineteen, she engaged him in an intimate conversation about her potential suitors and a few complaints about her parents' restrictions. Aaron listened with interest. It was important to LaVonne whether one young man was taller than the other, and how well he sang in church and what he smelled like. This was fascinating for Aaron. He wondered how Helen would like his smell. He thought about how he must have smelled in army camp and was glad she hadn't been there evaluating him.

LaVonne scrubbed and whittled at Aaron's mishmash face and finally had him looking halfway presentable. "I guess you'll do, considering," she said with a laugh.

Later that morning, something struck him. "Ma, where's Nattie?" he asked, wondering why she wasn't helping in the kitchen. "I haven't seen her or Gabe yet." Aaron began to stand, when he was stopped by a tortured glance from his father, who was stoking the fire against the November cold.

"They ran away, Aaron."

"They … they what?"

"They just up and left us after all the years we've looked after them!" Robert scowled and shook his head in disgust. "It happened a few months ago. They didn't show up for morning chores one day. Naturally, we were concerned they might be sick, so we checked their cabin. They had cleaned out and snuck away. Only a bit of furniture was left—the ungrateful wretches!"

Glen, who, along with Fannie, had just come for a visit with Aaron, added, "We've been struggling along for a while now, just trying to get all the work done."

"But why would they leave? I know that a lot of slaves took off, but it's hard to believe Nattie and Gabe would do it. We took such good care of them."

"Maybe some Yankee abolitionist stole them," Robert replied. "You know those Quakers have stolen slaves for a long time. They help get them into the North and then sneak them from place to place and into Canada, where they can't be returned." Robert continued, spitting out disdainfully, "Those Quakers call themselves Christians, and then they steal other people's property."

Fannie took a small step to stand behind Glen's shoulder to block her face from her brother-in-law. She couldn't abide this discussion but knew she wasn't allowed to react.

Robert paused a moment and then stated his firm conviction: "I'll tell you our mistake. We should never have taught them to read and write. That caused all the trouble. If they couldn't read, they wouldn't have known what was going on and wouldn't have gotten such sinful ideas." After a moment, Robert added, "But I wonder how they are. I just don't see how they can get along without us to take care of them. I pray that God will look after them and bring them back home. I think about how they might be out there someplace starving to death, or shipped to a cruel master."

Aaron could only nod as his father continued, "Do you remember when that radical, John Brown, tried to take over the federal arsenal over at Harpers Ferry and arm the slaves into a rebellion? Not long after that, I found a newspaper in Gabe and Nattie's cabin that laid out the whole story. I suppose they stole other newspapers from our houses too. I should have whipped them for having the paper, but we couldn't imagine them being taken in by abolitionist trash. Yes, we should never have allowed them to read."

Fannie bristled but again knew a response would be condemned by the men of the house. It had been her idea to teach the slaves to read and write—her calling, she'd termed it—based on her secret wish that Nattie's children could have the same opportunities her own had. She knew it was nonsense to imagine Negroes could somehow have the rights of whites, but her husband and Robert had respected her desires and let her teach, thinking it would do no harm.

Robert added, "Of course, there were lots of ways they could've found out what was happening. For one thing, they heard a lot of our conversations. I don't think we ever tried to hide anything from them." He paused and then added, "We didn't have any reason to question their loyalty. When they went into town with us, they talked to other darkies. I guess there's no telling how those ideas got into their heads. Anyway, I sure miss them. The ladies have a real tough time without Nattie. And you know how we relied on Gabe. But you're back now. As soon as you get some meat on your bones, we'll put you to work. We talked about it and decided not to buy another slave until things settle down."

Aaron didn't realize how much he missed Nattie and Gabe until he walked around the barn and saw their empty cabin. Gazing at the lonely little shack, he cursed Lincoln for invading the South and for forcing Maryland to stay in the Union—and, yes, even for taking his arm.

The next day, Robert saddled Smokey so Aaron could ride to the Prentiss farm. As he turned into Helen's yard, the dogs barked their welcome, and from the house emerged a beautiful person, one that electrified every nerve in Aaron's body. He swung down from Smokey's back with as much one-armed grace as he could muster, dropped the reins, and faced Helen across the expanse of Smokey's rump.

Helen didn't say a word. Tears flooded her cheeks. She hadn't seen the man she loved for nearly thirty months. He looked so different—so haggard, so weak—and without the arm she had told herself over and over that she must ignore. Still, she did her best to not look shocked or react in horror.

Tears pricked Aaron's eyes too as he held her awkwardly. They stood close together until Helen's mother stepped onto the porch with a louder-than-necessary cough. Aaron greeted her warmly, and they discussed his homecoming in a general way. For two hours, Aaron stayed and helped Helen with her household tasks. He then rode home, delighted by the reunion with the one he had loved and still loved.

The next day, Aaron awakened to the sun's warm morning rays streaming through the bedroom's eastern window. He lay there thinking, knowing that somewhere inside his body the happy-go-lucky, charming Aaron still lived. But he found it hard to relax or feel safe. Yes, he was changed. He had killed many men and had walked across dangerous fields, afraid he might be the next to die. Now he could hardly walk on the family farm for fear someone might be aiming a rifle at him. Twice during the night, he had jerked awake in a cold sweat after dreaming of an enemy soldier about to shoot him; once the enemy soldier had been his best friend.

He got up and went to the mirror. He wanted to be the Aaron everyone loved, the one everyone thought was so handsome, but his reflection showed what he felt—staring back was an angry, embittered, shrunken, one-armed man. Happiness seemed to be a mask he could put on, only to have it slip from his brow and expose the naked truth. He hated what he saw and envisioned putting his fist through the cloudy, battle-cracked glass to destroy the ugly image. He lifted his eyes to the mirror again and lectured himself. *Appearance is not what makes a man; what counts is what is inside.* But what was still inside?

After breakfast, he asked LaVonne to help him make a nice picnic basket for two. She cheerfully obliged. Devin hitched the one-horse family carriage, and soon Aaron was hurrying off, trying to control the reins with his one hand.

Helen was hanging the last of the wash on the line as he pulled the carriage into the yard. The sheets flapped in the cool November breeze like the billows of a sail, wafting the scent of soap, as she peeked around the laundry with a gorgeous smile. Aaron's heart fluttered.

"I don't suppose you know anyone interested in a picnic, do you?" he asked, resting his arm across his knees.

"Hmm …" She smiled, her cheeks dimpling. "There aren't many folks around. I don't suppose you would be content with li'l ole me?"

"I guess you'll have to do," Aaron said with a shrug, and then he jumped down from the carriage and kissed away her playful scowl. She laughed and then raced inside to fetch her bonnet and ask her mother for permission. Aaron tipped his hat when Helen's mother peered out the window. He helped Helen into the carriage and then gathered the reins and gave a smart slap to the rump of the bay gelding.

The sun warmed as they drove down the country lane. Eventually, they stopped by the creek, spread a blanket on the grass, and munched heartily on crusty sourdough bread, apple butter, and green gage plums, washing them down with freshly pressed cider.

Strolling beside the Antietam, they spoke of the weather, of their families, and of other goings-on in Sharpsburg. Aaron described the many places he had seen in Virginia and North Carolina, carefully avoiding the war and focusing on trivia. Helen nodded and smiled, but her heart heard his omissions and ached for everything he kept hidden.

The November sun was setting as Aaron rode the carriage back to the Prentiss farm, Helen laying her head on his shoulder as they drove in silence. After greeting her family, Aaron hurried home. On the way, he realized that, during a few moments with Helen, he had felt like his old self again. He softly sang "The Girl I Left Behind Me," rejoicing that the girl he'd left behind had become the sweetheart he came back to.

As the weeks wore on, Aaron returned more and more to music. He could still play his harmonica, and he had been able to adapt the trumpet to his one arm. Playing music enabled him to escape and feel like his old self again.

One afternoon, he and Helen sat in the Haskins family's living room, entertaining the littlest children. Helen's beautiful soprano went well with Aaron's baritone, and all were enjoying familiar songs and children's choruses. Sometimes Aaron burst out with brilliant notes on his trumpet. He let the children try the harmonica, and they all laughed cheerfully.

Later, after the children left the room, Aaron began picking out the melodies to familiar songs with his right hand on the piano. He sang softly, "Should old acquaintance be forgot, and never brought to mind …" Helen smiled, sat next to him, and played the accompaniment with her left hand.

Later, he reached up to straighten the music and knocked the entire stack to the floor. Helen giggled, but Aaron jumped up, eyes flashing and face red with embarrassment. He asked in a frustrated tone, "Don't you have the decency not to laugh at me? I can't help it that I don't have an arm!"

Helen became solemn. "I'm sorry, Aaron. I wasn't laughing at you. I was laughing because we were caught in a snowstorm of paper."

Aaron turned from his pacing. "Well, it wasn't very nice of you!"

After an awkward pause, he mellowed. "Helen, I'm sorry. I'm not upset with you. I'm upset with myself. I want to give you a great life someday, but how can I provide for you when I can't even straighten piano music?"

Helen went to him, took his hand in both of hers, and pressed her forehead into his shoulder. As she felt his anger subside, she looked into his eyes. "Aaron Haskins, you *can* provide for me. You are a wonderful man, the man I want to spend the rest of my life with."

Aaron cut her off. "No, you don't! You say that, but how do I know you aren't just being kind to me because I got hurt? I'm not even a whole man anymore!"

Helen looked directly at him. "Listen to me, Aaron Haskins. I know you are a different person than the boy I knew as I grew up. I know the war hurt you, and you will carry those scars forever. But I also know that you are just as loveable with one arm as you were with two. I love you, and I want to spend the rest of my life with you no matter what. I don't pity you, but you pity yourself. You need to stop and realize how foolish you're being. Don't push away my love just because you're not content with yourself." She paused and then said, "Aaron I think you should quit feeling sorry for yourself."

After several moments, Aaron responded. "I'm sorry. I love you and want to spend the rest of my life with you. But you're just so special, and I want you to have a wonderful life. I don't know if I can provide for you like someone with two arms could, and—"

Helen cut in. "Aaron, I don't care. We'll always be able to get by just fine, and I don't need any more than that. I don't need any of your self-pity. You're a fine man, and whether you have one arm or two has nothing to do with it."

Aaron couldn't answer. After a few moments, he pulled her close, and they remained for a long time in the comfort of their embrace.

Joel sat in his Belle Isle tent, reading a letter from his mother, telling him that Aaron was home and that he seemed to be doing quite well with one arm. The news was pleasant, but it brought envy and frustration and guilt. *Does Aaron know who shot him?* Still, Joel felt deep joy for his best friend and the family. In response, he wrote this brief letter:

```
Dear loved ones,

I was happy when I got your letter saying
that Aaron had come home. I hope I get to
come too before long.
Give everyone my love, and tell Aaron to
enjoy being back home. I know he will. I
hope to be out of jail before long. I don't
know when it will happen, but I'm sure it
won't be very long.

Joel Haskins
```

CHAPTER 21

Aaron with Mr. Williams, November 1863

Aaron visited Martin Williams, Johnny and Lawrence's father. He brought Willie and Stephen to play with Martin's young grandnephew, Cyrus, who quickly started gushing his story.

"Before the battle in Pennsylvania, the Rebel army came through Hagerstown, you know. I was over at my friend Joshua's house, and we watched them go by. First came the cavalry. Every man was riding a horse, and there was so many I couldn't hardly believe my eyes! We figured the Union army must not have any cavalry at all, 'cause it looked like the Rebs had all the horses in the world! Then rows and rows of foot soldiers come after that—"

Aaron attempted to interject himself into the story. "You know what, Cyrus? I was one of those foot soldiers. So was your cousin Johnny."

Cyrus barely acknowledged the interruption. "Then we found out that Joshua's pa, who's an important man, was being sent for by General Lee himself. General Lee! His pa said we could go along!"

Willie's eyes widened. "You got to see General Lee?"

Cyrus nearly bubbled, and he jumped up and down. "Oh, I didn't just see him! I talked to him and everything! Joshua's pa was giving him some directions and road names. The general saw us and asked if we wanted a ride on his horse. He lifted both of us up and said we was generals!"

Willie was jealous. "Oh, I wish I could have gone."

Cyrus was delighted at Willie's disappointment. His eyes blazed. "Then, the next day, Ma wanted me to take some raspberries to a fellow she knew who was an officer, so I did. I was going into his tent when who should walk by but General Lee! He said, 'Well, I do believe I have met your little friend before.' He remembered me!"

The other boys howled in envy. Cyrus invited them to play army, saying he would be General Lee and the other boys would be privates, as Martin invited Aaron into the parlor for coffee. Aaron usually loved to watch his younger brothers play, but he could only turn away when they began making sounds of guns firing, and dropping to the ground "dead." After more than two years, he knew war wasn't a game.

Martin spoke abruptly. "Aaron, I could hardly bear it when my Sarah died. Happened just after Lawrence. I think it must have been the shock. She had been a little sick, but she got much worse when we got the letter."

Aaron's heart grieved for the awful price Martin's family had paid. First, his boys had sneaked away to muster in, and then he'd had to face the death of one son and, later, the loss of his beloved wife from the grief of it. It was almost too much to bear.

Martin continued, "After you were wounded, you were taken to Williamsport, weren't you?"

"Yes, but I was pretty much out of it, I'm afraid."

Martin scratched the head of his red setter. "Right after the battle at Gettysburg, I heard a rumor that the Confederates were retreating this way, apparently fixing to cross the river at the same place you'd come over a few days earlier. I heard that a lot of men had been wounded and were being brought back to Williamsport to cross."

"Well, you heard right. I was one of them."

"That next week, I rode over to Williamsport. I saw mile after mile of ambulances coming into town. The blacksmith said there were seventeen miles of ambulance wagons coming between Hagerstown and Williamsport. Can you imagine a wagon train that stretched seventeen miles?"

"I don't know how anyone could measure the miles, but I know there were a lot of us."

"I looked into the wagons the best I could, wondering if Johnny or you might be there somewhere. Did you know that it was the same after the battle here at Sharpsburg? Joel was looking for you then."

"I'm just so very sorry about Lawrence. I was with him when he died. But I'm really glad Johnny wasn't hurt at Gettysburg. He started the charge toward Cemetery Hill right beside me, but I don't know what happened after I was shot."

"Johnny retreated, along with everyone else, and he wasn't wounded. He wrote me later that the ambulance wagons went ahead of them by a different route. He was involved in some fighting as they came to Williamsport, but the Federals didn't push them too much, I guess. He wondered what had happened to you."

Martin paused a few moments and then continued softly, "You said you were pretty much out of it following the battle at Gettysburg. I can tell you what went on, if you want to know. My cousin lives in New York, and he sent some clippings from the *New York Daily Tribune*. He knows my boys took the Rebel side, so he needles me when things go the Union way." He went to the pantry and came back with several envelopes from which he extracted clippings.

Aaron scanned the headlines: "REBEL INVASION," "The Fighting at Gettysburg," "The Severest Actions of the War," and "Heavy Losses on Both Sides."

He could only mutter, "Well, they sure got that right." He continued down the headline list. "'The Potomac Army Covering Itself with Glory,'" he read aloud. He snorted. "They mean 'covering itself with gory.' Sounds like a Northern paper all right. You just can't believe them." He didn't know if he wanted to read more but was drawn by the next headlines, dated July 6: "The Great Victory," "The Rebel

Army Totally Defeated," and "Its Remains Driven into the Mountains." Further down the headline column was "Its Retreat across the Potomac River Cut Off."

Aaron thumbed through several other articles and stopped with satisfaction on a July 14 dispatch announcing, "Last night, under cover of the intense darkness, General Lee crossed his entire force into Virginia."

As they talked, Aaron learned that Johnny was still in Fifty-Sixth Virginia but hadn't seen any major action since Gettysburg. Aaron gave the sad father some details of Lawrence's death at Charlottesville. Martin thanked him, and after clearing his throat, he looked down at the table and murmured, "I'm so proud of both my sons. I'm proud of you too, Aaron. Thank you for your sacrifice. You're a great example. You three are all real heroes."

"Well, the cause is worth a big sacrifice. Your own sacrifices are to be honored too. It makes me boil to know that we've had to lose so much just proving what our ancestors already proved—tyranny must be put down. The people won't stand for having their rights trampled on. Remember the saying from the American Revolution: 'Live free or die.' I want to live free, and I would give a lot more than an arm when a tyrant is taking our freedoms away."

After a pause, Aaron changed the subject. "Martin, do you know Mrs. Isabella Jennings? She's Helen's aunt, a fine widow who has a keen interest in dogs and bakes the best dark molasses bread in the county." Aaron studied his nails calmly.

"Hmm ..." Martin said he had never had the pleasure of making the lady's acquaintance. But Aaron thought maybe his friend's posture straightened and eyes sharpened as he asked, "What kind of dogs?" It seemed that there might be some hope for this man who had suffered so unfairly.

As Aaron gazed out the window, he saw a figure approaching. As it came closer, he detected a limp and a gray beard that almost reached the middle-aged man's waist. Martin and Aaron stepped outside. As Martin approached the gate to greet the stranger, Aaron's heart suddenly raced; something about the man was wonderfully familiar.

"Thomas! It's great to see you." Martin thrust out a hand to the man and guided him through the gate. "I hoped you would come by."

The stranger ignored the greeting, looking straight at Aaron. "I know you! Weren't you in First Maryland?"

"Yes, yes," Aaron responded in wonder. "And you're Thomas, aren't you? 'Doubting' Thomas Thomas?"

The two men embraced. It had been so long. Then Thomas looked at Aaron's stub. "You were injured at Gettysburg. Hundreds of injured were brought to Williamsport. I was there helping. I saw you. I even helped with your amputation. I thought it was you, but you were pretty much out of it, and I had to move on quickly to help the doctor with the next man. There were so many ..."

Aaron stood in amazement. "It's great to see you. I remember you well from the camp near Winchester. But you disappeared at Manassas. What happened?"

"I was injured—shot in the leg. They took me to a hospital in Richmond, and I mostly got over it. Then I decided to stay and help. When Lee's army crossed the Potomac, before the battle here in Sharpsburg, I came west and settled in Williamsport. I learned that Lawrence and Johnny Williams lived close by, so I came to meet Martin. I planned to get over to your house soon so I could see you again."

Aaron and Thomas talked warmly for a long time. Aaron said, "After you helped saw off my arm, I spent a couple of months in that Richmond hospital too. Did you meet a nurse named Tatiana—Tanya, that is?"

"Why, yes, I did. She seemed like a fine woman. She helped me a lot."

Aaron returned to the main point, saying wistfully, "I remember we all thought the war would be over in a summer, but you knew better. It's been a long time."

The men stood together, lost in a momentary silence, each contemplating his personal tragedy and nurturing the hope for peace ahead. What would the future hold?

It might have seemed odd to a passerby—three men standing on the porch talking of peace while three boys scrapped in the yard, dreaming of war. To Aaron, this war was tragic, but it was a necessary evil. *I wish we didn't fight our enemies, but sometimes we have to force them to do what is right. I regret that doing this may cause a lot of heartbreak, such as Mr. Williams losing Lawrence and me losing my arm, but good can come if we are willing to make the sacrifice.*

Standing on Martin's porch as the afternoon sky deepened, Aaron began to feel a sense of healing. He realized that it was time for Mr. Williams to heal too. Now he knew all too well how right Thomas Thomas had been in doubting that the war would be over before both sides had paid a price beyond comprehension.

CHAPTER 22

Andersonville, Spring 1864

Joel shivered in the soft Georgia rain. Along with several hundred other prisoners, he climbed stiffly from the cattle car and shuffled to the east, as directed. *This is May 24, my twenty-fourth birthday. I wonder if I'll ever have a twenty-fifth.*

His twenty-fourth birthday was a horrible day. He had heard that when the Confederates moved prisoners south, conditions got even worse—as they did for slaves who were sold down the river into the Deep South. He had also heard of Andersonville, the most notorious and feared of all the Rebel prisons.

A man named Captain Henry Wirz spoke for several minutes, but Joel could have summarized the speech in a few seconds. In commanding Andersonville, Wirz had a chance to repay the "damn Yank scum" for starting the war and for what they were doing to the South. He would make sure more Yanks died in prison than in battle.

Along with James McNally and Randolph Litchtenberg, his two

friends from Belle Isle, Joel soon found himself among tents made of mud bricks, clay balls, army blankets, old clothing, and oilcloth. Some men lay under hut dwellings, peering up like ancient turtles from their crusted shells. Many men's eyes bulged from gaunt faces. Joel trembled with gut-wrenching despair.

The guards ordered the new prisoners to find open spots and sleep on the ground. Sleep that first hungry night came as brief moments of relief from the stiffness, pain, stench, and loud sentry calls of "Aaaall's well." All was not well for Joel. He was terrified.

The next morning, he anxiously awaited breakfast and then discovered that roll call came first. His detachment included 270 prisoners, divided into squadrons of 90 for ration distribution and then into 30-man messes. The guards gave out no rations until each man in the squadron was accounted for, dead or alive. If one man missed roll call, the entire detachment forfeited that day's food.

Joel's empty belly gurgled in anticipation as some new friends shared their fire, showed the men how to cook the cornmeal, and gave them small pieces of tin stovepipe for plates in exchange for part of their one ounce of meal. Joel contrasted this with home, where the food was prepared by his wife or mother. He was deeply depressed, and he envied Aaron. At that moment, he would gladly give an arm to be surrounded by his loving family.

The horrible day slowly extended into a horrible week and then a horrible month. Yet the old Joel began to return, and one day, he and his friends from Belle Isle decided to walk around the prison.

Andersonville was a large rectangle; a twenty-foot perimeter inside the walls was a prohibited area. The guards watched carefully for men near this "deadline," because they received thirty days' furlough for wounding a man in the illegal space and sixty for killing him.

Joel was amazed at how many prisoners had something for sale.

"Here, buy some wood."

"Come here, soldier. I'll sell you a nice coat for only four dollars."

"Look over here. You can buy some sarsaparilla beer for only ten cents a glass."

"Do you want some tobacco? I have some of the finest for you."

"Here, buy some eggs—only twenty-five cents each."

"Come on, soldier, place a bet. You can double your money."

Joel said to a man near him, "I don't understand. Who are these men? They look just like prisoners."

The man wheezed through his corncob pipe. "Well, you're right. They're prisoners, except for the subtler up there with the wagon. He's a Reb who makes money selling to the prisoners. But these peddlers are prisoners, same as us."

"Where do they get the things to sell?"

"Sometimes they buy them from the subtler and sometimes from prisoners. Prisoners who work outside sometimes get rewards. Then they sell them to these peddlers, who sell to their fellow prisoners."

"I didn't know any prisoners worked outside."

"What I mean is that they have jobs such as carrying dead men out or taking men to the hospital just outside the prison or getting wood. Things like that."

"Oh, I see. But where do the prisoners get money to buy the things?"

"Some have money when they come from the outside, but most don't have it for long. Some get it from gambling with other prisoners or doing jobs such as burying the dead outside. We got ourselves a community of workers."

As they wandered farther through the crowd, they heard bits of the latest news.

"The Raiders did it again last night. My friend's head was pounded to pieces. Those crooks have no feelings at all."

"Who?" Joel asked. "The guards?"

"No, no," said a young man with a hideous black-and-blue bruise across half of his face. He looked about sixteen but was scarred for life. "The Raiders are prisoners, all Union men like us. They attack their fellow prisoners, steal from them, and beat them if they resist."

"Don't the guards here try to stop them?"

"They don't care, I guess. Saves 'em bullets. The only thing they come in here for is to search for tunnels now and a'gin."

The three men continued walking south, and the smell got even worse as they neared a large swamp. They learned that a stream—ironically misnamed Sweetwater Creek—entered the compound's west side and then spanned out and became a nauseating open sewer. The prisoners used the water upstream for drinking, midstream for bathing, and downstream for an outhouse.

One day, Private Tom Hanson, to whom he had given a little cornmeal for the use of his pan, told Joel of his brother, who had joined the Union army at sixteen and had been killed at Chickamauga.

"Since he was too young to muster in, he wrote the number eighteen on his shoe soles. That way, he could honestly swear that he was 'over eighteen.'"

"Nice ploy. I'm sorry he died, though."

Tom said he hated the Rebels even more since then. Once Tom started talking, he didn't stop. He raved on and on as Joel thought of Aaron and tried to say that, yes, maybe Rebels were horrible generally, but some might be good men. Tom would have none of it. The words continued to tumble from his lips in hateful streams.

Soon, a middle-aged volunteer who gave out the food sat down and said in an amused voice, "Tom, you still making sure all seceshes go to hell?"

Tom shot a look at his adversary. "They don't need my help; they'll get there on their own."

The newcomer introduced himself as Mark Nash, and he continued what was apparently a familiar argument. Tom expressed himself clearly: God was in charge of the war and would punish the guilty South.

Nash's response could have come from Joel's mother. "Both sides argue as though they're Old Testament Israel, with God on their side. But Jesus Christ condemns the hating and killing on both sides. Sometime read what the New Testament says of the early Christian church. They refused to hate and fight."

"Yeah, and look where it got them. About all of them got strung up. Pacifism just isn't practical. It doesn't work. It's stupid."

After a few more minutes, a Confederate guard who often manned the nearby tower joined the group. Mark Nash knew this confused Joel. "Bartlett and I are friends, neighbors. I volunteer here, trying to help those in need. Sometimes Bartlett comes, and we chat while he's off duty."

"Yeah," the guard added to Nash's point. "In a way, we're on the same side—both trying to take care of you prisoners."

"It seems kind of strange, though," Joel said to the guard. "Why do you care to talk to your enemy?"

"No reason not to. I'm not fighting you in here. Maybe if I'd met you on the battlefield I wouldn't have been so nice." He smiled, looking sideways at Mark as though they'd shared a thousand jokes over their differences, and continued, "Has Nash been preaching to you about his perfect, peaceful world?"

Joel paused a bit and then said, "He was just telling us that both sides always think they're right, but in God's eyes, both are likely wrong when they try to kill each other."

"Horse pucky! One side is right, and the other is wrong. In this fight, it's easy to see which is which. God wants the South to beat the Yankees to hell. And for you Yanks, it's a mighty short trip."

Tom responded, "You Rebs always think you know it all. Before I was captured, my chaplain preached a sermon telling why he was fighting for the Yankees. He said that he visited a cemetery and saw hundreds of graves and thought of the widows and orphans and brokenhearted parents the Rebel soldiers had caused. He said it made his revolver feel warm in his pocket, and he regretted that he was a chaplain rather than a fighting man."

This reminded a nearby prisoner of his own chaplain. "When I mustered in, the chaplain quoted something from the Bible: 'Out of the South the whirlwind cometh.' Man, was he right. The reverend recruited sixty men on the spot, including me, and by the next day, he had at least a hundred."

After a pause, Tom said, "Yes, that chaplain was right, Bartlett. God is going to deliver your army into our hands. The whirlwind came from the South, but the North is going to stop it."

"Not so," said Bartlett. "The God of Israel won't let the North burn the South and steal our slaves."

Tom said, "What you say is so ridiculous. My chaplain told us that God was with General Abraham, General Moses, and General Joshua and would bring victory to the Union just like he led His people into the land of Canaan."

Eventually the battle waned and ended with no victor. "Why don't we play a game of poker, men?" Bartlett asked, relieving the tension by removing a dirt-stained deck of cards from his haversack. Joel played for a while, glad for the distraction.

That night, a slice of moon peeked through the clouds and filled Joel's heart with longing. *I can just see that moonlight rippling in Antietam's waters. I would give anything to be home. Belle Isle at Richmond seemed far from home—but now I am much farther. I guess it must be a thousand miles! It might as well be a million.* His tears and moaning joined the choir that stretched around him as he looked over thousands of sleeping prisoners. In the morning, most sat up, but some lay still, waiting with infinite patience for the wagons that carried off the dead.

The Confederate guards, along with their prisoner assistants, kicked each sleeping man in the ribs until he expelled a groan or made some motion to indicate that he still lived. If the prisoner didn't respond, the workers hefted the body into a wagon and continued on their rounds.

Joel, James, Randolph, and a newcomer named Saul Ramsey slept spoon-fashion in order to stay protected in their little shebang. Each man lay on his right side, the four warming one another with the closeness of their bodies. After an hour or two, one would call out, "Switch," and they would all turn over onto their left sides.

Often Joel could not get to sleep. He constantly felt lonely. As he lay awake, he thought of Amy and Braden. Over and over he imagined what the little one looked like, and he spent the nights in deep despair. For Joel, Andersonville was a hellhole.

One day, Joel saw a group of hungry men swatting at low-flying swallows, with occasional success. For the skillful, the birds provided a lunch, which most ate uncooked. The feathers were then stuffed into sacks for pillows. Those who had money could buy fresh fruit and vegetables from an authorized subtler, but at staggering prices. Some men traded personal possessions for money or food. Prisoners who helped transport bodies to the deadhouse occasionally profited from change and other valuables they found in the dead men's clothing.

Joel was often overwhelmed by thirst. Like others, his mess dug four or five feet deep with stovepipes and railroad spikes. Their meager reward of bluish, sulfur-smelling water seemed better than going several hundred yards to Sweetwater Creek. They drank it, making faces as it burned all the way down. The water gave them the runs, but there was no place to run except Sweetwater Creek, and that took far too long. Mostly they used a bit of immensely scarce open ground and then buried their waste, with distinctly limited success.

One day, Joel watched as a group of Union Negro soldiers, prisoners from the all-Negro Fifty-Fourth Massachusetts Infantry Regiment, were herded into their midst. Some prisoners were killed outright because they were Negroes, but many were sent to Andersonville. The Rebel guards and most prisoners treated these newcomers with disdain. Even more than the Irish and the Poles, Negroes kept to themselves in an area near the south gate.

As the weeks passed, Joel became a good friend of Mark Nash, the volunteer with a kindred spirit. He was drawn to the man's peaceful nature and loving ways. One day, after distributing food, Nash approached Joel. "I guess there are more than twenty thousand prisoners here now, and others are coming all the time. The prison was built for half that many. Close to a hundred die every day. Some say that you have to harden yourself to get by here. I never have. I think it's killing me too."

"Why are you here if it's killing you?"

Nash sat on the ground, looking around at the broken, emaciated prisoners. "I volunteer to work here because I want to help people who are suffering. There are others, too, like the priests. Father Whelan brought ten thousand pounds of wheat flour to bake and give to prisoners. You know, Joel, things would be even worse here if it weren't for wonderful men like him."

He paused a few seconds. "It's hard to explain, but when I give water or food to a prisoner, I feel like I'm helping him. And I think it helps prisoners just to have a friend."

Joel fell into a wet-eyed silence, thinking of his mother. Nash said, "I know you agree with my questioning about whether war is the answer to this mess. I'll tell you what I think you should do. I think you should study the early Christians, Jesus's followers. I try to follow their example."

"But didn't they mess up too? Didn't Peter deny Him?"

"Yes. They were humans, just like you and me, just like the Yankees and Rebels. But they really tried to follow His teachings. I'll lend you a Bible, and you can read what He taught and how Peter and the others learned about love and justice. The early Christians refused to fight no matter what the cause, even for their own lives."

As Mark Nash paused, Joel commented, "You sound like my mother."

"Well, I think she's right. Think how much better the world would be if everybody obeyed His teachings like the Christians did for most of the first three hundred years. In fact, I think that if every Christian really obeyed Jesus's call to love our enemies, we would treat each other so well we wouldn't have any enemies."

Nash excused himself and returned to his duties. Joel watched him go, thinking, *That's very interesting. It makes sense. If we all loved our enemies, we wouldn't have any enemies. I wonder about this man. Is he profoundly wise or terribly stupid? It's hard to tell for sure. But I want to understand him.*

CHAPTER 23

Home, May 24 and August 23, 1864

As May 24 approached, the family planned a birthday party, and Helen was invited. She was waiting by the window when Aaron arrived in the rockaway carriage. After a few minutes with the Prentiss family, the two hurried out into a warm, beautiful spring afternoon. She was wearing a dark blue gown with a white lace collar. Aaron helped her into the carriage and drove down the lane to a beautiful spot along the flowing Antietam—the same romantic place he had picnicked with her just after he'd returned home six months earlier. She looked questioningly at him but waited as they stopped near the creek.

He climbed nervously from the carriage and helped her down without saying a word. As her feet touched the ground, he wrapped his arm around her and kissed her warmly and then sank to one knee before her.

"Helen Prentiss, what would you say if I asked you to become Mrs. Aaron Haskins?"

She smiled jubilantly as he repeated, "Will you be my wife?"

Aaron had no time to worry as she said, "Yes! Yes! Oh Aaron, I love you so." She knelt with him and held his face in her hands. The happy couple could hear the Antietam rippling joyfully, while the bluebirds overhead warbled their approval. Aaron led in a prayer for their life as husband and wife.

The couple clung to each other and kissed again and then headed to Helen's home. Aaron asked Helen's father if he could marry her and greatly enjoyed the overwhelming approval.

They then went to Aaron's home, eagerly anticipating their future together. When they entered the living room, Aaron announced triumphantly, "Everyone, meet the newest member of the Haskins family. Helen and I are getting married!" The family united in joyful approval and then dined together and celebrated Aaron and Joel's birthdays.

That evening, as he crawled into bed, a nagging voice marred the perfect day: *What about Joel?* Nothing would ever be completely right without Joel to share it. He longed to tell him the joy of his engagement. *How I wish he could stand beside me at my wedding, just like I did at his. But Joel isn't here, so I'll just have to remember everything about today so I can tell him when he gets home.* He tried his best to stop the thought there but couldn't keep his mind from adding, *That is, if he gets home.*

Little did Aaron know that on that very day, his twin cousin had been placed in a prison that was horrible beyond comprehension.

Aaron awoke with a start the morning of August 23, imagining his hands gripping Helen's slender bodice. His arm might have been gone, but nobody had told his brain.

He stretched awkwardly, the sheets tangling about his legs. *What a day! I'm going to marry the sweetest girl in the world.* For the next few minutes, he lay enchanted, imagining Helen's warm smile and how her face lit up when he called her name. *This will be the last day that I wake up alone*, he thought. *And tonight we will enjoy each other together in the new cabin my family built for us.* Stretching toward the edge of the bed, he imagined drawing Helen close to him that night—and every night.

He remembered when he'd first met Helen. They had played together as children, although she was two years younger. By the time she reached sixteen, he had begun to notice the way her golden hair would pull loose and rest ever so softly on her shoulder.

He silently dressed and tiptoed downstairs and out the front door. Closing the latch quietly, he leaned back and drew in the summer morning air, and then he slipped into the wooden clogs his father had thoughtfully bought for him because they didn't have to be tied. He felt compelled to take one more look at the cabin he and Helen would enjoy, so he walked over to the small building.

Helen and her mother had made dainty lace curtains to frame the windows, which contained nine square panes of glass each. Aaron liked how the random-width floorboards created a strange stair-step pattern. The boards peeked out from under a rug Helen and her mother had braided from strips of old cloth to put before the fireplace, which Aaron and his father had built. A table and four chairs sat beneath the other window; they had been gifts from Glen and Fannie, and Aaron could see the care with which his uncle had shaped and sanded each piece. Fannie had finished them by rubbing oil deep into each surface, and now they glowed in the early morning sunlight.

He looked across the creek to Joel and Amy's cabin. *Braden must still be asleep. How I wish Joel was here!* It seemed that some men were blessed while others were cursed. Aaron shuddered to think what was befalling Joel on this happiest of days. He breathed a prayer, hoping that fate was not dealing too harshly with his twin cousin. He often thought of his arm when he thought of Joel, but his love for his best friend overcame any feeling of blame.

He decided to get a cup of coffee before his mother awoke, but just as he opened the front door and slipped inside, she descended the stairs, humming a soft tune. She beamed at her son, hugged him, and patted his cheek with such maternal affection that he couldn't help but know that, in his mother's eyes, Helen was indeed the luckiest woman alive.

After breakfast, Aaron stood before the looking glass. He squared his shoulders and raised his chin, admiring how he had recovered since coming home. But his hair seemed wrong. He kept brushing it back, and it kept springing forward. He could hear LaVonne in the girls' bedroom. He knocked and asked, "Lovie, do you have anything to take care of this mess?" He held the wily strands between his fingers. "In my lifetime, I've seen you spend months on your hair. You must be an expert by now."

"Well, just for that remark," LaVonne said, "you're on your own. It won't be my fault that your head looks like a hen's nest. Maybe when Reverend Nathan asks Helen to say, 'I do,' she'll take one look at your hair and say, 'I don't.'" Walking out of the room, she added, "Did you read that one in the *Farmers' Almanac*? When is a man like a rooster?"

Aaron responded that he had no idea.

"When his hair is combed!" she shot back, laughing.

Aaron rolled his eyes and looked in the mirror again. His mother came up behind him and reported, "Your hair looks fine, dear. Besides, I know Helen doesn't really care what it looks like."

Aaron laughed and shook his head. "She's seen me look worse than this, and she loves me anyway. Amazing!"

"Stand back a little, and let me get a look at you." Abigail fiddled with the collar of his white linen shirt and straightened his thick black tie, saying with a smile, "You look so much like your father on our wedding day. What a great time that was!" She patted his tie, now adjusted to her satisfaction, and placed her left hand on his cheek. She repeated what she had said earlier: "Helen's a lucky girl."

"I'm the lucky one," he said, taking his mother's hand from his cheek and squeezing it in his.

"Well, you're both blessed by God. I guess it's more than luck."

Aaron agreed.

About noon, the Haskins adults filled their carriage, while the children walked the three miles to the Prentiss family's house. Several neighbors joined the two families. The crowd sat in the large living room, which was bedecked with garlands and bouquets. Aaron noted with joy that Mr. Williams and Mrs. Jennings were speaking quietly, and Isabella had a fine flush to her cheeks as she leaned to place a hand on Martin's arm. Thomas Thomas, who was seated with them, nodded and smiled. Aaron was thrilled to have him there.

Aaron, Robert, and Devin stood at the front. Reverend Nathan took his place, and two of Helen's sisters stepped in, along with her mother, Virginia. The minister watched Aaron's face as Helen came into view from around the corner of the door that led upstairs. Aaron's eyes shone, and the corners of his mouth turned up in a slow smile.

Helen wore a floor-length white gown of Swiss muslin that almost glowed. The bodice made a perfect oval around her curving neck, and her mother's cameo brooch was stylishly affixed at the hollow below her throat. A crown of dainty silk orange blossoms secured the veil that covered her face, and she clutched a bouquet of flowers with both hands. The dress's fitted midsection accentuated the bride's waist, while the skirt billowed out widely to the floor.

"We are gathered here today," began Reverend Nathan, "to witness the bonding together in holy matrimony of Aaron Haskins and Helen Prentiss."

Aaron deeply enjoyed the wedding ceremony, especially when he heard, "You may kiss your bride." He turned to Helen, lifted her veil, and gently kissed her soft lips. He looked into her clear eyes and felt a radiance of joy pour from every inch of his being. "I love you," he murmured softly, for her ears only.

"I love you," Helen echoed, spilling happy tears.

The two fathers gestured to the newlyweds to lead the way to the dining room. Aaron and Helen sat at the head of the table, and their parents, two grandmas, and special guests sat on either side. Others were in adjacent rooms and spilled outside to the shade of the cherry trees. Everyone congratulated the happy couple.

Then Aaron reached into his pocket and pulled out a precious stone. "Family and friends, you may remember what my father gave me when I left home. This stone represents the one in Genesis 28, when God made a solemn promise to Jacob. I have carried it for more than three years, and will carry it the rest of my life. It represents God's love and promise to me. Many times I have sung the song, especially the third verse. Each time, I hold the stone my father gave me." Aaron held up the stone, and his baritone filled the room:

Then, with my waking thoughts bright with Thy praise,
Out of my stony griefs Bethel I'll raise;
So by my woes to be nearer, my God, to Thee.
Nearer, my God, to Thee, nearer to Thee!

Grandma Haskins placed her well-worn hand on Aaron's arm. He noticed tears glistening as she said, "Oh Aaron, I feared I'd never see this day. I was so frightened when you were gone." She bent and kissed his forehead as he slipped his arm around her and gave her a heartfelt hug. Once again he felt her frail body and silently prayed that she would be with them for many years.

"I love you, Grandma Hazel."

"I love you too, and I'm proud of you. What a wonderful bride you have!" she said, wiping the tears from her eyes and smiling at Helen.

"Thank you, Grandmother Haskins," said Helen, "and thank you for the beautiful quilt you made for us! I love it. We'll treasure it always."

Grandma moved to Helen and squeezed her shoulders in an affectionate hug. "You're welcome, dear. I'm glad you like it. And I'm glad you're part of our family."

After a delicious meal, the Prentisses' slave, Lucy, and several neighbor women appeared with warm fruit pies, some accented with delicious almonds. About six thirty, Aaron helped his bride with her shawl and cloak. Everyone followed them to the door and bade them farewell as though they were leaving on a yearlong voyage. Aaron turned his bride toward their carriage. The couple paused only to shout one final good-night and, with a strong "Giddup," headed for their new home along the Antietam.

While Aaron cared for the horses, Helen got ready for bed. Very soon he came in, closed the door quietly, shrugged out of his coat, and walked toward her. He touched her face and gazed lovingly into her eyes, swept her close and kissed her soundly, and then led her to their bed.

She moved ever so slightly away to look up at him and then started to unbutton his shirt. She stripped it from his body. He cringed as her eyes glanced at his deformity. With a featherlight touch, she caressed his shoulder, and then, to Aaron's shock, she laid a soft kiss on the stub.

"I was afraid you would be repulsed by my arm," he said shakily. She only smiled, gazing up at him. "I'm glad you're not," he added, trembling with emotion and anticipation.

"The war hurt you, and the doctors patched you up. Well, no doctor is as good as a wife when it comes to taking care of her husband. Now it's my turn," she said with a brilliant smile.

For once in his life, Aaron could think of nothing to say, so he pulled his wife to him and kissed her breath away.

CHAPTER 24

Andersonville, Summer–Fall 1864

By July, the Andersonville multitude had grown to more than thirty thousand, stuffing the prison built for one-third that many with shrunken, half-living bodies that heard continual rumors of exchange for Confederate prisoners. Nothing happened. A few almost succeeded in escape attempts, tunneling with meager tools under the fence and outside, only to be shot on sight or captured by bloodhounds in the local swamps. Two men made it one hundred miles before Confederate bounty hunters, who were looking for runaway slaves and prisoners, won their thirty-dollar rewards.

Joel shuddered, horrified that the prisoners were not even safe from each other. The Raiders were a major curse, like foxes locked in the henhouse. None of the inmates had much, but what each had was dear to him, and these four hundred or more outlaws stole without conscience. They selected a victim, snatched his possessions, and clubbed anyone who moved to his defense. While most of the prisoners suffered from diarrhea, dysentery, and scurvy, the Raiders were healthier because they stole vegetables, flour, and fresh meat. They were well organized and armed, some carrying brass knuckles or even axes and bowie knives smuggled in by prisoners on work detail.

We're double victims—under constant threat from these contemptible beasts and under the control of Confederate guards who don't care. Joel kicked the mud in anger. The mud only added its rebuke with sharp pain in his bare toes.

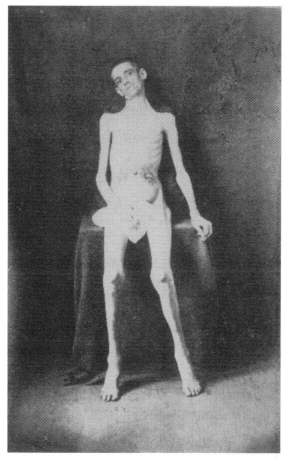

One morning, about twenty Raiders struck Joel's mess. A man advanced with a club, casting a dark shadow. Joel raised his arms to defend himself, but a blow to his chest knocked him down. Two men pounced, forced him to the ground, and stole the most wonderful possession he had ever owned—the timepiece Amy had given him, along with the lock of hair that bonded him to the one he loved most. He screamed and struggled but couldn't maintain the treasure. Others tried to help. James was thrown down, pounded mercilessly, and robbed of his eighty dollars.

When will it end? Why can't men who are fellows in suffering seek to help one another? Why do they sink us further into hell? I hate these men who deal in death.

Yet death was all around. At Andersonville, death was a fact of life; each day, hunger, disease, and Raiders took new victims, and the dead wagons carried out scores of far-too-young bodies.

Joel had taken to consoling himself by sitting in his shebang shaded by Grandma's comforter, staring longingly at Amy's picture, and rubbing the locks of her hair softly on his arm. Now he sat baking under a relentless sun, longing for his treasures. He was in torture.

Two days later, Mark Nash came again. "Look at me, Joel," he pleaded. Joel reluctantly looked at the volunteer's concerned face. Nash saw that Joel dangled on the edge of an emotional precipice. He had seen it before but had hoped Joel would be spared.

"Joel," he said softly, "tell me about it." His eyes again on the ground, Joel was silent. Nash waited patiently, and eventually Joel spoke.

"I hate these Raiders. I just hate them. I don't know how anybody can be so cruel." He paused, balled his fists, and pounded his leg.

Nash remained silent, knowing his friend wasn't done. His heart ached. Here was a soul in the depths of despair, a young man of enormous potential at the crossroads of his life. His was a cry of desperation, a pleading for answers to life's hardest questions. In spite of the men nearby, Joel cried out in anger.

"I'm sick of this! It doesn't make any sense. I hate this war. It made me a killer. I almost killed my best friend. Can you imagine how that feels? I want to go home, but I can't, and besides, I'm too scared for them to see the monster I am now. But I sit here day after day, just longing to kiss my wife and hold our baby."

Joel buried his face in his arms. "I can't understand it, but I can't figure out who to hate. They taught me at first to hate the Rebels, and

I did—all of them except Aaron. We were good; they were bad. But I know that some Yanks are evil, like these Raiders; some Rebs are good, like Aaron. It's just … too much for me."

Nash reached out to grasp Joel's shoulder. "I know you're steaming inside because of what they've done. I understand. Hating them might help for a while, but if you hate so much it destroys you, what's the point? We justify our hatred because of the bad things they do to us, and in doing that, we risk ending up as bad as the ones we hate."

Joel relaxed somewhat, thinking of what his friend had said. Mark waited a moment, emotionally holding the grieving man close to his heart. "Son, keep wrestling with these things until you know in your heart what's right and can come to terms with it. I've seen deep empathy in you. I see you struggling, trying to understand all this. But someday you'll understand that, down deep, in our innermost beings, we're all very much the same. Even the Raiders are more like us than they are different. That doesn't excuse them for the evil they do, but I mustn't allow my hatred of what they do to make me bad like they are."

Joel breathed deeply. He felt—for the moment, at least—the fire of vengeance had burned out and the ashes had been swept away by his mentor's words.

Nash said in parting, "Don't let them win, Joel."

Joel sat for a long time, thinking. *He's right. I mustn't let them make me just like they are. Who knows? Maybe someday I'll be able to speak to others with the patience and wisdom of my mother and of Mark Nash. That is, if I ever get out of this prison.* At that moment, it appeared that the only way out would be on the dead wagon.

During the next few days, Joel watched as a man named Key and several dozen other prisoners got the prison commander's permission to establish themselves as an official body that came to be known as the Regulators, an internal police force. On June 29, the Regulators engaged the Raiders in a terrible fight and captured their leaders. The prison authorities sanctioned a trial, run by the Regulators.

A jury drawn from the prisoners considered the evidence and handed down its verdict, releasing a few declared not guilty and sentencing several to sit in stocks. It condemned others to stand for hours with their arms extended overhead, held by thumbscrews. Some had to run the gauntlet, battered by their irate fellow prisoners. The court sentenced six Raider leaders to death by hanging.

Excitement buzzed among the massed prisoner-spectators as the prison gates opened. A small group of Union prisoners entered, playing the death march on musical instruments that nearby Confederate families had loaned for the ceremony. Behind stumbled the six condemned Raiders, surrounded by a Confederate guard detail and accompanied on horseback by Captain Wirz, the Confederate in charge of the prison. Father Whelan walked alongside, praying in Latin. Wirz then formally announced the delivery of the men to the Regulators, invoked God's mercy, turned his horse, and rode out. The Confederate guards followed.

The Regulators bound the six men's hands behind them. One broke free, ran, and staggered through the filthy latrine-swamp. Soon the prisoners captured the escapee and returned him to die with the others. Father Whelan gave the final sacrament, spending a few moments with each prisoner. Joel could see that some listened intently, confessed their sins, and received absolution. Then each condemned man had the opportunity to speak. Some stood stoically; some cried and begged.

Regulator officials then pulled cornmeal bags over the men's heads and adjusted the ropes on their necks. At the signal, the platform gave way, and the men dropped. The rope around the neck of the leader, "Mosby" Collins, broke. Blood splattered, but the condemned man still lived. As the officials marched him back up the scaffold and readjusted his rope, Collins pleaded, begged, said it was a sign from God, and offered $1,000 if his life was spared. Moments later, he dangled with the other five.

Two days later, the Regulators went through the Raiders' stored possessions. Among thousands of items, they found Joel's timepiece with Amy's lock of hair. He trembled with tears of joy, gazing at her beautiful face while feeling her hair against his arm. It was wonderful.

At night, his thoughts often went to his mother. Many times his mind conversed with her, asking questions and listening to her answers regarding the riddles of his torn life. He pondered a song his mother had often sung, one about her childhood memories, and now his own. He fought to remember the words, and they graciously came back from his mother's warmth.

> Precious mem'ries, how they linger,
> How they ever flood my soul;
> In the stillness of the midnight,
> Precious, sacred scenes unfold.
>
> Precious father, loving mother,
> Fly across the lonely years;
> And old home scenes of my childhood,
> In fond memory appears.
>
> I remember Mother praying,
> Father, too, on bended knee;
> Sun is sinking, shadows falling,
> But their prayers still follow me.
>
> As I travel on life's pathway,
> Know not what the years may hold;
> As I ponder, hope grows fonder,
> Precious mem'ries flood my soul.

Hope grows fonder, he mumbled in the stillness of many midnights—a stillness fractured by cries of men whose tears joined his own, and of gasping and snoring and the hourly "Aaaall's well." Yet the song brought his mother's presence. *Hope grows fonder!*

Early in September, many prisoners, including Joel, were moved out, headed to another prison away from an invasion of Georgia by a Union army. Joel's trainload included about eighty prisoners jammed into cattle cars. As the train lurched away, he grew frenzied. He felt the prickles of hysteria at the edges of his mind. *Oh Lord, I can't go on. I can't go to another prison. Help me find a way, oh Lord.*

He schemed and hoped, eyeing the thicket that lined the rails.

Some of the leaves almost touched the car as it crept through the bushes. The ground below seemed to heave and roll, beckoning to him. Like soft waves lapping at a creek's edge, it looked inviting—at least in comparison with another prison.

Eventually, deep into the night, the two guards became complacent. One cracked the door in order to relieve himself. As the guard fumbled with his trousers, Joel, his heart beating wildly, saw his chance.

Summoning all his feeble strength and throwing caution to the wind, he plunged through the half-open door. He curled reflexively as he tumbled onto the sharp rocks alongside the track, where he lay panting. He heard shots and yells from the train, but they gradually faded as it kept moving, unwilling to stop for one prisoner who would probably die anyway.

When all was silent and the ground no longer shook, Joel gasped in relief and unsuccessfully tried to stand. He lay in the darkness and began to laugh and sob. Every muscle ached, but, in that moment, he felt an overwhelming sense of victory. This was freedom like none other. He had escaped. He lay in a pile of rocks, scratched and bleeding, and smiled into the dark night.

"I'm free," he whispered in astonishment. "At least, I'm away from Andersonville and from the guards."

Free was an unreasonable thought. He was deathly weak and in the middle of enemy country with no food or water. Yet into his dreamlike state came his mother's soft voice, singing:

> As I travel on life's pathway,
> Know not what the years may hold;
> As I ponder, hope grows fonder …

"Hope grows fonder." I do have hope. Maybe when Mark Nash comes to Sharpsburg, I will be there to let him meet my mother!

CHAPTER 25

Georgia Plantation, Fall 1864

Joel knew not how long he lay helpless on the rocks, nearly unconscious, before he saw a young man, black as the moonless midnight, and heard a soft, pleading voice.

"Come on! Come on! You gotta hide. Come on! You're one of the Yankee prisoners, aren't you? I'm Jake. Come with me; I'll hide you."

Joel crawled to his knees, moving as much as his strength allowed, pulled along by the young man. He sighed with relief when he was finally laid down behind a rough log building.

"I'll go get help."

Joel only grunted in reply. The next thing he knew, he was on a cot with several Negroes leaning around him.

Joel saw that his benefactors were very dark and had kinky hair. "I found you by the tracks. We're slaves on Master Tyler's plantation. We know you're a prisoner, so we'll hide you." Joel just nodded with childish acceptance, barely able to understand through the strange accent.

Someone brought a bowl of soup. "Here, sip this. It's chicken. It'll be good for you." She seemed as familiar as Nattie, though she sounded much different. She tenderly tipped a spoonful of the delight into his mouth and laid a cool hand on his forehead as she brushed back his matted hair. She hummed softly, lulling Joel as he consumed what she offered. It was his first chicken soup in years, and it seemed like the best thing he had ever tasted. He thanked God that he was no longer in prison as the warmth trickled down his throat.

Joel took turns sipping hot soup and drinking cold water offered by a young girl who edged closer to the bedside to gaze down at him. Joel was not ready to speak, but he looked at her with a bit of a grin. She backed off shyly.

In the presence of these kind friends, Joel felt like a new man. *Well, not exactly new,* he admitted, *but a lot better than a few hours ago—or was it days? I don't know what will happen next, but at least I'm in the hands of friends, not enemies. Oh Lord, don't let this end badly. Don't let these folks get into trouble for helping me.*

Joel drifted into sleep, warmed and soothed by soup and safety. When he awakened, it was night. More sleep followed, then soup and water, and then sleep again. He dreamed of home. He was a child, and sick, and his mother was delighting him with chicken soup. His eyes opened again, and Nattie was mothering him, only it wasn't Nattie. Finally he was fully awake, and Jake was with him.

"Where are we?"

"This is Georgia, near the railway line. Did you jump off the train?"

Joel struggled to rise. Jake, who looked about sixteen, supported him and helped him to sit on the dirt floor against the log wall.

"Yes. I think we were going to another prison. I'm glad you found me and hid me. Aren't you taking an awful risk? What if your master finds out I'm here?"

"He'd beat us for sure. But I think we can hide you all right. The master never comes near the slave quarters, and the overseer doesn't come into our shacks."

Over the next few days, Benny, Jake's father, told Joel about life on a Southern plantation.

"The overseer calls me a hoe hand, and I'm not so busy this time of year. We grow cotton and corn mixed with cowpeas, and we have some sweet potatoes, peanuts, and a little sugar cane, for syrup."

Joel wished he could see the plantation, but that wasn't possible, so he contented himself with listening to the descriptions from those who worked the land. Benny said Master Tyler's was smaller than most, with about eighty-five slaves. Eighteen were called plow hands, mostly men and a few women, including Annie, Jake's mother. The plantation also had seventeen hoe hands, a carpenter, a stock tender, a cook for the overseer, a scullion—or kitchen helper, Benny explained—and a man who mostly raked leaves used for fertilizer. Others served inside the master's plantation house and the overseer's residence. The rest were children and those too old to work.

Benny said Master Tyler spent nearly all his time away. The white overseers were usually in charge, and they changed nearly every year. Some were kind, others very cruel. Benny lamented the floggings some gave when slaves fought among themselves, injured their mules, didn't work hard enough, or got too dirty.

"When I was a boy, my mama told me that a few weeks before I was born, she was working in the field, picking cotton. She got behind, and the overseer started shouting at her."

Benny paused as if he could see it happening. "It makes me sick even thinking about it. There I was, inside my mama, and the overseer came to her and beat her across the back with a stick. She told me it hurt her something awful, but that wasn't the only time she was beaten. She said she just wanted to protect me, so she curled over her belly as he whipped her. He could do anything he wanted to, of course."

Joel expressed a quick "That's horrible, Benny."

"Most of the overseers weren't that bad, though. Most of them didn't beat the slave women who were going to have babies, as most of them were most the time; it might even have been the master's babe the women carried. The masters want slave women who can bear lots of children, 'cause it gives them more hands to work or sell. I remember one woman who birthed nineteen children, but only six lived. Still, she was a favored one because she raised six work hands for the master, and he sold them for a lot of money."

Then Benny chuckled, showing gaps in his teeth. "One thing, though. The master always makes sure the overseers don't give slaves dangerous work. If a risky job needs doing, they hire a poor white, because if a slave is killed, it costs $500 or $1,000 to buy another. If a white worker dies, well now, it doesn't cost them anything."

After several weeks, Joel felt stronger and anxious to do more than hide. Many times as he lay in bed, he felt fearful that the overseers would rush in, arrest him, send him back to prison, and hurt the kind slave family that harbored him. He wondered about further escape, but he was still very weak; besides, where would he go that wasn't Confederate territory? So he had to content himself with his conversations with Benny and Jake. He was delighted they trusted him so completely that they would openly share so much.

Sometimes other slaves came, and they all sang together. The songs were different and delightful—"Dixie's Land" and "O Susanna" and lots of spirituals. *Aaron would love this,* he thought, *playing the banjo and singing with these people.* Then guilt struck him like a shaft of cold steel. *Aaron can't play the banjo anymore.*

Joel had much time to think and to pray. Although his slave hosts could not read or write, their master had given them a Bible. He read the new Bible often, focusing on Jesus's instructions to the disciples and how they related to the war he had just fought. It seemed obvious that Jesus didn't want hatred and war.

Joel thought much about how important love and forgiveness could be. It seemed clear that Christians should love their enemies and treat them in a way that would not make them want to fight back.

Then he had a new thought: *Suppose the early Christians had acted like most Christians do today?* His answer to that question led him to write the following brief story.

DARKNESS AT NOONDAY

Written by Joel Haskins in December 1864

Peter heaved a deep sigh and sat against a rock. The cave was cold and foreboding but a welcome refuge from the hostile world outside.

"It's been a hard week but a good one," he said. "A lot of new believers have been won." As he talked, he idly inspected a long sword, one of several hundred weapons the believers had collected.

"Stephen is certainly God's choice for the job of food distribution. He has deep spiritual insights and a real sense of justice," James added. "His zeal may get him into trouble, though."

"Yes—and all of us," warned Barnabus. "It's getting more dangerous to be believers."

"The more the church grows, the more hostile the Pharisees get," Peter said. "Everything we have worked for is in danger."

"I agree! We'll have to fight soon," said Simon the Zealot. "I knew my revolutionary experience would be useful someday."

"But wouldn't fighting be terribly dangerous?" asked Thomas.

"Yes, of course. But against Christ's enemies, we have to take risks. Besides, we really don't have a choice. Remember, they want to take away our freedom to worship God as we please. We have to show force, or they'll think we're weak. Anyway, we'll move so fast they won't even know what hit them. How many of us are there?"

"Over five thousand, and even more women and children," Matthew estimated.

"Great! What an army! When the time comes,

a lot of us will fight with these swords and daggers. The rest will carry rocks. I figure that if we kill a few hundred, they won't cause us any more trouble."

"But what if they do?" doubted Thomas.

"Then we'll hit them again—over and over—and keep coming back to the caves. They'll never catch us. We can hold out forever. We'll teach them that aggression doesn't pay!"

Just then, John came running up, out of breath. "The Pharisees are arguing with Stephen!" he panted. "I think they're going to kill him."

"Now's the time to act! Let's go!" Peter exclaimed.

As quickly as possible, the weapons were distributed among the believers. After a brief prayer for God's blessing, they left the caves and advanced toward the mob surrounding the pit. One hundred yards away, they broke into a run toward the astonished Pharisees. With a roar of defiance and a clash of swords, the battle began.

Meanwhile, Stephen lay in the pit, already near death. He looked up into the hate-filled faces of the Pharisees. Then, contrasted beyond, he saw the tender face of Christ, the Lord. Stephen's own face shone with compassion as he prayed, "Lord, don't hold this sin against them," and went to be with Jesus.

The believers quickly won the battle. Suffering only a few casualties themselves, they killed hundreds of the enemy. Although they failed to save Stephen, they proved that they would not submit meekly, like lambs.

Peter, the rock, fought valiantly and killed a dozen or more. Then he directed his rage against a young man who had been guarding the coats of those stoning Stephen.

Saul of Tarsus was standing transfixed, nearly oblivious to the battle around him, his gaze on the radiant face of the man in the pit. Stephen's compassion moved him mightily, touching him like nothing in his experience. For a moment, he wondered if he too should follow Jesus.

Then, suddenly, an armed man lunged toward him. With a cry of fear, he grabbed a dagger and thrust it hilt-deep into Peter's belly. Instantly, Barnabas killed Saul with a rock to the back of the head.

The believers carried Peter to the caves, where they mourned their losses but celebrated their victory. They vowed to fight whenever necessary to protect their freedom to follow Christ.

It was only noon when the battle ended, but a strange darkness covered the land. Peter, now near death, shivered in the cold haze, mumbling that he heard a cock crowing in the twilight.

The strange gloom was so intense that travelers many miles away said there was absolutely no light on the road to Damascus.

Joel read and reread his story. *How sad it would be if this had actually happened. Yet it has happened. It has happened so many times, including this war, where Christians on both sides are killing each other. I'm so glad the early Christians loved instead of hated. I'm so sad that later Christians have rejected the peace of the early church.*

One day, General Sherman's Union army marched within a few miles of the Tyler plantation, and a group of cavalry foragers came directly across the farm. Joel was struck with the irony: he had become strongly antiwar, yet he was welcoming Sherman's warriors! He recognized that this was an imperfect world. He could do far more good by refusing to use Satan's methods, but sometimes evil accomplished good. Many of the wars of history had brought good results; still, Joel recognized clearly that the world would be better if good, peaceful means had been used. He felt renewed determination to follow the peaceful methods Jesus had taught His followers.

The slaves danced and hugged, and when they learned that the master and overseer had fled, they threw open the plantation stores to the invaders. Joel flagged down some of the passing cavalry and told them of his personal situation. They promised to find a horse he could ride, and Benny directed them to the plantation's stables.

"Well, I guess this is good-bye," Joel said to Jake, extending a thin hand.

"Yes. I'm glad we could help you," Jake said.

"Thank you, Jake, for rescuing me and for being my friend."

Jake smiled through his broken teeth and joined in Joel's good-bye hug. Many of the women expressed their good-byes, dabbing a few tears with the corners of their aprons.

Joel found Benny alone, sitting under a peach tree, dreaming of freedom. "Now that the Union army has come, you're free," Joel rejoiced. "Can you imagine?"

"Yes," Benny said. "We're free." He said it with rejoicing in his voice. "I don't know what we'll do, though. We'd like to go to the North, where our dark skins wouldn't matter, but they won't let us come along with the army. So I guess we'll stay here and try to run the plantation ourselves, since the master is gone."

Joel grimaced sadly at Benny's naive belief that color made no difference in the North, but he said nothing. He wished he could help the family. He was afraid the master would return but didn't mention that either. He felt a strange mixture of joy and guilt. He was going home, he hoped—an absolute delight. But the slaves had to stay—for what, they knew not.

Joel reached out and shook Benny's hand—the first time Benny had been allowed such equality with a white man. And Benny broke another rule—he looked Joel straight in the eye. Then the two men embraced. Benny felt accepted as a human being. The two parted, hoping to meet again someday.

Joel rode with the Fifteenth Corps through small towns and woods, helping drive thousands of cattle, horses, pigs, and mules, all stolen from plantations by Sherman's forces. As it moved along, the Union army also destroyed the railroads by heating the rails and twisting them around trees. Some of the soldiers laughed and called the metal "Sherman's neckties."

One day, thirty or forty Negro men, women, and children approached the brigade. An officer went out to meet them, and Joel listened to the conversation.

"What seems to be the trouble, boy?" said the officer to an older Negro who appeared to be the leader. He tipped his hat back on his forehead and shaded his eyes.

"Well, sir, we heard that since you came through and beat the Confederates, sir, that we are free."

"That's right," said the officer.

"Well, we want to come with you up north."

"I'm sorry, boy, but we're under orders to only take darkies who will be useful to us. I'm sure you won't have any trouble from your white folks—they all ran off, and I don't know if they'll ever come back. You just go on home and keep working those fields so your family will have enough to eat."

"Yes, sir. Thank you, sir," said the leader of the disappointed slaves as he herded the group of family and friends back the way they had come. The officer turned and noticed Joel watching.

"That's what Lincoln's great plan is going to do to us." The officer pointed his chin in the direction of the retreating slaves. "When this war is over, darkies will be streaming into the North, and we won't know what to do with them. He wanted to free the slaves to help us win the war, but I doubt that he has any idea what he'll do with them." He rode away without waiting for Joel's response.

Slowly, the army progressed, and on December 22, Savannah fell to the Union. An officer said that General Sherman had wired President Lincoln to say that Savannah was his Christmas present.

Joel longed for home. Suddenly, he had an idea. Mail call had just been announced. *It will be taken on a Union vessel.* Joel approached the man who was collecting mail. "Sir," he said, "I'm a Union soldier and have been a prisoner since the big battle in Pennsylvania. I want to go to my home in Maryland. Could I ride with you in the mail boat?"

"Ah, surely, son," the old mail carrier replied, twirling his white mustache tips. "I'd love to have another hand on board. Can you read, lad?"

"Yes, sir, and I'm willing to work hard for you. Just please take me home!"

The mail carrier nodded and handed Joel a sack full of letters. "I can help you, son. I'll arrange it all with the captain of the Fifteenth Corps. Here, can you carry this for me?"

Within two days, Joel was on a boat headed north. *Annapolis,* he thought with a sigh. *Annapolis, Maryland! I'm going home!*

CHAPTER 26

Sharpsburg, February 1, 1865

Glen Haskins pulled off his gloves as winter's evening sun dropped behind the barn, casting a long gray shadow in the golden light. *It's been a long day—time for me to quit.*

He rubbed his eyes with dirty fingers, but as he stared ahead, a specter appeared. He blinked to focus as the ghostly form raised its arms. Glen trembled. "Joel?" The bearded apparition ran closer.

"Pa! Pa!" it shouted, arms waving, coming at an ungainly gallop.

"Oh Joel, Joel!"

Joel wrapped his arms around his father's neck as they crashed together. "Oh, it's true. My son, my son ..." Glen wept, pressing his son closer, as a missing piece of his heart began to ease back into place.

"Yes, Pa. It's me."

"We thought you were still in prison. How did you get out? But wait. I can't keep you from your mother."

"Fannie! Fannie! Come see who's here!"

Fannie hurried to the door and flung it open. Joel moved toward his mother, looking her full in the face. His presence so shocked her that she reached for the porch railing to steady herself. She couldn't speak; she just nestled her head on his chest, running her hands up and down his back.

She whispered, "Do you know how I've prayed for this day?"

Joel held his mother. "Oh Mama, I have too. I've prayed so much."

Fannie stepped back to look at her son, whom she hadn't seen for more than twenty-seven months. His eyes looked the same, but she was overwhelmed by his shrunken body; his long, ungainly hair and beard; and his tattered trousers. She shook a little, feeling a bit faint.

Then, recovering herself, she said to Joel, "But you want to see Amy and Braden."

"Yes, Mama. And today is Braden's second birthday!"

"Of course, Joel. They're at home. Amy's probably putting him to bed." Fannie beamed at the thought of her son's reunion with Amy and felt pleased that he remembered his baby's birthday. She squeezed him again and turned him toward his own home.

Joel opened the door and stepped into the warm world of more than two years ago. Amy turned at the sound, her face cast in the glow of the fire. She screamed and launched herself into his arms. She almost shuddered as she clutched his frail frame, her heart broken with what had happened to the one she loved. She quickly adjusted to this supreme moment as Joel held her against his bearded face, kissing her again and again.

Joel stepped back and took her hands in his. He raised her palms to his lips and kissed them gently and then studied the face he had adored in his timepiece and dreamed of touching. Neither said a word; they were both lost in the glory of the moment, each fulfilling the dream that had lingered so long. Then Amy cried out, "Joel! You have to see Braden! Oh, I've waited so long for you to see him." She took his hand and led him into the kitchen, where their two-year-old sat in his infant chair, eating peaches.

This was the best moment of Joel's life. He looked at his son for the first time, enthralled by his presence. He had longed for him each day at Andersonville and before. Now here he was. Joel was ecstatic.

Braden was not. He looked at the stranger quizzically. "Mama," he babbled, pointing his spoon as though asking, "Who is this barbaric-looking creature? And why have you let him into our house?"

Amy released Joel's hand and hurried to Braden, wiped away the peach juice, and lifted him. His round pink cheeks and wide dark eyes continued to captivate his father.

Amy held Braden out to her husband. "Braden, this is your papa. Can you say 'Papa'? Braden, say 'Papa.'" The little boy hid his face in his mother's loose hair.

"Braden," Amy scolded mildly. "I'm sorry, Joel. He's just so shy. It's going to take a little time, I suppose."

Joel longed for his son and tried to take him from his wife, but Braden clung to his mother, rejecting the stranger. When Joel reached out to force him into his arms, the toddler whimpered and then cried aloud.

Joel demurred. "I guess I should wait until I've shaved and had some time to get acquainted. I don't want to scare him."

Amy nodded agreement. "Well, at least you can help me put him to bed."

Later, Amy shaved Joel and clipped his long, scraggly hair. Then he approached his wife. For them, it was another wedding day. Once again, she was a lovely bride. He stroked her hair softly and let his hands fall to her shoulders. She sighed with pleasure at his intimate touch. She removed his shirt, struggling to not be repelled by his emaciated body, and looked into his soul instead. She loved the real Joel no matter how shrunken the body that housed him. Everything in her screamed to make it better, to fix it all. She would, she promised herself. Joel could see she was struggling not to look away from his emaciated body—the ribs protruding, his belly sunken in, his arms as skinny as young saplings.

He pulled her close and pressed his cheek against hers. "I missed you so much. I told you I would love you forever, and I will."

Amy embraced her husband and repeated, "Forever!" Joel softly touched his wife's breasts, which he had longed for all these months. He looked at her beauty and desired her deeply. He came to her and she to him. A twenty-seven-month chasm had been bridged. Togetherness had been restored, and now they united as husband and wife.

The next morning, the family crowded into Glen and Fannie's home. Joel delighted in talking with the children. He especially enjoyed his littlest sister, Kylie, who was now seven. She told him of her kittens and rabbits. He couldn't keep from remembering her kitten Fuzzy, who had been a casualty of war right there on the farm, but he didn't mention it and neither did she.

He also delighted in Chelsea and Stephen and Julia. His sister Grayce, a fine artist now eighteen, drew him a wonderful picture of little Braden. Soon the cousins began arriving. He enjoyed them all. He felt vaguely pleased when Uncle Robert and Aunt Abigail greeted him warmly. He had long feared how they would react to the family traitor.

When Aaron and Helen walked through the door, Joel held his breath, wanting to turn away, wanting to run and hide. Aaron strode to Joel and put his arm around his cousin, and the two embraced. They had both been swept into the storm of war and now sought to find each other amid the devastation.

Aaron broke the silence, saying, "Joel, it's been so long. I missed you. We've a lot to talk about. One thing I'll bet you didn't know. We have a new baby named Clay!"

Helen presented the tiny child to a delighted Joel.

Soon the family had a special noonday welcome-home meal. Joel sat at one end of the big table, where everyone could look at him. He noticed the way Aaron functioned with his one arm and marveled at the skill he had developed in only nineteen months. Later, the family had a delightful time of prayer, thanking God that both cousins were home.

That night, Joel and Amy lay entwined and then slept two hours until Braden awakened them with hungry cries. After Amy fed their son, the couple talked in the darkness. Amy laid her head on Joel's narrow chest and placed her hand lightly over his heart. He leaned against the headboard, stroking Amy's hair; then he softly rubbed her back. His heart felt near to bursting as he enjoyed this simple moment with his wife. In all his years, he had never had a more peaceful moment than lying in his own bed with his wife in his embrace and their child sleeping in the nearby trundle bed.

"Joel, my husband—it's hard to believe you're home. I'm so happy. I just can't believe you're here after so long without you. I'm so glad God protected you."

Joel felt a sense of comfort, of release. He had promised himself that he would tell no one what he had done to Aaron. Yet somehow, deep down, he knew that he and Amy could never be complete again if he didn't confess his guilt. It would always keep them apart, and she would never know why. He shuddered. Oh, the lovemaking was wonderful, but spiritual intimacy depended on being completely honest.

"Amy, Gettysburg was a horror," Joel said, turning onto his side to look at her. "I suppose it's partly the feeling every soldier must face after war. I was part of so much slaughter." After a brief silence he said, "I—well, I saw things you could never imagine." He stared upward, seeing the carnage in the shadows on the ceiling. "I did things that I don't know if I'll ever forgive myself for."

"Joel," Amy started, ready to tell him everything would be fine, that it was just a part of war. But he wasn't ready for her comfort.

"No, Amy, I have to tell you this," he said, cutting off any words she might have uttered, clutching the pillowcase with white knuckles. "You know that I killed a lot of men." He turned and looked into her innocent eyes. He saw nothing but gentleness and love, and he realized anyone who hadn't been there could never really understand. "I watched them fall, and I shot again. I don't know how many men I killed at Gettysburg. I didn't even care after a while. I did it to protect myself and my fellow soldiers. We were all part of a team, and I couldn't fail them. They would kill and die for me, and I would kill and die for them."

He paused and then added, "And the enemy was the same. They screamed, they bled, they died. We were from different sides, but death was the same." Joel was in the throes of his memories, and he grasped Amy's wrist. He felt that if she could just understand, he might have healing.

"Each time, it could have been me. Oh Amy, sometimes I just can't understand why I lived while so many other men died. It just isn't fair." He started sobbing and gasping so violently that he couldn't speak. His head ached, but he finally quieted enough to continue. "Of course, I know it was war. In war, people let their worst selves take over. They do things they would never do in peacetime."

Joel hesitated for several seconds, and then, in the arms of his wife, he continued. "That day, I shot a man. Then I guess I fainted or something. I think maybe I got hit in the head with a rifle butt. Anyway, the Rebels captured me. I think I was so confused I just walked into their camp, or I guess I might've walked back with them as they retreated. I don't know. It was strange. They were retreating, yet, at the same time, they captured several of us Yankees."

Amy looked at him in the shadowy moonlight. Joel stared back blankly, seeing his wife yet seeing himself on the battlefield at the same time. She swallowed and braced herself for what he would say. Like it or not, he was confessing his darkest sins.

"Amy, I shot Aaron."

Amy jerked. Her face twitched for a moment as her mind reeled with the truth. Fear raced through her as Joel continued. "Aaron saw me just as I saw him, and he stopped and didn't fire. And somehow I shot him instead. I just couldn't stop. I should have stopped, but I didn't stop." They were both silent for a moment, unconsciously hearing the popping logs in the ebbing fire.

Then Amy asked, "Does Aaron know?"

"No. Well … he might. I don't know. Yes, I think he probably does know." Amy pitied her husband as his shoulders hunched, trying to protect himself from the truth.

"But did he see you do it?"

"I don't know. I think so. It was so smoky. He was about to shoot me, and I think he may have recognized me and refused to shoot. I realized who he was, but I just couldn't keep from pulling the trigger. It was terrible. I had the gun pointed right at his chest, and I guess I tried to pull it away. I thought I killed him, but maybe pulling it that little bit saved his life. I don't know. It all happened so fast. I just thought he was an enemy about to shoot me, and I acted as fast as I could. Amy, I didn't want to die, so I shot him first … I shot him first." The words came out in a tortured whisper.

Amy took his hand in her own and laced her fingers with his. "I'm glad you told me, Joel. I don't know how to explain, but I could tell you were holding something back. I was afraid you had some problem with me."

"No, it could never be you," Joel said, wrapping his other arm around her. "It's me."

"But you've told me now," Amy said. "That's all you need to do."

For several minutes, Amy rubbed his head and then his neck and then softly stroked invisible patterns on his face with her fingertip. Joel relaxed; his fear and worry dissipated, and desire took their place. He moved to her and touched her softly. They concerned themselves only with their happiness and the pleasure each could give in intimate, shared physical and spiritual love.

Joel was home—forever.

CHAPTER 27

Fannie and Joel, February 14, 1865

Fannie rushed to Joel and Amy's house and barely stopped to knock. "Joel! Joel! The slaves are free! The slaves are free! Papa was in Sharpsburg today, and Mr. Litchfield told him that Congress has passed a law setting all the slaves free! Well, at least it has passed the House of Representatives and will be voted on by the states. But it will pass. The slaves are going to be free!"

Like his mother, Joel was overjoyed. They went to the creek bank and sat together, pondering the news and giving thanks to God. Neither could resist expressing frustration that war had been the instrument, but they were both glad that something good had come from all the killing. Then Fannie said, "I haven't really had a chance to talk with you since you came home. I so missed our talks while you were gone."

Joel smiled and snatched a long blade of grass. "I missed them too. I thought of them every day in prison. Many times I imagined that you were with me, sharing my pain." He reached out and squeezed his mother's hand.

She trembled as her son continued. "You gave me hope and comfort. I even had conversations with you, telling you of my grief and imagining your answers. Mama, do you remember the song you used to sing? 'Precious Memories, How They Linger'?"

"Oh my, how well I do." She smiled and then started to sing. He joined her. "How they ever flood my soul. In the stillness of the midnight, precious, sacred scenes unfold."

Joel almost shed tears as they sang the second verse: "Precious father, loving mother, fly across the lonely years, and old home scenes of my childhood, in fond memory appear."

The mother and son sat together, almost as close physically as they had long been spiritually. He told her some of the horrors of prison life and then sang gently, "As I ponder, hope grows fonder."

Looking deep into her brown eyes, he said, "I found it hard to hope, but I felt your presence, and my hope did grow fonder—and stronger. I'm so glad I'm home with you."

The two locked hands and watched the shimmering sunlight glinting on Antietam's rippling waters. After a few moments, Fannie said, "I knew it was awful for you. In your letters, you never really said much of how you felt, but I knew." She looked at her son for his reaction. "Of course, I know the letters were censored and you probably couldn't say everything you wanted to. But you told us some things. I know you've suffered a lot of terrible experiences. Do you feel like the war changed you much?"

Joel's face twitched. He didn't want to answer. He wanted to run away. But her love bound him stronger than any prison wall.

"It was terrible. War is so cruel. I never should have gone. I told myself God wanted me to fight and my cause was His cause. Lots of people said God was on our side, and I wanted to believe it, so I did. Yet Aaron had said the same thing about the Rebel side."

"What do you believe now, Joel?"

He inhaled like a man getting ready to dive into a deep sea and slowly released the air in one long breath. He looked at his mother as she stared back softly. Her unconditional love reassured him. He felt its power to cure, and he longed for healing.

"You know, Ma, all I saw out there was rage and destruction. I never met God in war. I think we met Satan instead. It was like we all turned our backs on heaven and marched into hell, cursing God along the way—saying we were acting in His name, but cursing His love by hating our enemies." He thought a moment and then added, "And it's so easy to hate. It's so easy for our leaders to get us to hate and fear our enemies."

This led Joel to tell his mother of Mark Nash. "He knows a lot about Christian history. He told me something you had said before I went to war—that for most of the first three hundred years after Jesus's time on earth, the Christians followed His teaching about loving their enemies and refusing to hate and kill. Mark believes that Jesus's movement suffered a major blow when Constantine made Christianity the religion of the whole empire. I remember him saying that Constantine sort of turned the Prince of Peace into a god of war. After that, Christians marched into crusades under the banner of the cross, and Christian nations fought one another, each thinking Jesus was on their side and that Satan was on the other Christian nation's side."

"Joel, what you're saying reminds me so much of what George Fox, the first Quaker, said in England a couple hundred years ago. Fox discovered that he didn't have to follow the ways of the Christian nations that were always fighting. He said that Jesus Himself could speak to our problems and help us to love rather than hate. Fox said he saw an ocean of darkness, but it was overcome by an ocean of light—Jesus's light!"

Fannie paused and then added, "Of course, it wasn't just the Quakers. Some others had shared their closeness to Jesus, like St. Francis of Assisi and the Mennonites and Brethren. Fox said that if we really lived like Jesus taught, and refused to hate and kill, Christianity would become a very powerful force because people in all countries wouldn't feel hated. They wouldn't fear us if we all acted like Jesus and treated each other with love."

Mother and son sat for a long time in a worshipful silence. She was thankful and proud of her son. This would be one of her most precious memories. She knew it would be a precious memory for Joel, too.

That evening, Joel milked Bessy for the first time since he had come home. He leaned his forehead against the warm cow and breathed in the familiar barnyard smell. He had missed it so much while in prison. He even squirted some milk into his mouth, as he had done when he was a boy. As he finished, he saw Aaron walking around the back of the barn and greeted his cousin.

Aaron came inside, waving his pitchfork. "Hello, cuz," he called.

"Hello, Aaron," Joel said cordially, picking up his bucket and stool.

Aaron saw Joel's nervous manner and asked, "What's the matter, Joel? You're as skittish as a cat in a thunderstorm." Aaron flashed a smile as he leaned against the pitchfork.

Joel shifted his shoulders as though he had no idea what Aaron was talking about.

"You haven't been easy around me ever since you came home, Joel. Don't deny it. Do you still blame me for joining the Rebs?"

"I don't think it's because you're a Rebel, Aaron. I think it's just that—well, I think it's just that I went through some terrible times in the war." Joel paused, wishing he could tell everything, but the truth still terrified him. *Does Aaron know?* He couldn't say more. It was as if every time he wanted to tell Aaron the truth, he was suddenly barred access to the words. He was imprisoned by his own guilty fear, and it was a prison as corrosive as Andersonville.

Aaron crossed the few paces between them and gently placed his lone hand on Joel's shoulder. His empty sleeve dangled near his cousin's heart. "Joel, look at me. Joel?"

Joel forced himself to look at his cousin. Aaron stared into Joel's face for several seconds and then said softly, "It was you, wasn't it?"

"What do you mean?" Joel gasped in surprise, shrinking from Aaron's touch with a half step backward.

"You shot me."

Joel's face drained of color, and he bowed his head. He felt as if he would faint. But Aaron didn't seem angry. After a moment, Joel returned his gaze and nodded, not knowing what else to do. "Yes."

Aaron reached out, curled his hand, and embraced the back of Joel's head. Joel then did the same to Aaron. Waves of release flooded over both men as they held each other close.

"Joel, it's going to be all right. I forgave you over a year ago. I know you didn't mean to hurt me."

Joel looked at Aaron in astonishment. "A year ago?" he whispered. Aaron nodded.

"You forgave me?" Joel quivered as his knees threatened to buckle. His trembling shook tears from his eyes.

"Joel," Aaron said, again gripping his cousin's shoulder and supporting him with his good arm, "I know what battle is, and I know what it does to a man. I know it wasn't really you on that battlefield—not your heart and your soul."

Aaron embraced Joel again, allowing himself to be the stronger man, emotionally supporting his devastated cousin.

The tears streamed down Joel's face. He breathed the words "thank you" and released his guilt. His shoulders shook as the heavy burden lifted from them. Nearly twenty months of horror and unending pain departed.

Because of his wife, his mother, and his twin cousin, Joel Haskins was a new man, reborn in a stable with only the company of cows and mice, but they could have been angels and shepherds and wise men.

At that moment, Aaron changed too. For the first time since losing his arm, he was acting as the physical and emotional strength for someone in great need. He allowed himself to not be a cripple; rather, he let himself be the man he once was. With this change came a renewed power and sense of purpose, infused with a profound love for his cousin.

The best friends sat in the barn, reveling in each other's company for many minutes before they parted. As Joel entered his front door, he heard from across the creek an almost-familiar whistling, which sounded as though it came from one hand and a warbling tongue:

"Whoo-ee. Who-ee." It was anemic and much different, but he couldn't miss the meaning.

Joel laughed loudly, cupped his hands, and, for the first time more than two years, gave the beloved call: "Whooeee! Whooeee-ooeee-ooeee! Whooeee."

After fairly kicking in the front door, he grabbed Amy and whirled her into a kiss of joy. This was Valentine's Day, a day of love and peace. For Joel, it was the end of the tragic journey begun so long ago and the beginning of the life of his dreams.

Hope grows fonder—and stronger. Yes, even stronger than fear.

CHAPTER 28

Joel and Teacher, March 1865

Several days later, Joel saddled Buck and went to see his friend and teacher, Robert Arthur. The sun shone as he rode with his hat brim tipped to ward off the chilling wind. He entered the barnyard to the cackle of chickens and welcomes from Socrates, Sophocles, and Stophanese. With them was a new puppy Joel hadn't met.

Mr. Arthur stepped out, helped Joel tether Buck inside the small barn, and brought him into the house. They shared pleasantries and coffee.

"I see you have a new dog," Joel commented. "What's his name?"

"Well, somebody left him at the schoolhouse. The children were calling him Pluto, but when I brought him home, I changed his name to Plato."

Joel laughed heartily. "Socrates, Sophocles, Stophanese, and now Plato. Another philosopher."

Joel inhaled the fresh brew, enjoying the steam curling around his nose, thinking how much better it was than army coffee. He held his mug close, enjoying the heat and fragrance. He was glad Mr. Arthur gave him a cinnamon roll rather than hardtack.

As their conversation progressed, Joel called Andersonville "the worst prison in history." Mr. Arthur responded, "I'm sure it was as ghastly as you say. War prisons are appalling. Do you remember Joseph Hale? He was two or three years behind you."

"Yes, I remember him well," Joel said, wondering what Hale had to do with the subject.

"Well, I have some relatives in New York. My cousin was a guard at a prison at a town named Elmira. It's a Yankee war prison, and I'd been told that Joseph had joined the Rebel cause and was a prisoner there, so I asked my cousin if I could see him. He took me into the guard tower and called Joseph over, and I got to talk with him for a while. I found that it was absolutely horrible. Just terrible! The prisoners call Elmira 'Hellmira,' and for good reason."

"Well, I'm sure Andersonville was the worst prison ever. We practically starved to death. Some actually did."

Mr. Arthur understood. "Yes. Food is scarce in the South, and there must be pressure to feed the local people and the soldiers rather than the prisoners. But I doubt that the poorer Southern people got a whole lot more to eat than you did."

Joel was uncomfortable talking about the life he was trying to forget, and was casting around in his mind when he heard some rustling under his chair. He was surprised to see a small kitten crawl from beneath a sheaf of papers. Joel picked it up and petted it. It purred contentedly as it curled into the crook of his arm. "I see Socrates has an apprentice."

Mr. Arthur laughed, shaking his long gray beard. "Yes, I guess that's right. This little fellow adopted me a couple of months ago and has been living a high life of cream and academics ever since."

Joel told his teacher of the slave family that had rescued him and about General Sherman's army. "You wouldn't believe how many crops the Union soldiers destroyed and how many animals they stole. I was told there was a rule against the destruction, especially inside the houses, but I don't think Sherman's army paid any attention to it. It was as if a bunch of horrible giants had come storming through the countryside, hell-bent on destruction just for the sake of destroying. Right now, Sherman's troops are in South Carolina, and I bet they are doing even more damage there, since South Carolina started the whole thing."

Mr. Arthur grunted in response and said, "I read about Sherman's conquest. I think he is trying to destroy the South's morale—to make the citizens suffer and give up hope. He wants to make it a hell on earth."

"Well, he did that for sure." Joel paused and then said, "Mr. Arthur, before I went to prison, the war was mostly defensive on both sides. The Union tried over and over to take Richmond because it was the Rebel capital, but they were stopped at Bull Run, on the Virginia Peninsula, at Fredericksburg, and I don't know where else. The Rebs tried to bring Maryland into the Confederacy, but Lincoln stopped them right here in Sharpsburg. Then they tried to win their independence by marching into the Union, and I think they probably wanted to go clear to Washington, but they were stopped at Gettysburg."

"Yes, that's an excellent analysis," said Mr. Arthur.

"Well, I'm curious about why the North is winning now. Sherman and others have moved clear into the South and are now coming north. It looks like the war will be over soon."

"I agree. You know, Joel, there have been a lot of battles. A big one was when the Union took control of the Mississippi in a battle at Vicksburg at the same time you were fighting at Gettysburg. This gave the Union full control of the Mississippi, and that was very important. For the last two years, the Union has sent troops into the South many times with great success."

"But why have they been so successful? Why is the North winning?"

"Well, Joel, I think it's really rather simple. The Union has a bunch of advantages. It has over twice as many people. It has a better-developed industry, because the Deep South has mostly plantations, while the North has bunches of factories. Also, the Union has developed a much stronger military. And, as I said, it has control of the Mississippi River."

Joel said nothing, so the teacher continued. "I suppose it was inevitable with all the advantages the North had, but it took a long time."

"Man, isn't that the truth. It's been about four years since the whole thing started."

Mr. Arthur then turned the subject to Aaron, and Joel told him that the two had fought against each other at Gettysburg, although he didn't tell about their tragic meeting. Arthur said he was glad the two had reconciled and then added, "I remember reading about another family. The father is a brigadier general who went with Virginia, his home state. His older son graduated from West Point and was in the Union army. The father was so angry he removed his son's name from the family records. Another son stayed loyal to Virginia and to his father. Well, both boys were killed, and of course the father was devastated. I understand that he put up a monument to both of them, inscribed with the words 'God alone knows which was right.'"

Joel soon moved to his main point. "Mr. Arthur, I've been thinking about this a lot. It seems like almost anything would have been better than this war."

Mr. Arthur poured more coffee and then asked, "Have you figured out how it might have been avoided?"

"Well, I don't think war can be avoided unless people see it for what it is. I remember how excited Aaron was. And he wasn't the only one. A lot of other people here in Sharpsburg were just itching for action. I felt like a coward for not going right away. And a lot of boys who were with me in the Union army told me how everyone applauded them—how the old men made patriotic speeches, and the women made flags, and the girls gave them kisses as they marched off. I think that, in a way, we were in love with war. I even remember Aaron was afraid the war would be over before he got a chance to be in it."

Joel paused and then added, "I guess war will always have an appeal—that'll never change; but at least half those who fight end up as losers. And, really, both sides lose a lot."

Socrates turned over once again and began to gently knead Joel's cuff with his needle-sharp claws. Joel pulled down his wool coat sleeve to intercept the kitten's small movements and suffered a small scratch on his hand.

Mr. Arthur asked, "What do you think should have been done?"

"Well, it seems to me that the North needed to figure out how to reduce the South's fear. This would be true of any war, wouldn't it? Both sides feel threatened. Do you think it would have been possible for the government to buy the slaves and then give them freedom? Before the war, I mean. I think if the government had done that a few years ago, there would have been no war, and the Negroes would be a lot better off today—and so would I, and so would Aaron. I thought a lot about the problems for the freed slaves while I stayed with Benny and Annie. It would have been so much better if they had been freed peacefully and then given the opportunity to make a good life."

Joel took a swig of coffee and then continued, "They saved my life. I tried to figure out what would have been best for them. They didn't know what to do when Sherman's army freed them. I don't know what they did. They wanted to come north like I did, but the army wouldn't let them. I don't know what they would have done if they had gotten up here. I sure wish I could find out what happened to them, but there's no way." Joel drained the last bit of coffee from his mug and set it beside the chair.

Mr. Arthur sat back and gazed at his student through glasses that had slipped farther toward the edge of his nose. "Well, Joel, you've been doing a lot of thinking. Of course, what you say assumes that they would have been for sale before the war, and most of them weren't. I think you might be onto something, though. I really wish we had done what the British did in 1833, when they abolished slavery all over their empire."

Mr. Arthur stood to stoke the fire, tossing the ends of his muffler back over his shoulder. As he added new logs, he continued. "For a while, slavery wasn't very profitable. I think some of the owners might have been willing to sell their slaves if the price had been reasonable. Most plantation owners probably wouldn't have sold them, though, so it would have been necessary to pass a law forcing them to sell the slaves for a good price. This is already done when a state or county needs a piece of land to build a road or something. Remember when we talked about the Homestead Act, which gave land to whites? How about doing the same for all those who have been slaves? A lot of people would object to spending the tax money, but it would have been much cheaper than fighting the war, and the results would have been far better—for the whites as well as for the slaves."

"It'll be interesting to see what happens when the war is done," Joel said. "It looks like the North is going to win, and all the slaves will probably be freed. When I got home, I was surprised to learn that Maryland freed ours while I was in prison. Of course, Gabe and Nattie had already run away. But the Deep South is so poor right now, and so bitter, that I think things will probably not be good between the North and the South for a long time. The hatred created by the war will hurt even the freed slaves. I'm afraid that even if they're free, the white people who control the South will still treat them like slaves. And the Negroes won't have any power to make it any different."

The two continued to explore each other's minds, then talked of the local news, and soon settled into a discussion about the new Sharpsburg cemetery that was being developed.

"It was terrible around here, even long after the battle," Mr. Arthur said. "Did you know that at least seven hundred bodies were buried on William Roulette's farm?"

"My pa mentioned that. A lot of them were only half buried, or maybe their bodies were dug up by animals, right? It's the same on our farm, but not as many. I buried some of them right after the battle."

"While you were gone, I helped to bury, or rebury, a lot of soldiers. We made grave markers such as we could, but there were so many bodies. Your pa and Robert helped too."

Mr. Arthur scowled deeply and added, "Sometimes relatives would come and search—still do. We helped them the best we could, but hundreds of men had been buried in long, shallow trenches, and it was terribly hard to know who they were. Some were buried alone in the fields or in some of the churches' cemeteries. Who could know where a particular man was? But of course lots of relatives wanted to know, and we would at least try. I saw mothers and fathers weeping, hoping to find something that had belonged to their sons. I remember how one cried when we found a mangled, decaying body with a letter she had sent and a photograph of her family. It was almost more than I could handle." He paused; it was almost more than he could handle now, just telling Joel. He sighed, stood up, and returned the mugs to the kitchen. Then he added, "There's a plan now to make a new cemetery over near the Dunker Church, not far from Roulette's house."

At last Joel stood up to leave, cradling the kitten before setting it down in the chair he had vacated. "So what's his name?" Joel said, motioning with a jerk of his chin.

Mr. Arthur smiled and said, "Pax. I named him Pax."

Joel cast a sidelong glance at his mentor and then looked back to the little kitten. "Pax—peace. A strange name in strange times, Mr. Arthur."

"But maybe not so strange in the future, my boy. Not so strange at all, we hope. Maybe peace will sometime become a reality. Anyway, Pax is a good companion for Socrates, Sophoclese, Stophanies, and Plato." Mr. Arthur laid a warm hand on Joel's shoulder and helped him with his scarf and coat.

As Joel rode home, he remembered that Mr. Arthur had said that an understanding of history was the best platform from which to gain an understanding of life. He knew that following the model of his teacher would drive him toward that understanding. He thought that maybe someday he would go to school again and study history and maybe become a teacher; perhaps he could replace Mr. Arthur when he retired. The thought warmed him.

That evening, Joel looked to the future with hope, rejoicing in his budding friendship with his two-year-old son. He played with Braden and put him into his crib and then focused his mind on the good times ahead. He lay awake, knowing it wouldn't be easy. He knew his past would always be with him, but he vowed to do what he could to win his own war with his nation's Civil War.

Then, like the kitten named Peace, Joel yawned, cuddled closer to Amy, and fell into a tranquil sleep. How wonderful it was to be home and in peace.

CHAPTER 29

Aaron and Joel, Gettysburg, July 3, 1866

Exactly three years after their Gettysburg tragedy, with the guns of war now silent, Aaron and Joel rode east from Sharpsburg and then turned north. After several hours, they reached their destination. Once again they were in Gettysburg, Pennsylvania.

"I don't see why this should make any difference," Aaron said with a restless shrug of his shoulders.

"I don't either. Reverend Nathan has good judgment and gives good advice, though. I appreciate him for suggesting it. Who knows?" After eighteen months of watching the two young men catapult through emotions, their minister had recommended that they go together to the battlefield in an attempt to overcome the trauma that still occasionally obstructed their lives.

As the two men approached the Pennsylvania town, the terrain looked foreign. Then, with help from some townspeople, they began to get their bearings. They rode through the trees to Seminary Ridge, where they tied their horses and viewed the valley to the east.

"Do you see those trees way over there? That's Cemetery Ridge. That was our target," Aaron said. "Of course, I had no idea you were there."

"And I had no idea you were here, coming at me. I only knew the Rebel army was charging. I still shiver just thinking about it—me over there, and you coming after me from right here."

"I saw this long line of men defending the ridge," Aaron recalled. "I don't know what I would have done if I had known you were one of them. But we knew our duty, and we were going to do it."

"And we knew our duty, and we were going to do it too. It looked like a million Rebs were coming at us, determined to drive through us and right on to Washington. It was breathtaking."

"Well, you just about took my breath—forever," Aaron responded. Joel wasn't amused by his cousin's attempt at mirth, but he chuckled.

Aaron noticed the changes caused by the battle three years earlier. Many trees were battle-scarred. Some fences were still down. Scores of graves were visible, some with the occupant's name or initials and army unit marked on crude headboards.

The cousins walked in reverent silence, remembering three years ago. Presently they crossed the Emmitsburg Road. Silently they ascended the hill and reached the stone wall. Joel quickly found the spot he had defended at the corner where the wall veered east. Finally he commented, "I was right here. When we got the order to fire, I shot a man straight ahead of me. I still remember how he died." He paused, reliving the horror. "You must have been close to him."

"Maybe. My friend Hiram Lott was killed in the first volley. Remember him? He was a year behind us in school and mustered into First Maryland the day I did. He was right next to me. We were shoulder to shoulder. Johnny Williams was on the other side of me. When Hiram fell, a soldier from the second line stepped into his place. We came on up to the wall, just about here. There was so much smoke I couldn't see anything very well. I knew the enemy was right here behind these stones." Aaron put his hands on the low wall, facing Joel on the other side.

"Yes, right here," Joel said. "We had been ordered to hold the wall no matter what."

"And we had been ordered to take the wall no matter what."

The cousins faced each other at the very spot their lives had been dramatically changed exactly three years earlier. Aaron finally asked, "Do you remember much of what happened?"

"It's strange, but I remember it better now than I did then. I know you were about to shoot me, and I shot just as quick as I could. I still remember the look on your face."

"I remember too. I was shocked when I saw your face. But just as our eyes met, you fired."

"Oh Aaron, I've thought about that for so long. I thought for sure I killed you. I don't remember what happened next. Everything just blacked away from me. Everything was going in circles, getting dimmer and dimmer. I passed out right here—right on this spot. Later, I discovered blood on my head. Do you suppose it might have been your blood?"

"Probably. I got up pretty quick, though. All of Pickett's men were retreating, and I guess I got back across the valley as fast as I could, along with the others."

Joel said, "All I can remember is that I heard someone tell me I was a prisoner. I've tried to figure it out, and I think I must have been unconscious for several minutes. I think maybe somebody else hit me on the head with a rifle butt—at least, my head ached for a long time, and maybe that's why it was so bloody. I guess I must have retreated right along with the Rebels. I don't know if they took me prisoner as they retreated or if I got clear across the valley and wound up in their camp. I really can't remember. But I thought I killed you, and I wanted to die too."

Aaron said, "I don't know how long I was unconscious. One strange thing, though—I seemed to imagine I was home. I even thought I heard a band playing 'There's No Place Like Home.'"

"I heard it too! It was real! Someone in prison told me later that a Union band played it as the battle was ending."

"Those bands sure do a strange job of picking a song," said Aaron. "But for too many, home was the graveyard."

Presently their steps carried them along the ridge to the nearby cemetery, where they wandered among the gravestones. Soon they found where President Lincoln had delivered the Gettysburg Address four months after the battle.

"Joel, looking at this place brings my anger back."

"I understand, Aaron. I know Lincoln had his faults. He wouldn't have been reelected if Sherman hadn't won at Atlanta on his way to the sea. But Lincoln tried very hard. Like so many soldiers, he paid with his life. I can't resent him. Maybe he symbolizes more than he really was, but I'm beginning to see him as a martyr for a good cause."

"And what good cause is that?" Aaron's hostility blazed.

"I think his desire to keep the nation together was good and—"

Aaron broke in with a caustic "And I suppose King George's desire to keep the British Empire together was good, and we shouldn't have declared independence."

Joel didn't know how to respond, so he ignored the interruption. "Well, even though Lincoln's purpose in freeing the slaves was to punish the South and win the war, I'm glad the slaves are free. Besides, I think that down deep, Lincoln had abolitionist hopes too, but he knew abolition wasn't politically possible before the war. But since slaves were property, and in wartime it's okay to take the enemy's property, it made it easy in the seceded states."

Aaron was livid. He pounded his fist and snorted. "We have a whole section of the country that's devastated and that will resent Lincoln and the North forever. Won't they take it out on the darkies? I wonder how much better off the slaves really are. I wonder how it will be for their children."

"I understand, Aaron. I think that Lincoln's method of freeing the slaves was about the worst way it could have been handled. But at least the slaves are free, and the nation is united again."

The two men sat quietly for a long time before Joel spoke again.

"You know that tomorrow is the Fourth of July? Thomas Jefferson and the others announced the Declaration of Independence ninety years ago tomorrow."

Aaron cut in harshly. "Yeah, and you think independence is bad. I still don't understand how he could use the Declaration of Independence from England as a reason for keeping independence from the South. If independence was good in 1776, why was it bad in 1861?"

Joel didn't feel like arguing any more. In silence, each thought about his own understanding of Lincoln. To Joel, Lincoln had wanted the United States to be a beacon, announcing freedom to the world. To Aaron, Lincoln had announced his sovereign right to use force to destroy a way of life. But whatever Lincoln represented, both twin cousins knew the men in the graves had given heroically—those from the North trying to preserve the Union, those from the South trying to create a nation they thought would return to the ideals of the Declaration. As Joel and Aaron silently pondered the dilemma, they stood and walked reverently among the fallen heroes.

After a time, they left the gravestones and found themselves back at the angle of the wall, gazing out over that once-bloody field. It was an eerie sensation for Joel; as he looked across the valley, he could see the hordes coming and smell the sharp tang of gun smoke. He shivered as they again were at the point they had met exactly three years earlier, trying to see through the fog of war. He reached out and touched the stones of the wall gently.

Aaron broke the troubled silence, admitting, "It's just so hard, Joel. Both sides thought they were right. I believe the South was right, but sometimes I have questions."

Joel rubbed sweat from his neck and responded softly, "I think maybe neither side was really right. Lincoln called the cemetery 'hallowed ground.' That's because so many brave men died. But I'm determined to find ways to hallow our nation without so many gravestones."

They sat silently on the stone wall. Presently Aaron said, "You know, Joel, I killed a lot of men. But do you remember that Christmas night we spent together on the Rappahannock, when I told you about the first one I killed? He was just a boy carrying a United States flag. I heard a song just before the war ended, and I keep hearing it over and over, and I think of that boy and his family."

"What song is it?"

Aaron hesitated, in pain. "Oh, you know—that one about the vacant chair—about the family that gets together for a family meal, but there is one vacant chair. I think about that boy and his family and the vacant chair at their table because of me."

"Well, yeah—but you can't worry too much about it, Aaron. You know—the war caused hundreds of thousands of vacant chairs all over the country, North and South. If you hadn't killed him, somebody else probably would have."

"I know. I know. I try not to think about it or to take it personally. But I keep wondering if that boy's name was Willie. The boy in the song was a flag bearer named Willie."

For several seconds, the men were wrapped in a solemn silence; then Aaron softly sang the heartbreaking words: "At our fireside, sad and lonely, often will the bosom swell at remembrance of the story, how our noble Willie fell, how he strove to bear our banner through the thickest of the fight and uphold our country's honor in the strength of manhood's night."

Aaron paused again and then said, "I know his name probably wasn't Willie. But I keep feeling bad for his family when they found out he was dead. But like you said, there were hundreds of thousands of vacant chairs."

Then he sang, "We will meet, but we will miss him. There will be one vacant chair. We will linger to caress him as we breathe our evening prayer."

Joel paused for a few moments and then said, "Vacant chairs have come from every war for thousands of years." He stopped and then added, "And there'll be vacant chairs for thousands more if we don't wake up."

He put his arm around his cousin. For a full two minutes, they remained silent. Then Aaron put his hand on Joel's shoulder and squeezed it. Joel looked at him with tear-filled eyes. "I'm so sorry I took your arm," he whispered. "You never say anything about it, but I know you miss it terribly."

"Oh Joel, I know you're sorry. I'm sorry too. I do miss my arm. Every time I try to help with the milking or carry something or make love to Helen, I miss it." He choked on the emotion rising within him.

Aaron tried to control his sobs but couldn't. His shoulders shook. "I miss it when I want to play the fiddle or the piano or do our signal to each other. I've learned to make music with one hand, but it just isn't the same. Oh, how I wish I could have my arm back ..." The twin cousins were together again, as close as in their boyhood.

Their tears washed the stones their blood had once stained.

When their tears were spent, they walked back through the valley of the carnage of death to their mounts on Seminary Ridge. Aaron said he felt now that he could be the kind of father he once had dreamed of being.

A month ago, Helen had given birth to Espen, whom they had named for her grandfather. He now told Joel the meaning of the name Espen: "bear of God." Helen's grandfather was a man of bear-like strength—a strong bearer of God's message. Now Aaron felt that he could help Espen live up to his name.

As they set their faces toward Sharpsburg, Aaron suddenly burst into song, with Joel quickly joining:

'Mid pleasures and palaces though we may roam,
Be it ever so humble, there's no place like home!
A charm from the skies seems to hallow us there,
Which, seek through the world, is ne'er met with elsewhere.

Home! Home! Sweet, sweet home!
There is no place like home!
There is no place like home.

Aaron's song was manna to Joel's starved ears. He followed with a favorite hymn, and the two sang together:

Guide me, oh thou great Jehovah,
Pilgrim through this barren land.
I am weak, but thou art mighty;
Hold me with thy powerful hand.
Bread of heaven, bread of heaven,
Feed me till I want no more.

Open now the crystal fountain,
Whence the healing waters flow.
Let the fiery, cloudy pillar
Lead me all my journey through.
Strong deliverer, strong deliverer,
Be thou still my strength and shield.

The twin cousins rode through the ebbing light and then through the dark of night as they journeyed back to their home along the Antietam. Each knew he could never be the innocent boy he once had been. The scars would never be completely healed. But each knew that the crystal fountain had been opened, and the healing waters were flowing.

They approached their home as the sun's first rays lit the Alleghenies ahead. It was the Fourth of July, Independence Day. The twin cousins had done much to gain independence from the horror of war.

The dark night was ending. The sun's morning warmth flooded their souls as a new day dawned with visions of faith and hope.

CHAPTER 30

Christmas 1866

The Haskins family awakened to a clear Christmas morning. The three mothers whose lives had been so changed by the war were slowly adjusting. Abigail and Fannie still lived with the terror each had suffered, knowing it would never be completely gone, desperately wishing it had never happened but now finding healing. The third mother, Nattie, was far up north, free from slavery but controlled by a white population intent on limiting Negro freedoms.

Christmas had always been precious to the Haskins, and that day the combined family gathered in the original house. Some special guests were the crowning joy of this Christmas Day. All the children had been taught by Mr. Robert Arthur, and having no family of his own, he joined the Haskins family. Aaron's friend Thomas Thomas still lived in Williamsport and was a special visitor.

The most exciting guest was Mark Nash, the only light Joel had seen in his dark months at Andersonville. Joel greeted him with hugs and tears of profound joy, delighted that he could rejoice with his one good memory from the horror.

The extended family sang "Nearer, My God, to Thee." Robert led in prayer, and the crowd enjoyed a grand feast and good company.

After the gift opening, Joel told the family again of the special role Mark Nash had played in his life, and he asked Mark to speak about Christmas. Mark said, "Jesus is the Prince of Peace, and He can bring peace to our hearts. That is the greatest gift we can ever receive."

Mark concluded his message tenderly. "You know, my dear Haskins family and friends, I came to deeply love and respect Joel. I can see that his family is wonderful too. Some of you took the side of the North, some the South. Some agree with me that the war itself was the problem and should never have happened. But I'm so thankful to come here to Joel's home and meet his delightful family. The important thing now is not which side you were on during the war. The important thing is that you are all together now, and I can see that you've accepted each other completely. You're a wonderful family."

Glen responded, "I'm thankful for your friendship to Joel when it was so needed. Mark, I'd like to invite you to come every year you can and always be a part of the Haskins family. And you know we feel the same way about you, Thomas, and our own Robert Arthur."

Later, Fannie uncharacteristically spoke out. "I want to share with you all a letter I received just this week. It's from Nattie."

Several gasped, but Fannie went ahead. "She sent it to 'Fannie Haskins, Sharpsburg, Maryland.' She says that after they left here, they went on the Underground Railway into the North, staying with many kind people on the way, including some of the Quakers and Mennonites and Amish I grew up with. She says ..." Fannie's voice stumbled as she tried to get out what came next. "She said my mother and father were among those who cared for them and helped them on their way." Fannie was now crying. "I'm so glad Nattie and Gabe and their children are free to manage their own lives."

The room was nearly still. Fannie, usually so peaceful, had introduced a major shocker, an issue that had torn the family apart. Would it do it again?

Then she added, "I know they are facing lots of hard times up north. Most Northerners treat Negroes about as bad as the slave owners did—lots worse than we did, I know. But I'm glad Carl and Sunny have a chance to make some of their own choices and to grow up in hope of seeing themselves as real people."

The room stayed still until Fannie spoke again. "You all know that I grew up in a family that was against slavery—they even thought it was sinful. I know that we treated Nattie and Gabe nicely. Glen, I love you so much, and I'm so glad you and Robert and Abigail were kind to them. But I've lived with this burden for almost thirty years. I thank you for being nice to me when you knew I didn't approve of slavery. I just want you to know I'm so very glad our servants are no longer slaves. I pray that God will help them overcome the prejudice they still face. Thank you, my dear family, for accepting me all these years and listening to me now. I love you and appreciate you so much."

Joel was about to give his mother a hug, when, wonderfully, his father beat him to it. Glen took her in his arms and held her close. "Fannie, my love for you is partly because you stand for right. I'm not sure Gabe and Nattie are better off without us, but I'm so thankful for everything you did for them, and for what you have said."

Soon Abigail and Robert joined. Neither said she or he thought the slaves ought to be free, but both said with their actions that they loved Fannie, accepted her, and were proud that she stood up for her convictions. Joel, and then even Aaron, hugged the huggers.

In a few moments, Joel said, "Do you remember that song Nattie used to sing called 'Run, Mourner, Run'? When I was with the slave family in Georgia, I learned that the song had a hidden meaning. The mourner was the slave; to run meant to escape. I guess Nattie's song finally came true."

Fannie thanked her beloved family and admitted that they weren't all in agreement about slavery, but they were all together in love. The Prince of Peace was being honored on His birthday.

After a few minutes, Braden came to Aaron and asked, "When are we going to sing Christmas songs?"

Aaron smiled. "Well, Braden, how about right now?" He pulled a black leather case from behind the couch, flipped open the center clasp with his one hand, and raised the lid like a jewelry salesman displaying his wares. He lifted his trumpet and began to breathe his life into its body. Now, three and one-half years after Gettysburg, he played beautifully with his lone hand.

Robert found his fiddle and joined in the fun. Joel played his harmonica. Abigail and Helen sat together at the piano and made it shout for joy. The rest of the family sang lustily.

Aaron still loved a hungry ear. He sang "God Rest Ye Merry Gentlemen" and then led as the family shouted their favorite Christmas carols. Stephen asked for "It Came upon a Midnight Clear," Kylan called for "Joy to the World," and LaVonne requested "Silent Night." Little Braden sang "Jingle Bells," and his solo delighted the family members, who knew Amy had taught him the song while dashing through the snow as they sleighed along Antietam Creek.

Aaron reached into his pocket and pulled out Bethel, the stone his father had given him before he'd left for war. He clutched it tightly and said, "Thank you, Pa, for giving this to me. I've carried it for almost five years now, and I'll carry it the rest of my life. It means so much to me. It is my solid rock." Then he sang gently, "On Christ the solid rock I stand, all other ground is sinking sand ..." He went to his father and gave him a big hug. "Papa, you can never know what this symbol has meant to me. Thank you so much."

The music continued as the family sang before the fire. Aaron again took the lead, and his music lifted everyone's spirit straight to heaven. Later, he and Helen played the piano together, and then Joel asked for "I Heard the Bells on Christmas Day." Aaron recalled the amazing evening exactly four years earlier when Joel had surprised him on the Rappahannock's bank. The former enemies now sang together, each with an arm around the other:

> I heard the bells on Christmas Day
> Their old familiar carols play,
> And wild and sweet the words repeat
> Of peace on earth, goodwill to men.

I thought how as the days had come,
The belfries of all Christendom
Had pealed along the unbroken song
Of peace on earth, goodwill to men.

Then in despair I bowed my head;
"There is no peace on earth," I said,
"For hate is strong and mocks the song,
Of peace on earth, goodwill to men."

Then pealed the bells more loud and deep,
"God is not dead nor doth He sleep,
The wrong shall fail, the right prevail,
With peace on earth, goodwill to men."

The family sat in silence for several seconds. The Haskins family knew that God was neither dead nor asleep. In their family, at least, war's horrible wrong had failed miserably; the wonderful right of love was prevailing. Within their world, they knew peace and goodwill; the long, cruel nightmare had in many ways ended.

Joel felt drawn to his mother's side. He told the family of his lonely nights at Andersonville. "Mama," he said softly, "I sang your song to myself and to you over and over on those dark nights. Would you sing it with me now?"

Arm in arm, they stood, their damp cheeks mirroring those of the family around the room. Together, mother and son remembered:

Precious memories, unseen angels
Sent from somewhere to my soul;
How they linger, ever near me,
And the sacred scenes unfold.

Precious father, loving mother,
Fly across the lonely years;

And old home scenes of my childhood,
In fond memory appear.

I remember Mother praying,
Father, too, on bended knee;
Sun is sinking, shadows falling,
But their prayers still follow me.

As I travel on life's pathway,
Know not what the years may hold;
As I ponder, hope grows fonder,
Precious mem'ries flood my soul.

Precious mem'ries, how they linger,
How they ever flood my soul;
In the stillness of the midnight,
Precious, sacred scenes unfold.

It had been a wonderful Christmas. It would be the family pattern for many memories still to be created as they traveled on life's pathway.

EPILOGUE

Federal Penitentiary, September 1918

"Federal penitentiary, ladies. Enjoy your stay. I'm glad it'll be a long one for you cowards."

Joel Haskins found himself in another Georgia jail more than fifty years after Andersonville. He cringed, recalling his earlier imprisonment. *At least this guard didn't call us "damn Yank scum."*

The new prisoners were soon surrounded. "Hey, old man, what got you in here? Murder somebody?"

"No. Actually, I'm trying to save lives."

"How long you in for?"

Joel shuddered. "A long time. Ten years."

Yes, and I won't get out. I remember that when I was at Andersonville, I thought I would die in a Georgia prison. I was right—just many years later and a different prison. When you're almost eighty, ten years is a life sentence.

The lonely memories of 1864 at Andersonville Prison returned.

Again he hummed the song he'd sung while in that Civil War prison, a song that now brought him face-to-face with his mother, who'd been in heaven for fifteen years. *Precious memories, how they linger ...* Heading those beautiful memories were Amy and their four children and fifteen grandchildren. Another precious memory was Aaron, who, along with Helen and their children, had been close friends through the years.

Aaron had managed to live a good life despite his missing arm. Joel marveled at how he found innovations for his beloved music. He'd had to give up the fiddle, but he could still make his trumpet shout and had learned a good one-handed harmonica. Fortunately, a missing arm did not affect his voice. Aaron remained the best singer in Washington County, at least in Joel's opinion. In spite of his impairment, Aaron was happy. Through the years, the twin cousins had remained the closest of friends.

He thought of his own life—how he and Amy and their children had moved temporarily to Georgia during Reconstruction, found Benny and Annie, and tried to help them cope with being free but still in the bondage of intense prejudice. He delighted in his memory of Jake, who had rescued him in 1864. Joel had been able to help rescue Jake by paying for a college education.

He thought about how he and Amy had moved north in the late 1880s; he would never forget his reunion with Nattie and Gabe, and his attempt to bring justice to both black and white workers. He never ceased to regret the Civil War and what it had done to Aaron, to himself, and to America. Although pleased that slavery had ended, he observed the bitterness of the Southern whites and the degradation of the Negroes in all parts of the country. He often thought about the harsh Jim Crow system of racial segregation that had extended slavery's legacy. The United States remained a two-tiered society. Now, sitting in prison again, he pondered a what-if.

I wonder what would have happened if the Southern part of the Democratic Party hadn't split off in 1860 and allowed Lincoln's election with less than 40 percent of the popular vote? What if the Southern states had accepted Lincoln's presidency instead of seceding? What if part of the money spent on the war had been used by the government to purchase the slaves and give them education and jobs—maybe a Homestead Act for former slaves that would have paralleled what had been done for whites in 1862? What if people thought more about preventing wars and less about fighting them? What if we tried as hard to create the conditions for peace as we do to demonize the enemy and excite fearful people to war? What if our country spent as much time and money learning about peaceful solutions to conflict as teaching men to fight?

He recalled feeling deeply concerned when Americans had been easily persuaded that they should go to war with Spain in 1898. He was frustrated that the same was true of the war being waged in 1918. As always, both sides considered themselves right. German soldiers marched into battle with belt buckles inscribed with the words "God is with us," while Americans, many of them Christians, marched in parades, waving banners that declared, "Hell is too good for the Hun." Chaplains on both sides preached that their side was God's side. It was all too familiar for Joel. As a naive young man, he had believed the same lies, and so had his enemy cousin.

Joel's concern peaked when his twenty-year-old grandson Lester enlisted and was killed in France. Joel had felt his convictions flare into a bright fire of protest. He spoke out more forcefully against the war and encouraged young men to consider carefully whether they should kill for this or any other cause.

He often asked questions similar to those he had asked his mother: "Has the United States government ever done anything you thought was a mistake?" The audiences always laughed. He followed with "Suppose that getting us involved in this war was one of those mistakes?" Some people got his message, but most seemed to believe that it could never be a mistake to kill others to defend one's country. He often asked Christian audiences the types of questions he had asked his mother: "Who is your commander in chief—President Wilson or Jesus Christ?" and "What if Jesus didn't want us in this war?" and "If you lived in Germany, who would be your commander in chief—Kaiser Wilhelm or Jesus Christ?" Then he would explain that certainly nations would go to war, but if all Christians followed the loving example of the early

Christians, the impact would be so great that there would be far less fear, less hatred, and less war.

Joel admitted he was violating the US law that in wartime no one was allowed to resist the war effort in any way. The court sentenced him to ten years in the federal penitentiary in Atlanta. Even in prison, though, the government could not still his pen. He wrote a true story about his grandson Lester.

> On a Sunday morning in 1918, Christians in churches all over the United States were praying for victory and the safety of their soldiers. So were Christians in Germany. A brave young American marine named Lester Haskins was crawling the enemy lines to signal back the position of some machine-gun nests. He succeeded; the nests were destroyed. Lester thrilled as enemy bodies flew into the air.

> Coming back, he was shot by a German sniper. The sniper thrilled as Lester fell dead. My daughter cried lonely, bitter tears when she learned of her son's death. So did the loved ones of the Germans in the machine-gun nests.

> Likely, Lester, although a dedicated Christian, had given no thought to the moral implications of the war. He was just fulfilling God's purposes in defending his good nation by killing those from a bad nation.

> The German soldiers wore belt buckles inscribed with "God is with us." Kaiser Wilhelm called it "a defensive war that has been thrust upon us," and the German purpose "to protect the place that God has set for ourselves and all coming generations." The Germans felt they were fighting a righteous war on behalf of their Christian nation.

Yet can it really be possible that God wants His people to kill each other because their nations believe their opponent is evil? Can both sides be pleasing God? How were Lester and the Germans to know if they had good reasons to kill each other?

Under the circumstances, I don't blame Lester for doing what he did, nor the sniper who killed him for doing what he did. Each believed his country was fighting a just war against an evil enemy.

Today my grandson and the German sniper may be fellowshipping together around God's great white throne. I wonder what they are saying about the cause of their deaths. I believe they agree that there are better ways than war to solve our problems. They are saying we should put less effort into learning to kill and more into learning to make peaceful, victorious solutions for both sides.

Joel knew that, like the early apostles, he was in a dungeon, though not as horrible as those of Rome or Andersonville. In spite of the men in nearby cells, he opened his mouth, and out burst a song he had learned shortly after the Civil War:

> What though my joys and comforts die?
> The Lord, my Savior, liveth.
> What though the darkness gather round!
> Songs in the night He giveth.
> No storm can shake my inmost calm
> While to that refuge clinging.
> Since Christ is Lord of heaven and earth,
> How can I keep from singing?

> What though the tempest loudly roars,

I hear the truth; it liveth.
What though the darkness round me close,
Songs in the night it giveth.
No storm can shake my inmost calm
While to that rock I'm clinging.
Since love is lord of heaven and earth,
How can I keep from singing?

I lift mine eyes; the cloud grows thin;
I see the blue above it;
And day by day this pathway smoothes
Since first I learned to love it.
The peace of Christ makes fresh my heart,
A fountain ever springing.
All things are mine since I am His—
How can I keep from singing?

Joel sat down, still pondering the song. *I hear the truth; it liveth. What though the darkness round me close, songs in the night it giveth … The peace of Christ makes fresh my heart …*

Joel felt a deep sense of joy. For him, the light of Christ would overcome the darkness of Satan. His heart overflowed with a promise Jesus made in John 8:32: "Ye shall know the truth, and the truth shall make you free."

He thought deeply, *I will live and die convinced that I should never go to war, nor do anything that makes others hate and want to kill me. For me, this is truth.*

Then, with firm conviction, the old man stood, gripped the bars of his cell, and smiled as a deep peace washed over him. Inside those prison walls, Joel Haskins was a free man.